Ujurak straightened up, raising his snout. "No," he replied; his voice was stronger now and more certain. "I don't know exactly what is wrong, but I know one thing for sure: This isn't the end of our journey."

"It *is* the end, Ujurak," Toklo protested. "It has to be. There's nowhere else to go." He gestured with one paw at the sea below. "This is as far as we can travel without getting our paws wet."

Ujurak gazed down at the stretch of wrinkled gray water with the encroaching ice glistening on the horizon. Then he looked back at Toklo. His brown eyes were pleading for one of them to understand what he was saying. "I know you must be right . . . but if this is the end, then why don't I feel it?"

SEEKERS

Book One: *The Quest Begins*

Book Two: *Great Bear Lake*

Book Three: *Smoke Mountain*

Book Four: *The Last Wilderness*

Book Five: *Fire in the Sky*

Book Six: *Spirits in the Stars*

MANGA

Toklo's Story

Kallik's Adventure

Also by ERIN HUNTER

WARRIORS

Book One: *Into the Wild*
Book Two: *Fire and Ice*
Book Three: *Forest of Secrets*
Book Four: *Rising Storm*
Book Five: *A Dangerous Path*
Book Six: *The Darkest Hour*

THE NEW PROPHECY

Book One: *Midnight*
Book Two: *Moonrise*
Book Three: *Dawn*
Book Four: *Starlight*
Book Five: *Twilight*
Book Six: *Sunset*

POWER OF THREE

Book One: *The Sight*
Book Two: *Dark River*
Book Three: *Outcast*
Book Four: *Eclipse*
Book Five: *Long Shadows*
Book Six: *Sunrise*

OMEN OF THE STARS

Book One: *The Fourth Apprentice*
Book Two: *Fading Echoes*
Book Three: *Night Whispers*

EXPLORE THE
WARRIORS WORLD

Warriors Super Edition: Firestar's Quest

Warriors Super Edition: Bluestar's Prophecy

Warriors Super Edition: SkyClan's Destiny

Warriors Field Guide: Secrets of the Clans

Warriors: Cats of the Clans

Warriors: Code of the Clans

Warriors: Battles of the Clans

MANGA

The Lost Warrior

Warrior's Refuge

Warrior's Return

The Rise of Scourge

Tigerstar and Sasha #1: Into the Woods

Tigerstar and Sasha #2: Escape from the Forest

Tigerstar and Sasha #3: Return to the Clans

Ravenpaw's Path #1: Shattered Peace

Ravenpaw's Path #2: A Clan in Need

Ravenpaw's Path #3: The Heart of a Warrior

SEEKERS
THE LAST WILDERNESS

ERIN HUNTER

HARPER

An Imprint of HarperCollinsPublishers

The Last Wilderness

Copyright © 2010 by Working Partners Limited

Series created by Working Partners Limited

All rights reserved. Printed in the United States of America. No part of
this book may be used or reproduced in any manner whatsoever without
written permission except in the case of brief quotations embodied in
critical articles and reviews. For information address HarperCollins
Children's Books, a division of HarperCollins Publishers,
195 Broadway, New York, NY 10007.
www.harpercollinschildrens.com

Library of Congress Cataloging-in-Publication Data

Hunter, Erin.

    The last wilderness / Erin Hunter. — 1st ed.

       p.   cm. — (Seekers ; [#4])

    Summary: The four bears finally arrive at the legendary Last Great
Wilderness, thinking it is the end of their long journey, but they discover
that their true mission has really just begun.

    ISBN 978-0-06-087133-8

    [1. Bears—Fiction.   2. Fantasy.]   I. Title.

PZ7.H916625Las   2010   2009020696

[Fic]—dc22   CIP

                                                      AC

Typography by Hilary Zarycky

20 BRR 10 9

❖

First paperback edition, 2011

Special thanks to Cherith Baldry

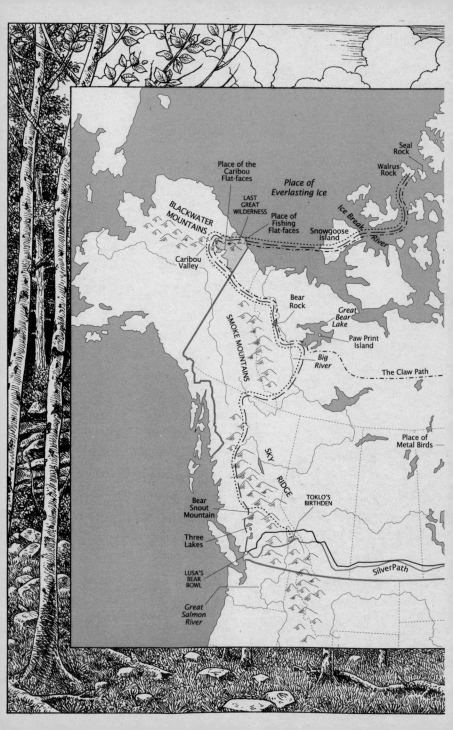

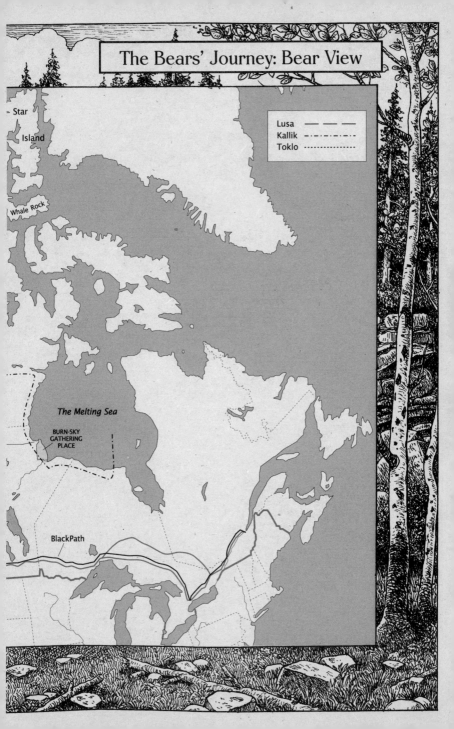

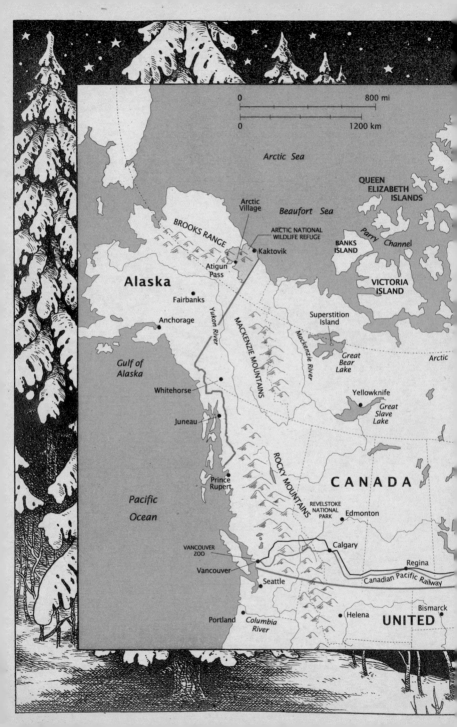

CHAPTER ONE

Ujurak

Wind buffeted Ujurak's fur as he plunged down the mountain slope toward the rolling foothills below, where the caribou were grazing.

It was late burn-sky, and after the recent rains the air was filled with delicious smells. Ujurak drew them in with every breath: scents of prey, of green growing plants, and underlying it all the salt tang of the sea.

As he bounded down the slope he glanced around at his friends. The white bear Kallik raced beside him, her stride as smooth as flowing water, her twitching nose sniffing the air. After so many moons of traveling through dark forests and over sunbaked rocks, Ujurak wondered if she could smell the sea-ice at last, the smell of her home.

He heard a *whoomph* and glanced back just in time to see the black bear Lusa tripping over her own paws in her haste to keep up. She rolled several bear-lengths before scrambling up and continuing to pelt downward. She was the smallest of the four bears by a lot now, and she seemed to run two strides for every one of theirs, but she was never outpaced for long.

And charging ahead, his tufty ears flattened by the wind, was the brown bear Toklo—always out in front, always the first. Warmth welled up inside Ujurak. Toklo had trusted him enough to come with him all this way, so far that Ujurak could hardly remember the mountains where he had met Toklo and then Lusa. Suddenly he wanted to be able to remember every pawstep, picture every day they had spent walking, walking, walking, all the way to the edge of the world.

Because finally they had reached their journey's end. They'd found the Last Wilderness.

Down on the grassy hills, the caribou raised their heads as the bears hurtled toward them.

"Watch out!" Ujurak snarled. "Here we come!"

Toklo glanced over his shoulder. "They're too big to hunt, feather-brain!" he called.

Ujurak huffed at him. He wasn't really going to hunt the giant caribou; strong as he was, he knew he was still small enough to run right under the bellies of the longest-legged creatures. He was just enjoying the feeling of unstoppable running, his paws skimming over the grass with a satisfying hiss, the fur along his flanks slicked down and rippling in the breeze he had created.

They had reached the foothills now, swerving down the gently swollen slopes until they rushed straight into the herd of grazing caribou. Close-up, the horned beasts were huge, and they swung their heavy heads to glance lazily at the bears, unafraid of Ujurak and his companions. There were so many of them, Ujurak couldn't see to the other side of the herd once he was on their level. All he could see was a forest of legs as thin as sticks, topped with pale, hairy bellies. The caribou's pelts gave off a powerful musky scent that made Ujurak puff and wrinkle his nose.

Toklo darted to one side and led the bears out of the herd, sending the caribou scattering. The valley opened up in front of them again, and Ujurak blinked in the bright sunshine. A vast green plain unrolled at his paws, dotted here and there with clumps of dark spiky grass with still, silvery water just visible between the stalks. Through his wind-watering eyes, Ujurak could see patches of white where flocks of geese had landed to feed in the damp grassland.

This is the wilderness Qopuk promised us. Enough to feed us all, space for every bear, no sign of flat-faces or firebeasts or BlackPaths . . .

Ujurak felt a sharp pain in his belly. The journey through Smoke Mountain had been a hard one, with little prey, and the sight of the geese awakened his hunger. He swallowed as his mouth filled with saliva. The grass blurred beneath his front paws as he pushed himself faster, thinking of nothing but a meal of tasty, plump goose. . . . Then Ujurak felt his legs tingling and saw his forelegs begin to lengthen and grow thinner; his pelt prickled as his brown fur transformed into a rough gray pelt.

Wolf!

His snout grew longer and he could feel his vision narrowing, the edges darkening as he focused on a single flock of geese on the plain. *One flock.* The sounds around him faded to insignificance and all he could hear was the geese directly in front of him honking and yakking, their noise growing louder and louder.

His stride lengthened. He felt swift; as he raced past Toklo he thought he heard the brown bear growl. But the sound seemed to come from far away. It meant nothing to Ujurak. The hot reek of the geese engulfed his senses. His tongue lolled as he pinpointed his prey: a fat white bird feeding at the edge of the flock. *One goose.* He could almost feel his teeth sinking through its feathers, crunching its bones. He smelled its blood and heard its heartbeat.

Kill . . . one bite into warm prey . . . then feed.

The plain whirled past him in a blur, his paws hardly seeming to touch the marshy ground. He reached the edge of the flock; the birds flew up in a storm of flapping wings and terrified squawking. Snarling, Ujurak leaped on his chosen prey. His fangs closed on its neck. He shook the goose. It battered him with its wings, then went limp.

Ujurak proudly lifted his head with his prey dangling from his mouth. *Feed now. . . . Taste blood. . . .* But something was gnawing at his mind. He couldn't eat yet. Reluctantly he turned and began trotting back the way he had come.

Ujurak felt his rangy wolf body begin to swell and thicken; brown fur replaced the shaggy gray pelt, and his footsteps grew heavier. His heartbeat slowed as the wolf's hunger for blood died away.

Gradually he began to notice the plain around him again.

The geese were settling a little way off, their raucous cries fading. Ujurak could hear the rattle of wind in the reeds and the splashing paws of an Arctic fox as it darted from one clump of bushes to another. He blinked in confusion as he saw three other bears approaching him, just coming off the foothills onto the plain. Black, brown, white . . . he felt that they ought to be familiar. *Why can't I remember who they are?*

"Ujurak!" The small black bear bounded forward to meet him. "That was a great catch!"

"Uh . . . thanks . . . Lusa." Ujurak's confusion vanished as he stood in front of her and dropped the prey at Lusa's paws. Of course he knew who she was, and the other two bears padding up to him were his friends Toklo and Kallik. The long legs he had as a wolf had rapidly outdistanced them. "Come and share," he invited them.

Toklo growled his thanks as he tore off a part of the goose and retired a couple of paces to flop down and eat the newkill. Ujurak waited for the two she-bears to take some before he settled down to eat, too. The goose was a fat one, and there was enough to share among all of them. It tasted delicious, warm in Ujurak's belly.

"Thish ish—*mmmm*—won-erful!" Kallik said, chewing enthusiastically. She raised her head and sniffed at the air. "Can you smell the ice? Soon the sea will freeze closer to shore, and I'll be able to get back to the white bears' feeding grounds."

"But . . . there's no . . . shelter . . . on the ice," Lusa objected, her mouth full of juicy meat. "The wind will blow you into the sea."

"No, we dig dens in the snow," Kallik explained. "Then we curl up together, and it's so cozy!" Ujurak saw a shadow of sadness creep into her eyes, and he wondered if she was remembering her old life with her brother and mother. Kallik blinked, and the shadow vanished. "And we hunt for seals through holes in the ice. You've never tasted anything as delicious as seal!"

"I'll settle for the brown earth under my paws, and the prey I can catch on it." Toklo jerked his head toward a distant ridge that was thickly covered with trees. Ujurak could see birds wheeling over it and sensed the throbbing life of small animals under the branches. "That's the best sort of place for brown bears—right, Ujurak?"

"Right," Ujurak replied.

"Look at all those trees," Lusa said, pawing a feather from her muzzle. Her dark eyes sparkled with anticipation as she looked across at the tree-clad ridge. "I love sleeping in the branches, with the sound of the wind and the bear spirits close by."

Toklo tore off another mouthful of goose flesh. "What—mmm—I like about . . . this . . . place," he said, gulping it down and swiping his tongue around his jaws, "is no flat-faces. No BlackPaths. No firebeasts. No flat-face dens."

"Just open land and sea, wherever you look," Kallik said.

"And all the prey we can eat," Toklo added.

Lusa sprang to her paws. "What should we do next?" she

asked. "I want to find a tree to spend the night."

"Let's rest for a bit." Toklo batted a paw at the eager little bear. "There's plenty of time."

Ujurak finished eating his share. He was enjoying listening to his friends as they chattered excitedly about their new home. He had brought them here, to a place where they could be safe and well fed and away from flat-faces for the rest of their lives. He was licking his paws, feeling his belly full of warm meat, when a soft voice sounded inside his head. He stiffened as it whispered: *Not the end.*

Ujurak lifted his head, his pelt prickling as if it were crawling with ants. He quietly rose to his paws and stepped away from his friends, pretending to drink from a pool of water. He flattened his ears and listened in case the voice came again.

He had heard this voice before.

Many moons ago it had spoken to him one cold night under a blaze of stars. *Follow the Pathway Star,* it had said, and when he had looked up he had seen one star twinkling more brightly than the rest. He had chosen to ignore the voice at first. But it had whispered to him in the quiet moments as he curled up to sleep and before he rose in the morning. *You will not travel alone,* it had told him.

"What do you mean? There's nobody here." Ujurak had looked around, seeing nothing but the forest stretching into shadow, as if he were the only bear in the world. *They will find you,* the voice promised. Then he met the brown bear Toklo, and his question was answered. He'd started to listen to the voice after that. If ever he had doubted the journey they were making, the voice inside his head urged him on, soft and insistent. Over time, he'd thought he'd figured out who it was, reaching to the edge of his memory, the very first things he could remember.

Ujurak lapped the ice-cold water from the pool. Above, a single star glimmered faintly in the dusky gray-blue sky. *Not the end,* the voice whispered again.

I don't understand! Ujurak protested silently, gazing up at the Pathway Star.

Then, over the mountains, he saw a tiny black dot moving in the sky—no, there were three black dots. They moved closer, following the line of the ridge, and he could hear a distant buzzing. The dots grew bigger and he saw the flash of evening sunlight on hard silver. *Metal birds,* he thought with alarm. He glanced back at his companions. They hadn't noticed the dots in the sky. They were too busy arguing about which was better to live in, trees or caves.

Ujurak watched the metal birds fly away into the distance. The clatter of their wings faded, echoing on the still air. Ujurak's fur prickled. Metal birds were flat-face things— firebeasts of the air. So what were they doing here? Like Toklo had said about this place: *No firebeasts. No flat-faces.*

Ujurak looked at his friends again. Lusa cuffed Toklo, pretending to be angry with him when he said that trees were too full of twigs to be comfortable. They looked so happy. Ujurak felt his heart pounding in his chest.

But I have brought them here—to this place, he told the voice inside his head. *There is nowhere left to go.*

Not the end, said the voice.

Then what am I supposed to do? Ujurak begged.

He listened for an answer. But all Ujurak could hear was the sound of the wind in the long grasses and the call of a gull.

CHAPTER TWO

Lusa

Lusa stood at the top of a grassy hill, gazing across the plain. A cold wind flattened her fur against her face and made her eyes water. It brought with it the scents of ice and fish. In the distance she could just make out the white edge of the ocean. Shivering, she thought of the ice that Kallik longed for so much. That wasn't where she belonged—her home was here, among the trees and the long, sheltering grass.

"We've made it!" she murmured.

Her quest was at an end! She had come through all the dangers and hardships of the journey, and now she was safe here with her friends, a truly wild black bear at last.

The sun was rising, throwing Lusa's shadow out beside her. The night before, after feasting on the goose that Ujurak had caught, they had made their dens at the edge of a patch of stunted thornbushes. Lusa felt rested and energetic after spending the night among the gently tossing branches, knowing her friends were sleeping below.

"Hey! Fluff-brain!" Toklo bounded up beside her, butting

her gently in the shoulder with his snout. "Are you dreaming, or what? I've called you three times!"

"Sorry," Lusa replied, playfully pushing Toklo in return. He was so much bigger than her, it was like trying to shift Smoke Mountain.

"I've caught a couple of hares for us," Toklo went on. "But if you don't want your share, we can eat it for you."

"Don't you dare!" Lusa yelped.

Toklo loped off toward the bottom of the rise where Kallik and Ujurak were waiting beside his newkill. Lusa followed, puffing as she tried to keep up. They had grown fast over the last moon, and Lusa was more than a head smaller than the others now—with Kallik the biggest of all of them.

When they had finished eating, Lusa cleaned her face with her paws and sat up straight, feeling the wind tug at her ears. "What should we do now?" she wondered out loud.

Toklo shrugged. "We've arrived, haven't we? We can do whatever we want."

"Then we should explore!" Lusa decided. If this was her new home, she wanted to know every pawstep, every scent, every bush where berries grew.

Toklo and Kallik stood up at once, ready to set out, but Ujurak didn't seem as eager. Still, he didn't object as they trotted through the long, whispering grass, keeping to the line of the foothills. Geese fluttered up from patches of shallow water as the bears went past, only to settle again almost at once. Lusa's belly was comfortably full; there was no need to hunt now. When they were hungry again, there would be plenty of prey to be caught, and hopefully some tasty leaves and berries for her. She didn't like eating meat all the time, and her mouth watered as she thought of picking fruit from the trees on the mountains.

It seemed strange to think about having a choice of what to eat. *I'd almost forgotten what it was like not to have to worry where the next meal's coming from.*

There were plenty of places to make dens, too. Trees for her, holes between rocks or under tree roots for Ujurak and Toklo, and soon there would be the ice for Kallik. Lusa let out a long sigh, letting go of the tension from the many moons of fear and anxiety.

"Race you to that rock!" Toklo exclaimed suddenly, pointing with his snout toward a rounded gray boulder half-buried in the ground. He propelled himself forward, powerful muscles pumping under his thick brown fur; Kallik raced after him, hard on his paws, but Ujurak hesitated, his head tilted back as he studied the clouds.

"Hey, Ujurak!" Lusa called. "Are you going to let those bigger bears beat you?"

Ujurak jumped, as if his thoughts had been far away, then turned and pelted after his friends.

Lusa scampered behind them, knowing she didn't have any hope of winning but enjoying the sensation of strength in her muscles and the certainty that they wouldn't have to travel anymore. She was a wild bear now, and this was her home. If only Ashia and Yogi could have come with her.

Toklo reached the rock a snout-length before Kallik. "I've

won!" he yelled. "I'm the fastest!"

"You had a head start!" Kallik leaped on the young grizzly
and pushed him over; brown and white pelts brushed as the
bears wrestled, grunting and slapping each other with their
paws.

Meanwhile Ujurak scrambled up onto the boulder and
gazed around, toward the distant sea and over the rolling hills
they had just left. Lusa thought he looked anxious, as if he was
searching for something and couldn't find it.

*What's gotten into his fur? We've finally made it to the place he's been
searching for. He should be happy!*

"Ujurak, are you okay?" she asked.

Ujurak blinked at her, almost as if he didn't recognize her.
"What? Oh, sure, Lusa, I'm fine."

Lusa wrinkled her nose. There was a tasty scent hanging in
the air, something plump and juicy mixed with the cold tang
of stone. She rested her front paws on a smooth round rock
at the foot of the boulder and pushed until it started to shift.
"Help me out here, Ujurak! This is a trick that Miki showed
me in the forest beside Great Bear Lake."

Ujurak leaped down and helped Lusa turn the stone over.
They both jumped back as it rolled away to expose a nest of
fat, wriggling grubs.

"Try them," Lusa invited, taking a mouthful. They were
much nicer than meat, which felt heavy in her stomach. One
quick bite and juices flooded her mouth. There were enough
grubs here for a moon! Perhaps she could find a sleeping tree
with friendly bear spirits nearby.

She was distracted from planning her new home by a bark of surprise from Toklo as he and Kallik rolled over and slammed into a low-growing thornbush. An Arctic hare that had been sheltering under the branches sprang out of cover and fled; Toklo broke away from Kallik and pounded in pursuit. He cornered the hare against an outcrop of rock and killed it with a single expert blow.

Lusa bounded up with Kallik and Ujurak, and stood looking down at the limp body of the hare. Its dark chestnut pelt was flecked with white, reminding her that leaftime was drawing to a close; soon the snows would return.

"Good catch," said Kallik. "But I'm still full from that goose."

"It's okay, we can bury the hare until we're ready to eat it," Toklo pointed out. "That's what brown bears do. I once found a stash that another bear had left in the woods."

Kallik nodded. "That makes sense."

It felt strange to Lusa that they had to decide what to do when they had too much food. *But it's a good problem,* she decided. *Much better than looking for food and not finding any.*

Toklo had just begun to scrape a hole in the ground when an Arctic fox darted forward from the bushes, right under his paws, and snatched up the hare.

"Hey!" Toklo swung around threateningly. "That's ours!"

The fox was already racing away, the prey dragging on the ground between its front paws. Toklo set off in pursuit, but the fox squeezed down a hole and vanished with a flick of its brown-and-white tail. Toklo jabbed his front paw into the burrow, but the fox was obviously out of reach, because Toklo soon came padding back. "Stupid creature," he grumbled.

"It doesn't matter," Lusa said, giving Toklo's shoulder a friendly poke with her snout. "We'll catch more when we're ready."

Dark clouds had begun to gather above the sea, and an icy wind whipped in, bringing with it the tang of snow. Kallik drank it in deeply, raising her muzzle and taking powerful long breaths. "The ice is coming," she murmured.

Lusa and the others followed Toklo as he padded over to a pool. Lusa dipped her snout to drink from the ice-fresh water. It tasted different from the water farther inland: sharp and salty, with a trace of fish. Lusa wasn't sure she liked it, but Kallik gulped it down.

"This feels almost like home," Kallik said. Her voice grew eager. "Come on, let's go to the shore. I want to dip my paws in the sea!"

Toklo lifted his dripping snout from the pool. "You mean you want the water to freeze your fur off?" he teased.

"Cold is *good*," Kallik insisted. "Please come! I really want to go down to the sea today."

"Come on, Toklo," Lusa put in. She could see the longing in Kallik's eyes. "It'll be fun."

Toklo shrugged. "Okay. It's not like we have anything else to do."

The bears set off with Kallik leading the way, her pace

quickening as they neared the glimmering line of the ocean. The wind grew stronger as the land flattened in front of them, sweeping in from the sea with a spatter of sleet that stung Lusa's eyes.

Kallik still kept on going, her head lowered into the blast, but Toklo stumbled to a halt, and after a moment's hesitation Lusa and Ujurak joined him.

"Hey, Kallik!" Toklo called out. "We can't go down to the sea now. This wind is too cold. And it's blowing my fur off."

Kallik paused, looking back over her shoulder. "The wind is great!" she protested. "Can't you smell the ice in it?"

"But we're not like you," Lusa told Kallik. "The ice isn't our home. Let's stay here in the hills for a while, until the weather's better."

"But—" Kallik began.

She broke off as Lusa touched one paw to her shoulder. "Just for now," Lusa whispered. She knew what was going to happen: The bears would split up, each finding his or her own perfect place to live, and she might never see the others again. They had reached the end of their journey, but Lusa didn't want it to be the end of their friendship, too. "Wait until the ice comes back," she pleaded.

Kallik hesitated, then gave a reluctant nod. Lusa saw her glance longingly back at the sea before she followed her friends toward the hills once more.

There weren't many trees in this direction, Lusa noticed sadly, but there were plenty of low-growing bushes and outcrops of rock that could provide shelter from the freezing wind. The caribou grazed on the tough moorland grass, throwing up their heads and snorting with dismay as the four bears padded past.

"They're really restless," Lusa commented. "I wonder if something's disturbed them."

"*We've* disturbed them," Toklo responded, baring his teeth.

"No, I think it's something else," Kallik murmured.

The whole herd was shifting like waves rolling over a beach, but they didn't seem to be going in any particular direction. They would feed for a while, then raise their heads, pace away for a few bear-lengths, then settle to feed again. A weird clicking noise came from them every time they moved.

"What's that funny noise they're making?" Lusa asked.

"They do it every time they walk." Ujurak eyed the caribou with interest, distracted from the uneasy brooding that had worried Lusa earlier.

"It's coming from their feet!" Kallik exclaimed, after watching for a moment longer. She raised one of her paws and flexed it curiously. "Why do caribou's feet click when bears' don't?"

"Who cares?" Toklo asked. "Maybe it's so we can creep up on our prey without their noticing. Their prey is *grass*. You don't have to sneak up on grass."

They wandered on, while the sun hauled itself almost to the height of the mountains before it slowly began to sink again. Days didn't last long here—not like when they'd been by Great Bear Lake, where the sun had barely dipped below the horizon before rising again.

"Hey, Toklo!" Lusa called. "How do you like the idea of sinking your teeth into a caribou? We'd never be hungry again!"

Toklo halted and scanned the nearest of the herd with a gleam in his eye. "No, I already said they're too big . . ." he muttered. His claws scraped the ground as if he was imagining how it would feel to rake them across a caribou's hide.

"I think you could do it," Ujurak told him.

Toklo blinked as a look of pride spread across his face. "Well, maybe a small one . . ."

Lusa noticed that he was eyeing the herd with much more interest now as they padded on. There were caribou calves among the herd, grazing beside the full-grown adults. *I bet Toklo could catch one of those.*

On the other side of the caribou, the ground sloped up more steeply and vanished into a dark growth of trees. The branches rippled in the wind, as if the whole hillside were the pelt of a huge animal.

"Look at the forest!" she exclaimed, jerking her snout in that direction. "Please can we go check it out? Please?"

"Looks good," Toklo agreed. "I could find my own territory there." His eyes focused with a gleam of determination. "Any bear who crossed my border had better watch out!" He gave Lusa a playful nudge. "I might let annoying black bears visit, though. Just to make sure they didn't starve."

"You can be annoying yourself!" Lusa bared her teeth at

him in a mock snarl. "I can look after myself, thank you very much. Miki showed me lots of tricks in the forest beside Great Bear Lake."

"That scared little cub? The one the white bears took?" Toklo's voice rose in disbelief.

"Miki knew a lot," Lusa assured him. She shot a sidelong glance at Kallik, trying to warn Toklo not to remind the white bear of how her brother, Taqqiq, and his friends had stolen the little black bear. Kallik still loved Taqqiq, whatever he had done. "He showed me what sorts of berries were the best, and how to find grubs underneath stones. . . ."

"Berries . . . grubs?" Toklo growled, though his eyes still shone with amusement. "That's no sort of food for a bear."

"It's the best!" Lusa argued. "And ants . . . I never imagined that ants could taste so delicious."

"I'll settle for goose, thanks," Toklo said. "Or caribou." He eyed one of the herd that was clicking nervously past. "You're right, that would really fill our bellies."

"I'm hungry for seal," Kallik murmured, gazing back down the hill to where the white sea-ice glimmered on the horizon. "You don't know how exciting it is, crouching beside a hole in the ice and waiting for the seal to come up for a breath!"

"Exciting?" Toklo muttered into Lusa's ear. "If sitting all day freezing your fur off is exciting, then I'm a goose!"

Lusa gave him a stern look. "Doesn't the seal know you're there?" she asked Kallik.

"Not if you're really quiet," the white cub replied. "Then

when it appears, you have to be so quick, to drag it out and kill it before it can get away." She heaved a long sigh. "Seal meat is the best thing ever. . . . I can taste it now. I can't wait for the ice to come back!"

Seeing the glow in her eyes, Lusa knew she had to feel happy for her, though a prickle of apprehension ran down her spine. The day when they would follow their separate paths couldn't be far away.

"I love building a snow cave and curling up inside it," Kallik went on. "It's so cozy to listen to the wind whistling outside and know you're warm and safe. And swimming with beluga whales—"

"Swimming with *whales*?" Lusa's fur bristled with alarm. "Isn't that how your mother died?"

"No, it was an orca whale that killed Nisa. Belugas are different." Kallik's eyes clouded with memories, making Lusa sorry she had asked the question. *Bee-brain! Think before you open your big mouth!* "The beluga won't hurt you," Kallik went on, brightening a little. "I wish I could show you the ice, Lusa. You'd love it."

I doubt it, Lusa thought, gazing out at the silver shimmer on the edge of sight. Just the idea of all that emptiness made her ache inside. How could that ever feel like home? *Not a tree in sight! I'd get blown away like a leaf, if I didn't freeze into an icicle first!*

"I think forests are best for black bears," she told Kallik.

"They're certainly better for brown bears," Toklo declared. "I'll mark out my territory before the snow comes, and then I'll dig myself a nice warm den and settle down to wait for the sun to come back." He yawned as if he was ready to close his eyes right now. "Then I'll wake up and find a river, and catch all the fish I can eat. That's the best way for bears to live—isn't that right, Ujurak?"

The smaller brown cub jumped. "What?"

Lusa realized that Ujurak hadn't said a single word while the rest of them were remembering their homes and making plans for the future. "Is something wrong?" she asked.

Ujurak's puzzled brown gaze rested on her. "I . . . I don't know," he began uncertainly. "I mean, yes, something is wrong, but I'm not sure what it is."

Toklo gave an exasperated sigh. "Ujurak, your brain's full of fluff! We're here; we've made it. This is a good place, with all the prey we can eat and not a flat-face in sight. This is the end of the trail."

Ujurak straightened up, raising his snout. "No," he replied; his voice was stronger now and more certain. "I don't know exactly what is wrong, but I know one thing for sure: This isn't the end of our journey."

Lusa remembered uneasily that when Ujurak had first looked down at the plain from the slopes of Smoke Mountain, he hadn't been sure that this was the place they were looking for. Now he seemed to have made up his mind. She felt even more uneasy when she remembered the dream that had come to her in the mountains, the dream that told her that she must save the wild. She had managed to push it out of her mind for a while, but Ujurak's doubts had brought it back.

"It *is* the end, Ujurak," Toklo protested. "It has to be.

There's nowhere else to go." He gestured with one paw at the sea below. "This is as far as we can travel without getting our paws wet."

Ujurak gazed down at the stretch of wrinkled gray water with the encroaching ice glistening on the horizon. Then he looked back at Toklo. His brown eyes were pleading for one of them to understand what he was saying. "I know you must be right . . . but if this is the end, then why don't I feel it?"

CHAPTER THREE

Toklo

Toklo let out a huff of exasperation. "Stop being such a worry-face!" he exclaimed, giving Ujurak an affectionate shove that almost carried the smaller bear off his paws.

"I'm not a worry-face," Ujurak protested. "It's just . . ."

His voice trailed off. Toklo shook his head in confusion. He had never truly understood Ujurak's impulse to keep traveling, following his invisible path past places that would make great territories.

"You know what?" Toklo snorted. "You've never known anything but traveling. So you can't imagine what it's like to settle down." Ujurak had never talked about his BirthDen or his mother, and something had stopped Toklo from asking about them. Did he even *have* a mother? And if he did, was she a bear or something else? "It'll feel good, I promise," he assured Ujurak. "Just think—we can make our own territories here and catch a tasty caribou, or a goose, anytime we want. We won't be hungry ever again." Surely that was what mattered most of all, after they'd nearly starved in the mountains

and been hungry enough to steal flat-face food that Lusa
found? Had Ujurak already forgotten what hunger was like?

"Maybe you're right," Ujurak muttered, not meeting Toklo's
gaze. "But I can't help what I feel. There's something tugging
at me, telling me that we have to go on."

"Well, tell it to go on its own!" Toklo huffed. "Can't you see
how great this place is?"

"We don't have to talk about this now," Lusa broke in. "It's
more important to decide where we'll make our dens for the
night. If we don't hurry up, it'll be too dark to see where we're
going."

Toklo let out an irritated snort; it was especially annoying
because he had to admit Lusa was right. The sun was going
down; this wasn't the time to stand around arguing. "Okay,
let's go," he said.

He led the way to the top of a ridge in the foothills. Beyond
it the ground sloped down into a wide valley. At the valley's
head he could just make out a waterfall, tumbling down from
the mountains. On the floor of the valley the waterfall split
into countless narrow channels flowing swiftly past a scattering of rocky islands.

"That looks like a good place," said Kallik. "If we swam out
to one of those islands, nothing could sneak up on us."

"And there might be fish," Ujurak added hopefully.

Once they reached the edge of the river Toklo could see
that they wouldn't have to swim. The fast-flowing stream
ran clear over brown pebbles; when Toklo waded out, it came
scarcely halfway up his legs.

The others followed. "The water's freezing!" Lusa squealed, bounding through it and throwing up fountains of spray.

Toklo veered away from her. "Watch it! You're soaking my fur."

They headed for one of the biggest islands, a grassy stretch in the middle of the river with a ragged circle of large boulders covering the upstream end. Toklo flopped down gratefully in the shade.

"Let's rest. We can fish in the morning. And explore the woods," he added when he saw Lusa looking expectantly at him.

His friends settled down around him. Lusa was soon snoring, her paws wrapped over her nose. Ujurak yawned, flattened the grass to make a smoother spot to lie on, then followed her into sleep. Kallik stayed awake longer, her snout raised and her gaze fixed on the sky, but at last her head drooped and her eyes closed.

Toklo found that he couldn't sleep. He watched the river turn to red as the sun sank toward the horizon, then fade to the color of storm clouds as the last rays of light shrank behind the mountains. He wriggled, trying to find a position that would send him to sleep. But the ground beside the rocks was soft and grass covered; there weren't any loose pebbles digging into him to keep him awake. No, it was the scent of the caribou herd, still trailing tantalizingly from the hills they had crossed, that was stopping him from going to sleep. So much food, all in one place, clicking its way into his thoughts.

I'd be fine on my own, he thought. He could picture himself as a full-grown bear, striding across his own territory, marking the trees to warn off other bears. He could almost hear himself roar as he challenged his rivals and hunted down prey. He couldn't lie still a moment longer, trying to sleep. He needed to prowl! This was his home now; he could go wherever he wanted, hunt whatever he chose. Careful not to rouse his sleeping companions, he rose to his paws and waded out into the river.

The surface of the water was a sheet of rippling silver touched with white foam where the river splintered against rocks. The only sound was the gurgling of the current. Toklo took in deep breaths of the clear mountain air, enjoying the icy touch of water against his legs. He felt exhilarated to see night falling again, after so many moons without true darkness. He could feel his dusty pelt being washed clean by the river, his pads soft and cool on the smooth round stones, so that the moons of journeying faded away.

His grumbling belly brought him back to reality. Bending his head, he studied the water and soon spotted the dark gray flicker that betrayed the presence of a fish. He settled himself more comfortably, legs braced against the current, and waited.

The flicker came again. This time Toklo struck, plunging his snout into the water a little downstream of the glimmering shadow. His teeth met in a plump, cold body, and he straightened up with a wriggling fish in his jaws. Toklo gulped it down where he stood, remembering that other river—a single great tongue of water, much wider than this one—skylengths away from here, where he had been swept off his paws trying to catch his first salmon and nearly washed up in the jaws of Shoteka. So much had changed since he had been abandoned by his mother and had met the strange cub Ujurak. He wasn't the same bear anymore.

Swiping his tongue around his jaws, he looked up at the sky and spotted the star-bear, shining alone in the dark sky.

I felt like him once, Toklo thought. *The other animals fought with me or drove me away. I was lonely and miserable, just like he is.*

But not any longer, he told himself. He was bigger and stronger now. He had proved himself at Great Bear Lake, where he had accepted the challenge to swim to Paw Print Island and defended his territory there against his old enemy. Toklo's claws rasped against the pebbles on the riverbed as he remembered how Shoteka had fled, defeated and disgraced. Having the island as his territory had made Toklo feel proud and strong and independent. He wanted that feeling again.

He glanced over his shoulder to where Ujurak was sleeping at the foot of a boulder, his nose resting on his paws. *I promised him I would look after him, and I have,* Toklo thought with satisfaction. *We made it together, all the way to this place where we can live well and safely, just like brown bears should.*

Even so, Toklo couldn't help feeling slightly uneasy. Ujurak kept insisting that the journey wasn't over. Would the smaller bear be able to survive if he continued the journey on his own?

Toklo shrugged. *He'll get over it, once he understands what a good place this is. I couldn't save Tobi, but I have saved Ujurak.* He nodded to himself. His mind was made up, and he was glad to realize that he didn't feel any sadness. The time was right for him to go it alone. Wading out of the river, he settled down beside his friends; their muffled breathing soothed him as he drifted into sleep.

We'll say good-bye soon, he thought drowsily. *I'm glad to have known you all, but it's almost time for me to leave.*

CHAPTER FOUR

Kallik

Kallik opened her eyes on darkness shot through with silver. A couple
of bear-lengths away, the river splashed between the smooth
gray rocks, its surface flashing with the reflections of moon
and stars. Around her lay the humped shapes of her friends,
snoring softly in deep sleep.

Excitement filled Kallik's belly, powerful as the surge of
the river. She wasn't sure what had roused her from sleep, but
she felt as if something momentous was about to happen. She
looked up and saw Silaluk, the great star-bear, blazing out
from the blue-black sky.

Was it you that woke me?

She stared at the glittering ice spots that surrounded Silaluk, wondering which one of them was her mother's spirit.
The thought that Nisa might be looking down on her filled
her with happiness. "Thank you for bringing us safely to this
wonderful place," she whispered. "I know I would never have
made it without you."

Thinking back on her journey, the struggle from the melting

Frozen Sea through the land of sunbaked earth and stones, Kallik still found it hard to believe that her quest was over. She had been alone then, drifting like a piece of broken ice on the waves. Only her determination to find her brother and the unfailing light of Silaluk above her had kept her trudging on. Sadness welled up inside her as she thought about Taqqiq. She had been so delighted to find him beside Great Bear Lake, and even happier when he had agreed to join her and the others on their journey.

"But it didn't work out," she whispered out loud.

Taqqiq hadn't been able to get along with the other bears, and with every step away from the lake his conviction had grown that it was wrong for him to be traveling with them. Finally he had decided to go back to the lake and tried to trick Kallik into returning with him.

"He wanted to be with me," she murmured. *But not enough to stay,* she added silently.

Kallik let out a long sigh. There was nothing more she could do for Taqqiq; it was unlikely they would ever meet again. That part of her life had to be frozen deep inside her, locked in a block of ice. But at least now she knew that her brother was alive and that he could fend for himself.

"Good-bye, Taqqiq." She whispered the words to the empty air. "May the spirits be with you."

Exhaustion swept over her, and her eyes felt heavy. She closed them again, letting herself sink back into sleep. In her dreams she bounded tirelessly across the ice while her mother's face shone down on her from the sky, her eyes filled with love.

* * *

When Kallik next woke, the ice spirits had faded from the sky and a red band of mist hung over the horizon. The other bears were already awake and had padded down to the water's edge, black shapes outlined against the milky light. Kallik rose to her paws, gave her pelt a shake, and headed over to join them.

Toklo stood in the river with the water flowing around his legs, staring intently at the surface. Lusa and Ujurak were both crouched on the bank, each gnawing at a fish.

Lusa looked up as Kallik approached her; fish scales were clinging to the fur around her jaws. "Toklo caught a fish for me," she announced. "He'll catch one for you if you like."

Before Kallik could protest that she could catch her own, Toklo plunged his snout into the river and pulled out a glossy salmon. He tossed it to the bank, where it gasped and thrashed in front of Kallik's paws. She planted one paw on it and bit it hard behind its head to kill it quickly.

"You can have this one if you want," she told Toklo, looking up.

"No, you have it," Toklo said. "I can catch another."

Kallik hesitated. She didn't want Toklo to think that she couldn't find her own food. But she could see how proud he was to be providing for his friends. Besides, the smell of the fish was too enticing for her to wait for long. "Thanks!" she said, squatting down to eat.

The fish was plump and succulent, its scent and taste bringing Kallik's dreams of the ice and ocean back to her mind. "I have to go to the ocean today," she announced.

"What?" Toklo glanced up from studying the current. "Have you got bees in your brain? We're heading into the hills, remember? Lusa wants to check out the forest."

"I know. I'm sorry," Kallik said. "But the ocean is my home, just like the forest is yours." Her voice quavered. "And I haven't seen it for so long."

Lusa gulped down the mouthful she was chewing. "I understand. I'll come with you," she said. "We can go to the forest tomorrow."

"I'll come, too," Ujurak added quietly.

Toklo waded out of the river with another fish in his jaws and crouched down to feed, tearing into the flesh with enormous bites.

"Toklo, are you coming to the ocean with us?" Lusa asked.

Toklo blinked at her, almost as if he hadn't heard the question. "No, I don't think so," he replied at last. "I want to check out the caribou."

Lusa flashed a swift glance at Kallik.

Is this where we say good-bye? Kallik wondered.

"Okay," Lusa said. Kallik thought she was trying to sound cheerful, and not succeeding very well. "I guess this is it, then. I . . . I hope you find a good place to make your territory."

"Don't be such a fluff-brain," Toklo mumbled around a mouthful of fish. "I'm not going anywhere. I'll see you later."

"Oh—I mean, great!" Lusa's eyes brightened as she bounced to her paws.

Leaving Toklo to finish eating, Kallik, Lusa, and Ujurak waded across the river and followed along the bank as it wound gently down to the plain. Kallik's paws tingled. She felt as if every step was leading her closer to the ice: The ground smelled of it, and she could taste it in the pool of water where they stopped briefly for a drink.

As the view opened up and they could see the plain once more, they disturbed a flock of snow geese. The birds went whirling up into the sky, filling the air with the clamor of their wings and their harsh cries.

Kallik paused to watch as the flock formed into a ragged wedge shape and flew off across the open ground. Her excitement rose as her gaze followed them and she saw the edge of the ocean, the blue waves stretching to the horizon where she could see the tempting shimmer of ice.

"Come on!" she called to Lusa and Ujurak. "It's not far now!"

She quickened her pace until she was bounding along, with her friends panting after her, splashing through the river's wandering channels. Mounds of tough, springy grass grew up to the water's edge, delicate wildflowers dancing among them. High in the pale sky, a golden eagle hovered.

The light strengthened as the sun rose, turning the surface of the water to dazzling silver. The darkly forested slopes were far behind them now, and Kallik shivered with anticipation at the cries of seabirds coming from up ahead. As the river neared the ocean, she left the bank and struck across the shore at an angle until she could stand at the very edge, with seawater lapping at her paws. The air was laden with the scents of ice and fish.

"Home . . ." she whispered.

Narrowing her eyes, Kallik peered at the ice in the distance. Its frosty glimmer merged with the haze at the bottom of the sky. *Can I swim out to it yet?* she wondered. *It seems very far away. . . .*

"Kallik . . ." Lusa said nervously behind her.

Kallik turned her head to see Lusa and Ujurak backing away, staring at something farther along the shore. Following their gaze, she spotted another white bear with two half-grown cubs, trundling along the shoreline toward them. For a moment a pang of sorrow stabbed at her belly. *That should have been Nisa and Taqqiq and me. . . .*

Lusa and Ujurak, wary of a strange bear so much bigger than they were, scurried to take shelter behind a nearby thornbush, but Kallik stayed where she was until the she-bear and her cubs came up to her. "Greetings," she said, dipping her head respectfully to the mother bear. "Are you going onto the ice?"

The she-bear's eyes widened in shock as she gazed at Kallik. "You're so thin, young one!" she exclaimed. "Where have you come from?"

"From another sea, a long way away," Kallik replied. "The ice melted there, so I crossed the land to Great Bear Lake, and then to here. I was looking for the Place of Everlasting Ice."

"You have come so far!" The mother bear breathed out the words in amazement, while her two cubs stared at Kallik as if she were Silaluk herself, come down from the sky. "I've only ever met one other bear who made that journey from the other

SEEKERS: THE LAST WILDERNESS   35

Frozen Sea. Her name was Siqiniq; she was very wise."

"I know Siqiniq!" Kallik exclaimed joyfully. "I met her at Great Bear Lake. She was my friend."

The mother bear dipped her head. "I'm glad to hear Siqiniq still lives. I was only a cub when I met her, but I've never forgotten her. How did you manage the journey?" she went on. "So many skylengths, and alone!"

"I wasn't alone," Kallik replied. "Not all the way. I had friends with me." She pointed with her snout toward Ujurak and Lusa, who were peering out anxiously from behind the thornbush.

The she-bear flinched, instinctively stepping between them and her cubs, who huddled behind their mother. "A brown bear and a black bear?" she growled. "What are they doing so close to the sea? Those kinds don't often come down to the shore."

"They won't try to hurt you, or your cubs," Kallik assured her. "They're just waiting for me and they've helped me come all this way. But now I think my journey's at an end." She turned again to gaze out to sea. "I've found what I was searching for. The Place of Everlasting Ice."

Was the ice closer than when she had first seen it? Kallik wasn't sure, but her longing to swim out to it, to be part of that cold, white world again, was so strong that she could taste it. "Are you going to the ice?" she asked the she-bear.

"Not yet," the she-bear answered. "I'll wait until my cubs are stronger first."

Kallik eyed the two cubs. They looked strong to her

already, plump and healthy, so different from the wretchedly thin bears she had seen on the shore of the Melting Sea and at Great Bear Lake. With their mother to take care of them, they were sure to reach the ice soon.

Longingly Kallik gazed out at the ice again. Its pull was overwhelming; her ears filled with the murmurings of the ice spirits, the sound of ice crystals forming in the water. The ice seemed to have drawn closer already. Kallik felt as if she could stretch out her snout and touch it. Her paws carried her into the sea; she could feel the cold touch of the waves as they lapped around her legs. Her excitement rising, she waded deeper into the icy water.

Then she halted abruptly as a huge paw rested on her back. "Wait, little one," came the voice of the mother bear. "The ice will soon return."

The whispering of the spirits faded, drowned by the cries of seabirds and the rush of wind in Kallik's ears. She became aware once more of the wide stretch of open sea that separated her from the ice.

Kallik wrenched herself free from the lure of the ice. She was standing several bear-lengths from the shore, the waves washing against her belly fur. Beside her, the she-bear watched her with worried bright eyes.

"Sorry," Kallik said hoarsely, beginning to head back to shore. "You're right. I'll wait." Wading out of the sea, she shook water from her pelt and dipped her head to the mother bear. "Thank you."

"You're welcome, young one," the mother bear replied.

"Maybe we will meet again, on the ice."

"I hope so," Kallik replied.

Calling her cubs to her, the mother bear trudged off along the shore. With one more curious stare at Kallik, the cubs followed, their stubby tails bobbing as they scampered over the stones. Kallik glanced across to where Lusa and Ujurak were still peering anxiously from behind the bush.

"Are you okay?" Lusa called.

"Fine," Kallik replied, plodding up the beach to join them.

Their concern for her filled her with warmth, but she knew that however much she loved them, the pull of the ice was stronger. For the first time, she realized that when the ice came close enough to the shore, she would be able to leave them without regret.

My path is different from theirs, she told herself. *Soon I must go where they can't follow.*

CHAPTER FIVE

Lusa

Lusa, Kallik, and Ujurak turned back toward the low hills. Lusa kept close to Kallik's side and her anxiety gradually ebbed away. For a few heart-stopping moments she had thought that her friend was going to leave her forever and swim out toward the glittering ice on the horizon. Relief had flooded over her when Kallik had turned back.

But she'll go as soon as the ice reaches the shore, a small inner voice nagged at her.

Lusa pushed the thought away. She would deal with parting from Kallik when it happened, and not before. For a while they wandered along, following the line of the shore. Ujurak bounded down to the water's edge to sniff at a piece of wood washed up on the pebbles, only to bounce out of the way as a bigger wave surged in and swirled around his paws.

"I'm soaked!" he exclaimed, trotting back toward his friends, scattering shining water drops from his fur.

Kallik nudged his shoulder with her snout. "Now do you know how wonderful it is to have your paws in the ocean?"

Ujurak wrinkled his nose. "The water doesn't taste very nice," he commented, licking droplets from his muzzle.

Kallik snorted. "You don't have to drink it!"

Gradually they veered inland, heading back toward the hills, stopping where the pebbly beach gave way to scrub so they could strip a thornbush of its berries. Halfway through her second mouthful, Lusa realized she could hear a tremendous rattling and clacking coming from beyond the ridge.

"What's *that*?" Kallik barked.

"Let's go see!" Ujurak bounded ahead, halting at the top of the slope. "Look!" he exclaimed as Lusa and Kallik scrambled up beside him.

Lusa stared down into the next valley at the moving river of caribou, massed so close together that she could hardly see the ground they were walking on. The loud rattling was coming from their feet as they headed away from the coast, many times louder and faster than the rattling from the lazily ambling caribou they'd seen the day before.

"Where are they all going?" Kallik asked, tilting her head to one side. "There's nothing chasing them."

Lusa shrugged. She had no idea what could have prompted the herd to move off all together like this. Did they feel Ujurak's urge to travel, or the powerful pull that was drawing Kallik back to the ice?

"Toklo will be disappointed," she said. "He wanted to hunt them."

While she was speaking, she spotted a flat-face den at one side of the valley. It was built of tree trunks, and it blended so well into the landscape that Lusa hadn't noticed it until now. Her heart began to race. She gave Kallik a nudge with her snout. "Look over there."

Kallik's eyes stretched wide with dismay. "That's a flat-face den! There aren't supposed to be any flat-faces here."

Looking more closely, Lusa spotted flat-face pelts strung on a line at one side of the den, and a wisp of smoke coming from a round thing like a tree stump on the roof.

"There's something odd . . ." she muttered.

Snuffing the air, she figured out what was different about this den. There was no smell of BlackPaths around it, or the heavy scent of the flowers flat-faces grew in their gardens. The den didn't just blend into the valley because it was made from tree trunks; it didn't even have a distinctive flat-face scent. "Maybe these flat-faces aren't dangerous," Ujurak suggested hopefully.

"Aren't flat-faces always dangerous?" Kallik huffed.

As they stood peering down at the den, the door was flung wide and a young flat-face cub burst into the open. He was pointing at the caribou herd and yelling something in a high-pitched voice. An older female flat-face followed the cub outside, along with a broad-shouldered flat-face male. All three of them wore pelts made of the same gray-brown fur as the caribou; the little cub had a brightly colored pelt on his head.

The female flat-face called the cub back to her, and all three of them watched the herd as they walked past. Lusa, Ujurak, and Kallik crouched side by side in the long grass, their gazes fixed on the little group.

"They haven't seen us," Kallik whispered. "Do you think we should go?"

"I can't see any firesticks—" Lusa began, breaking off when she noticed a familiar shape lying in the shadow of a rock not far from the flat-face den. *Toklo!*

Ujurak spotted him at the same moment. "There's Toklo," he announced cheerfully. "Let's sneak up on him and surprise him."

"Not in front of the flat-faces, fluff-brain," Lusa retorted.

At first she thought that Toklo was asleep, but then she noticed that his ears were alert. He was watching the caribou, muscles tensed, ready to spring into the hunt. But before he could move, Lusa noticed the little flat-face cub running toward the rock where the brown bear was hiding. With his gaze fixed on the caribou, Toklo hadn't seen him.

"Ujurak, look!" Lusa exclaimed, her heart beginning to thump with panic. She remembered the time when Toklo had been so desperate for food he had almost attacked another flat-face cub. What would he do now if the little flat-face interrupted his hunt? "We've got to do something!" she went on. "Ujurak—"

She swung around toward her friend, only to see a young caribou hurrying down the slope to join the herd, his feet clicking briskly. Horns were sprouting from his head as he trotted away.

"Oh, no!" she exclaimed, annoyance mingling with her fear. "Ujurak's done it again!"

Turning back to the rock, Lusa saw that the young flat-face had scampered up to Toklo and was reaching out to him. Toklo looked up in surprise, then stretched out his muzzle toward the cub. Was he preparing to launch himself forward? Lusa and Kallik were too far away to do anything. Lusa dug her claws into the ground, flinching at the thought of Toklo's jaws closing on the cub's paw, but all the grizzly did was to sniff suspiciously at the little flat-face's fur coat. The flat-face cub didn't look scared at all.

"Toklo doesn't know what to make of him," Kallik commented, amusement in her voice.

Lusa's heartbeat steadied as she realized that Toklo wasn't going to hurt the cub. He was pressing himself back against the rock while the little flat-face patted him with one paw, letting out happy cries. Lusa snorted as she imagined Toklo huffing with vexation. He was trapped, helpless as a rabbit, by a tiny flat-face!

At the same time, the last of the caribou herd disappeared up the valley; the clattering sound died away and only the trampled ground showed where they had passed. Toklo had missed his chance of prey.

The flat-face cub turned away from Toklo and scrambled up to the top of the rock. Suddenly he tottered and fell over, letting out a loud cry. Lusa could see a rip in the pelt that covered his hind legs, and blood trickling out of it. Toklo leaped backward in alarm.

Panic surged up in Lusa. "Oh, no—the flat-faces will think Toklo hurt him! They'll get their firesticks and—"

She broke off as the male flat-face sprinted over to the squalling cub and swung him up into his arms. He glanced at Toklo, but didn't shout at him or try to hurt him. Instead he carried the cub over to the old flat-face female and spoke to her for a few moments while the young one's howls grew quieter. Then he carried the cub away, around the corner of the den.

"Now what's he doing?" Lusa wondered out loud.

She found out a moment later when the two flat-faces reappeared, riding on top of a very small firebeast with a spindly body, like the skeleton of a deer, and two very thin round paws; the big flat-face sat up straight, holding the antlers of the firebeast, while his cub clung on behind. Lusa could see scarlet blood soaking into the pelt around his leg, and she could smell the salty tang on the breeze. The male waved to the older female; then he and his cub disappeared up the valley in the wake of the caribou.

"Great stars! What was that?" Kallik gasped, her eyes wide with astonishment.

"It looks like a . . . a sort of a firebeast without the fire," Lusa replied, aware that it wasn't much of an explanation.

Kallik shook her head. "Flat-faces are weird."

The female flat-face had gone back into the den and closed the door. Once she had gone, Lusa and Kallik bounded down the hill to join Toklo.

"Well done!" Lusa yelped as she bounced up to the big grizzly cub. "You were really kind to that young flat-face."

Toklo huffed in embarrassment. "Little pest. I was about to

catch a caribou, but the cub messed things up. He smelled of caribou," he added. "He's lucky I didn't eat him instead!"

"You don't mean that," Lusa said, hoping she was right. "Though I was a bit worried you might mistake the cub for a caribou at first."

"No chance," Toklo muttered. "He was far too noisy. Definitely a flat-face!"

He rose to his paws and stood facing toward the head of the valley, in the direction the caribou had gone. Taking a deep sniff of the air, he growled, "We should follow them. One of those would feed us for days!"

"But you can't—" Lusa began, remembering that Ujurak had joined the herd.

"Why not?" Toklo interrupted. "We should go after them while there's still a chance of catching up. What if they're leaving here for good?"

Lusa exchanged a glance with Kallik. "You can't hunt the caribou," she explained patiently, "because Ujurak is one of them."

Toklo let out a snort of disgust. "Then he'd better watch out!"

Without waiting for a response, he charged off up the valley after the caribou.

CHAPTER SIX

Toklo

Snuffing up the enticing scents of the caribou, Toklo followed their trail along the valley. Steep mountain slopes reared up on either side, while in the valley bottom the trail wound between ponds and stretches of marshy ground. Toklo gazed around him and breathed in the mountain air. *This is the right sort of place for bears!* He was aware of Lusa and Kallik padding after him, but he didn't wait for them to catch him. He was concentrating too hard on his prey.

Soon the trail joined another river, the bank heavily rutted with caribou hooves. The valley twisted and turned; sometimes Toklo caught the sound of the caribou's clicking hooves and thought he was about to see them at last, only to find that around the next bend the sound faded again.

Pausing briefly, Toklo studied the caribou hoofprints, trying to judge the speed of the herd from the depth of the prints and the distance between them. In the heart of the herd he spotted smaller prints; water flooded his jaws as he imagined bringing down a young caribou and feasting on it.

Toklo set off again, bounding faster in pursuit of the herd. Rounding yet another bend, he halted at the sight of a flat-face denning area: a group of dens made from the same neatly lopped tree trunks as the one farther down the valley where he had met the little cub.

"More flat-faces!" he growled, a shock of disappointment running through him. "I thought there weren't any here in the wilderness. But they get everywhere."

Trotting briskly down the track toward him was another brown bear; Toklo breathed a sigh of relief as he recognized Ujurak. No matter what he had said to Lusa and Kallik, he didn't want to mistake his friend for a caribou and kill him.

"Hi!" Ujurak called as he came into earshot. "Did you see all the caribou? Aren't they amazing?"

Toklo ignored the question. "How far away are they?" he demanded, bounding forward to meet Ujurak. "When did they pass through?"

"Oh, they're long gone," Ujurak replied. His eyes were sparkling; he had obviously enjoyed his brief journey with the herd. "You'll never catch up with them now."

Weasel-brain! Toklo thought to himself. *We're not just here to have fun. Don't you want a good meal?*

"That pesky flat-face cub," he grumbled. "If he hadn't gotten in the way, I would have caught a caribou."

"Ujurak, you're back!" Lusa greeted the smaller brown cub

as she and Kallik padded up. "What was it like, traveling with the caribou?"

"Great!" Ujurak replied, with a little bounce of excitement. "The whole herd of us, on the move together. Did you hear the sound we made?"

Toklo gave an exasperated snort. "Tell us something useful. Where are they going? Will they come back?"

Ujurak shook his head. "Not until next fishleap. They come here when the days grow longer, to feed and have their calves on the plain. The cold winds from the sea keep insects away, but just lately flies have been bothering them. I think that's what sent them off into the mountains."

"I don't know why we can't follow them," Toklo complained; he still felt furious that he had been cheated of the juicy prey. "They weren't going that fast when we saw them."

"Some flat-faces appeared with firesticks—"

"Firesticks?" Kallik interrupted, looking around worriedly. "Then we're not safe here!"

"They're a long way up the valley," Ujurak reassured her. "The herd stampeded, with the hunters after them. That's when I decided I'd better turn back into a bear, and I let them leave me behind."

"You have some sense, then!" Toklo butted the smaller cub with his snout, still irritated, but glad that his friend was safe.

"But what about these no-claw hunters?" Kallik still sounded anxious. "They'll be just like the ones who chased us on Smoke Mountain. We'd better get away from here."

"But I don't think these flat-faces were interested in hunting bears," Ujurak explained, sounding a little uncertain. "They weren't like those others. These had . . . animal spirits!"

Toklo stared at Ujurak. *What's the fluff-brain going on about now? Flat-faces don't have animal spirits!*

"What do you mean?" Lusa asked, tipping her head to one side.

"I'm not sure. I could just feel it," Ujurak replied, shrugging. "Come on, I'll show you."

He led the way to the top of a gentle rise from where they could look down on the flat-face denning area. Toklo followed the others reluctantly. If the caribou were out of reach, it was time to start looking for other prey, not to wander about close to flat-faces. From the crest of the hill he could see a large firebeast sleeping outside one of the dens, and a number of the weird little firebeasts, like the one the male flat-face and the cub had used. *Maybe they're firebeast cubs?* he guessed.

Beyond the firebeasts, several flat-face cubs were kicking something round back and forth to one another. Toklo twitched his ears at their high-pitched cries.

"What spirits have they got?" he muttered. "Mosquitoes?"

Ujurak ignored him. "Look down there," he said, pointing with his muzzle to where a female in a shiny red pelt was sweeping the patch of ground in front of her door. She pattered to and fro on flat paws, darting out her head as she jabbered in flat-face talk to an old male flat-face sitting outside the den next to hers.

"She has a goose spirit," Ujurak announced. "And the old male has a brown bear spirit."

Toklo stared at the male flat-face. He was plump, hunched up on his seat; his hair and face were covered in curly brown fur.

"He's not a bear!" Toklo exclaimed, thoroughly offended.

He would never have admitted it to the others, but privately he sensed an air of peace enfolding this place, something he had never felt before around flat-faces. There was no trace of the threat they had experienced from the flat-faces on Smoke Mountain.

Or maybe they're just good at hiding it, he thought suspiciously.

"We shouldn't be here," he said aloud. "It's time to go. Bears and flat-faces shouldn't be around one another."

"Don't be such a grump, Toklo!" Ujurak shouldered Toklo playfully. "This is fun!"

"No, Toklo's right." Kallik's eyes were wary. "Haven't we had enough trouble with flat-faces? We should go."

"But there's nothing to be afraid of here," Lusa put in. "I *know* there isn't. These flat-faces remind me of the kind ones who looked after us in the Bear Bowl."

"Oh, you and your Bear Bowl!" Toklo huffed.

Before any bear could reply, the door of one of the dens opened and the little flat-face cub from farther down the valley trotted out.

Lusa's eyes danced with amusement. "There's your friend, Toklo!"

Toklo glared at her. *I'll never hear the last of this. I almost wish I'd eaten the little nuisance!*

The cub looked happy again. His injured leg must have been treated, because he ran quickly over to the older cubs and started to chase after the round thing they were kicking between them. The male who had brought him there—his father, Toklo supposed—appeared out of the same den, with an older male flat-face following him. He was tall, with long gray head fur, and wore a caribou pelt fringed at the edges. The two males talked together, pointing at the playing cubs.

"I could watch them all day!" Lusa murmured. "I like the sound of their voices. Look at the little one—he's got hold of the ball! Now he's throwing it!"

The "ball," Toklo realized, must be the round thing the cubs were kicking. He wondered what it was for; it didn't look as if you could eat it. Memories came back to him of playing with Tobi before his brother became too weak. Oka had made up all their games to teach them things they needed to know. Maybe this flat-face game was like that. He tried to remember if he had ever seen full-grown flat-faces doing something with balls.

As they watched, the door of a larger den opened and another adult female appeared. She shook some flat-face thing that made a loud clanging noise, and called to the bigger cubs. At once they ran across to the den and filed inside. One of them scooped up the ball and took it in with him. The little cub ran back to his father, pointing upward at a squawking flock of geese that swirled overhead before flying across the valley.

"Let's go now," Toklo said as the last of the cubs disappeared and the door of the den closed behind them. "I've had enough of this. And I'm hungry!"

CHAPTER SEVEN

Toklo

Toklo glanced back at Ujurak as he began padding down the hill, away from the flat-face dens, in the direction the geese had taken. The smaller cub looked reluctant to leave.

"Come on, Ujurak," he growled, sounding harsher than he meant to. "It's time to be brown bears, remember, hunting and building dens. Looking after ourselves."

"But I want to watch these flat-faces," Ujurak protested. "They're different, somehow."

"For stars' sake, flat-faces are flat-faces!" Toklo retorted. "We're wasting time!"

"Okay." Ujurak took one last glance at the flat-face dens, then bounded down the hill to Toklo's side. "Let's hunt."

Toklo gave him a friendly shove before leading the way through the valley, back in the direction of the coast. The lingering scent of caribou on the trail made it harder to detect other prey, but as they rounded a jutting spur of the hillside he spotted the geese again, feeding around a lake, their white feathers standing out against the tough grass.

"There." Toklo pointed with his snout. "Let's go."

On their way across the valley they kept low among the long grasses, wading a shallow stream and hiding behind rocks. But closer to the lake the ground flattened out until there was no other cover between them and their prey, no way of sneaking up without alerting the geese.

"We should get downwind so they don't pick up our scent," Kallik suggested.

"I know." Toklo sighed. The wind was blowing from exactly the wrong direction, and it was going to take forever to work their way around without being seen or scented. The geese could be long gone by then.

He signed to the others to stay back, then flattened himself to the ground as he tried to creep up on the geese. But before he could get near them, the whole flock rose flapping into the air, letting out raucous cries of alarm.

They flew a few bear-lengths, then settled again and began to feed. With frustration bubbling inside him, Toklo waited for his friends to catch up to him.

"Maybe we should spread out," Lusa offered. "That way, if they fly away from one of us, someone else might catch one."

"I suppose we could try," Toklo said grudgingly.

The bears separated so that they were creeping up on the flock of geese from different directions. But it didn't work. The geese spotted them long before they were close enough to pounce; they took to the air, and when they landed again they were still out of reach.

"This is stupid!" Toklo growled. His belly was howling with hunger by now; he was so angry with the geese, he could think of nothing but tearing into one and seeing the feathers fly. "We need another plan."

He beckoned to his friends with a toss of his head. "I have an idea," he began, when all three were clustered around him. "Ujurak, I want you to try a new way of hunting. Turn into a goose; then when you're in the middle of the flock, you can change back into a bear and grab one of them."

"Toklo, that's brilliant!" Lusa exclaimed.

"It's worth a try," Kallik agreed.

But to Toklo's dismay, Ujurak was looking uncertain. *What's wrong with the fluff-ball now?*

"I don't know. . . ." Ujurak sounded guilty, his brown eyes unhappy. "When I change, I . . . I really turn into the creature that I become. I think the same thoughts as they do and I feel what they feel. They're not prey anymore. I can't imagine hunting them."

"That's ridiculous!" Toklo snorted. "You're a bear all the time, right? Even when you're in the shape of something else? So you need to do what a bear does, and right now, bears are hunting these geese."

Ujurak shrugged doubtfully.

"Go on, Ujurak," Kallik begged him, her eyes sparkling. "It'll be fun!"

"Try it." Lusa poked Ujurak's shoulder with her snout. "I want to see you surprise those geese!"

Ujurak hesitated a little longer, staring at his paws, then took a deep breath and looked up. "Okay, I'll do it."

"Great!" Toklo was relieved that the smaller cub had come to his senses at last. He had to have this weird power for a reason, right? What better reason than helping to catch food?

Ujurak stood still for a moment, staring at the geese. Then his neck grew longer and thinner; his snout shrank and changed into a beak. His body became smaller, while his forelegs stretched out into wings. A ripple passed across his brown fur as it changed into white feathers. His hind legs grew spindly, with webbed feet instead of paws. At last, with a harsh cry, a snow goose took off, circled in the air above the bears' heads, and then flew over and alighted among the flock.

"I'll never get used to that," Lusa whispered.

Toklo kept his gaze fixed on the flock. They were feeding so close together, he was already uncertain which goose was Ujurak. And there was no sign of him transforming back into a bear again.

"What's he waiting for?" Toklo said irritably. "Can't he remember that he's really a bear?"

Kallik was scanning the flock, her eyes narrowed. "I think that's him," she said, pointing with her snout. "The big one, with the brown mark on his side."

Lusa shook her head. "I didn't notice any brown mark when he flew off."

Toklo scraped his claws on the ground. There was still no sign of any of the geese turning back into a bear.

"Toklo, do you think we should call him—" Lusa began.

A sudden clamor of honking and squawking from the geese interrupted her. The whole flock took off: not the short flutter to another feeding ground this time, but whirling high up into the air.

"Now what?" Toklo asked, exasperated.

"Look!" Kallik pricked her ears. "A wolf!"

Following her gaze, Toklo spotted the lean gray shape at the opposite side of the lake. It was stalking toward the flock, but as the birds rose into the air the wolf leaped forward, snarling, only to halt in frustration as the geese circled overhead.

I know how it feels, Toklo thought.

His annoyance grew when, instead of settling again, the geese formed into an irregular wedge shape and flew off, heading for the distant seashore. There wasn't a single one left by the lake.

"Ujurak's gone with them!" Kallik exclaimed.

"Oh, no!" Lusa's voice was filled with dismay. "I wish he wouldn't keep going off like this."

"Stupid squirrel-brain," Toklo muttered. "One of these days, he'll disappear and not be able to find us again."

Kallik let out a sigh. "Do you think we'd better follow him?"

"Maybe we should." Toklo broke into a gallop, chasing after the departing geese. "Come on!"

Lusa and Kallik bounded along by his side. Seeing the bears charging toward him, the wolf leaped back, startled, then turned tail and fled to the trees at the far side of the valley.

Good riddance! Toklo snarled inwardly. He remembered

being chased by wolves, back in the mountains with Lusa and Ujurak. It felt good to be big and fierce enough now to scare off a full-grown wolf.

"Ujurak! Ujurak!" he bellowed out loud. "Come back!"

CHAPTER EIGHT

Ujurak

Ujurak's wings beat strongly as he sliced through the sky above the lake. The wolf had dwindled to a gray speck at the edge of the water. Memories thronged his mind, though they were not his memories: bright, ravenous eyes, sharp teeth and snapping jaws, and the spattering of blood on white feathers. Vaguely he remembered a time when his own fangs had sunk into goose flesh, but it seemed as if that had happened to another creature, a long time ago.

Faint cries came from below; glancing down, Ujurak saw three small shapes bounding along in the wake of the flock. Black, white, and brown . . . Briefly Ujurak felt puzzled. He thought he should have remembered who they were, and why they were calling to him. But his confusion was swallowed up in the joy of his escape from the wolf, and the power of his wings as they cut through the air.

Around him the rest of the flock switched places and overtook one another until they were flying in a ragged triangle, heading for the ocean. Ujurak found himself about halfway down one side.

"Fly! Fly far! Leave wolf behind!" The honking cries of the geese surrounded him; Ujurak realized that the commands were coming from the lead goose and rippling from one bird to the next down both sides of the triangle.

"Fly far! Fly!" he croaked as the harsh cry reached him.

The hills fell away behind them and the coastal plain opened up ahead of the flock as the geese winged their way toward the sea.

"Feed well now!" Another command swept down the line of geese from their leader at the front. "Soon fly to other home! Feel sun on feathers!"

"Other home . . . sun . . . feed well . . ." As the geese passed the words back and forth, Ujurak could almost feel the warmth of the sun's rays soaking into his frail bird bones, and the longing to fly to this other home gripped him like a claw.

The sunlit vision distracted him so completely that he forgot to concentrate on his flying. A more powerful wingbeat sent him blundering into the goose ahead of him. Both birds fluttered and rolled in the air, trying to regain their balance. For a few dizzying moments the earth and sky whirled around Ujurak; he didn't know which way to fly. A third goose, following just behind, lost its rhythm, too, and flapped wildly to recover.

"Slug-brain!" the first goose hissed at Ujurak. "Did you just hatch, or what?"

"Slug-brain . . . slug-brain . . ." The insult rippled on down the line.

"Sorry!" Ujurak struggled to regain his place. Beating his wings to propel himself forward was a lot harder now that he was outside the wedge. Air currents tugged at him and buffeted him around the sky. With a massive effort he caught up to the rest of the flock and found another place within the wedge. Flying was instantly easier as he rode in the rush of air created by the goose in front of him.

The two others found places, glaring at Ujurak and then ignoring him. Ujurak reminded himself to stay out of their feathers once the flock landed.

Whirling behind the leader, Ujurak spotted an eerie shadow on the far horizon. It looked as if a storm cloud had sunk to earth. There were flashes of light inside it and some kind of solid structure that Ujurak couldn't see clearly.

"Bad place!" the goose leader honked as he veered away from it. "No food! Bitter water!"

"Bad . . . bitter . . ." the rest of the flock repeated.

"Noisy beasts! Landwalkers! Never go there!" the leader ordered.

"Never go there. . . ."

Ujurak didn't know what the geese were talking about, but their words called up a feeling of dread inside him. He remembered that the very first time he had set paw in this place—*Paw? Not wings?*—he had felt uneasy. He had known that this wasn't where the journey was supposed to end. Now the feeling of uneasiness intensified; all he wanted was to flee far away on strong wings so that he could put the ominous shadows out of his mind forever.

Instead he swooped down with the rest of the flock to land in a brackish meadow close to the water's edge. Seaweed was strewn all along the waterline; Ujurak's feathers prickled with anticipation as he spotted the tasty green and brown heaps, and he realized how hungry the flight had made him. He splashed across the muddy grass, shouldering his way through the crowd of geese, and began to feed.

Gulping down the first delicious strands, he remembered that there might be danger here, too. He raised his head, casting quick glances from side to side, all his senses alert for enemies. But he couldn't detect any wolves here; there were no bears close by, and no foxes either. No landwalkers. For the time being the flock was safe.

Ujurak lowered his head and tucked into the seaweed again. His pangs of hunger began to fade as he filled his belly. Then as he stretched out his neck to swallow a big clump of seaweed, he felt something hard hidden inside it. He retched, trying to get rid of it. Instead he felt a sharp pain as something stabbed into his throat from the inside.

Lowering his head, he tried to cough up the obstruction, and spotted a long, thin tendril trailing from his beak. It was clear and so fine that he had not seen it tangled up with the seaweed. Ujurak's throat spasmed and he broke into a burst of racking coughs as he struggled to free the tendril from his throat. Blood spurted out of his beak and the stabbing pain grew worse.

"Help!" he choked out. "I can't . . . can't breathe. . . ."

The geese around him turned to give him sharp, suspicious

looks, and when they saw he was in trouble they edged away from him. Ujurak realized despairingly that there was nothing they could do to help. He raised one foot in an effort to pull at the tendril, but the webbed pad swiped uselessly across it; unbalanced, he fell over on one side, flapping his wings in a panic.

A wave bigger than the rest washed over him, half lifting him as it retreated, washing strands of seaweed over him. The world was growing dark, clouds swirling around him.

Change . . . an inner voice told him. *You won't survive like this.*

Ujurak wasn't sure what the voice meant, but he stretched his limbs and soon his white feathers blurred, and brown fur flowed over his body. Still, his strength was ebbing fast. He gave one last hacking cough that shook his whole body, then let his head drop and lay limply in the surf, his blood flowing into the sea foam on the edge of the waves.

CHAPTER NINE

Kallik

Kallik pounded along the valley, desperately trying to keep the departing flock of geese in sight. Already they were almost a skylength away. Toklo ran beside her, while Lusa raced along a bear-length behind. Toklo had given up shouting for Ujurak to come back; he seemed to be saving all his breath for the chase.

Pebbles and gritty soil stung Kallik's paws as she ran in a wild zigzag, changing direction to follow the flock whirling above her. Her chest heaved as she fought for air.

What if they fly out of sight? Will Ujurak be able to find his way back?

The geese left the hills behind and flew on toward the coastal plain. They followed the line of the shore for a little way, then to Kallik's relief alighted on a smooth stretch of grass reaching down to the water's edge.

Thank you, Silaluk!

Toklo halted, and Kallik drew to a stop beside him. A moment later Lusa came panting up.

"What do we do now?" the little black bear gasped. "If we

just dash up to them, the whole flock will take off again."

"I know," Toklo growled. "Somehow we have to get closer to them. If we call out so that Ujurak hears us, he might remember he's a bear."

His eyes glittered with fury; Kallik was half-afraid of him when he was like this, but she knew that he was angry with Ujurak only because he was so worried about him.

"Maybe we're making a fuss about nothing," she ventured. "Ujurak has always come back before."

"That's right." Lusa's dark eyes sparkled. "He's been a gull, and an eagle . . . and do you remember, Toklo, when he was a mule deer and led the wolves away from us? That was before you joined us," she added to Kallik.

"Yes," Toklo snapped, still looking annoyed. "We had to wait forever for him to turn up again."

"But he *did* turn up," Lusa insisted. "And if he hadn't changed, we would have been wolf-prey. He'll remember this time, like he always has before."

Toklo snorted. "I just wish he'd remember he's supposed to be hunting for us."

"All right, suppose we creep up on him," Lusa suggested. "There are bushes and rocks we can use for cover."

"We can try," the young grizzly agreed.

He took the lead, treading softly from one clump of thornbushes to the next, as carefully as if he was stalking prey. Kallik and Lusa stayed hard on his paws. Eventually they reached the shelter of a dip in the ground where long grasses grew around a brackish pool. A stretch of open ground separated them from the flock.

Toklo dipped his snout into the pool for a quick drink. "This is where we have to show ourselves," he announced, shaking drops from his fur. "We'll run among the geese and call Ujurak's name. The rest of the flock will fly off, but if we're lucky, Ujurak will stay behind."

"And if we're not lucky?" Lusa asked.

"Then he can stay a goose for all I care!" Toklo retorted.

Lusa exchanged a glance with Kallik. "He doesn't mean it," she murmured.

Toklo snorted and burst out of the hollow, yelling, "Ujurak! Ujurak!"

"Ujurak, it's us!" Kallik cried as she raced after the brown bear with Lusa at her side.

As Toklo had predicted, the geese took to the air again. The sky seemed full of wildly beating wings. Kallik's heart slammed into her throat as she saw not a single white bird left on the seashore.

Then Lusa exclaimed, "Ujurak!"

She pointed with her snout, and Kallik made out a brown, humped shape lying in the surf; at first glance she'd taken it for a spit of sand. Now she realized it was a small brown bear, lying motionless on his side as the waves washed around him.

"What happened to him?" she panted as all three bears bounded toward him. "Did he fall? Did he forget how to fly?"

Toklo was the first to reach their friend, and nosed him carefully from snout to tail, while Kallik and Lusa looked on in horror. Ujurak hadn't stirred as they approached, hadn't even lifted his head to look at them.

"He's not dead," Toklo pronounced at last. "I can feel him breathing, but I don't know what's the matter with him."

Kallik bent down and sniffed Ujurak's sodden fur. His eyes were closed, and she had to watch carefully to see the faint rise and fall of his body as he breathed. Blood trickled from his mouth, dark and glossy against the seawater.

Then she noticed something shiny coming out of Ujurak's mouth along with the blood. She felt as cold as if an ice storm were blowing around her. "Look!" she whispered.

"What's that?" Lusa asked, stretching her neck to sniff the shiny stuff.

Toklo came up to see, and planted a paw on the shiny tendril. "He's swallowed something," he said. "I'll see if I can pull it out."

"No, don't!" Kallik flinched as Toklo swung around to face her, shock and worry flashing in his eyes. "Nisa told me about this stuff when we were together on the ice. It's called . . . fishing line. Flat-faces use it to pull fish out of the sea. Nisa told me it's really dangerous."

Toklo poked the line with one paw. "How do you catch a fish with that?"

"There's a hook on the other end," Kallik explained, blinking as she pictured what was happening to Ujurak right now. "I think Ujurak has it stuck in his throat. That must be where the blood is coming from."

"So what are we going to do?" Lusa squeaked.

"Don't pull it, to begin with," Kallik ordered. "That will just push the hook in deeper."

"Are we supposed to let him die in front of us?" Toklo growled.

"Of course not . . . Lusa, your paws are smallest. Can you reach down Ujurak's throat?"

"I'll try."

Kallik levered Ujurak's jaws open with her paws. When she tilted his head back—his eyes didn't open—she could see the line trailing down his throat, mixed up with scraps of half-chewed seaweed. Lusa tried to squeeze her paw into Ujurak's mouth, but it was clear right away that she couldn't reach far enough down his throat to find the hook.

"It's no use." Kallik let Ujurak's jaws close, and gently drew one paw down the side of his neck. He gave a muffled, rasping cough and then lay still again. Kallik stared hopelessly at Lusa and Toklo. Their friend was dying, and there was nothing they could do. Ujurak would know which herbs might help, maybe even how to get the hook out without hurting him more. But Ujurak couldn't help himself, and they were useless without him.

"We can't help him," said Lusa, echoing Kallik's thoughts, "but I think the flat-faces would know what to do."

"Oh, right," Toklo grumbled. "Like flat-faces would care about a bear."

"They will!" Lusa insisted. She sounded so certain that a tiny spark of hope flared up inside Kallik. "Back in the Bear

Bowl, there were flat-faces who healed bears. They took my mother away and made her better when she was sick."

"We're not in the Bear Bowl now, in case you haven't noticed," Toklo pointed out.

"And we don't know if there are any flat-faces who heal bears here," Kallik added, her spark of hope ready to be snuffed out.

"But we know they heal other flat-faces," Lusa retorted. "Remember the little cub who fell over and cut his leg? Later on we saw him running around, quite well again. That flat-face den where his father took him must be where the flat-face healer lives."

"And how does that help Ujurak?" Toklo asked.

But Kallik had already understood what Lusa meant. "If Ujurak can turn into a flat-face—" she said slowly.

"Then we can take him to the healer," Lusa finished, her eyes shining. "And the healer will help him."

Toklo grunted. "He was a flat-face cub when I first met him. But I don't know if he'll be able to change now."

Kallik nudged Ujurak's shoulder with her snout. "Come on, Ujurak, wake up! You have to be a flat-face."

Ujurak didn't move. Toklo shouldered Kallik aside and gave Ujurak a sharper prod. "Wake up!"

Ujurak moaned faintly and more blood trickled out of his mouth. His eyes flickered open, glazed with pain; he stared at his friends as if he didn't recognize them. A grating sound came from his throat.

"Don't try to talk," Kallik said, bending over him. "You're

hurt. But you have to turn into a flat-face so we can help you."

Ujurak blinked slowly, as if he didn't understand. Kallik peered at him, looking for the first signs of change, but he was definitely still a bear.

"It's no use; he can't—" Toklo began.

"He can and he *will*." Kallik wouldn't let any of them give up yet. "Come on, Ujurak. You know what a flat-face looks like. Please try."

"You don't have any fur, and your skin is pink," Lusa added, crouching down beside Ujurak on the other side from Kallik. "Your face is flat."

"Don't worry, we'll stay close." Kallik pressed herself against Ujurak's flank, feeling the cold of his sea-soaked fur. "We won't let the flat-faces hurt you."

A hoarse groan came from Ujurak. Very slowly, Kallik saw his fur start to melt away, until his body was patched with brown and pink. His legs grew thinner, twitching with pain as they transformed. Kallik watched with a mix of pity and wonder as her friend's forepaws stretched and divided, cramping into claw shapes. Ujurak let out another cry of pain, higher pitched this time, as his snout shrank and his ears twisted and flattened. At last the remaining patches of brown fur vanished, except for a tangle covering his head.

Kallik gazed down at the frail flat-face cub lying in front of her with the waves washing around him. He had lost consciousness again in the final stage of his transformation. His breath was faint and shallow. The fishing line still trailed from his mouth, with a froth of pink blood around his face.

"Come on," Lusa barked. "He'll die if we don't get moving."

"I'll carry him," Kallik offered.

"No, I will." Toklo stepped forward, looking stunned. Kallik could understand; Ujurak's transformations were usually so easy, and he looked as if he enjoyed them. This had been full of pain and had taken every last scrap of his strength.

"Okay, Toklo, lie down here," Lusa instructed him.

The grizzly cub obeyed. Together Lusa and Kallik pushed Ujurak onto Toklo's back. The brown bear rose to his paws with the pink flat-face cub draped over his shoulders; slowly and steadily he set off on the long trek back to the valley where they had seen the flat-face denning place. The sun was sinking, its sullen red gleams piercing through stormy gray clouds. Kallik knew instinctively that they had to get Ujurak to shelter before darkness fell. An injured flat-face cub, with no warm coat of fur, could never survive the cold night. That was the shape Ujurak needed to be in to be healed, but he seemed so vulnerable and frail in it!

She and Lusa plodded along on either side, ready to catch Ujurak if he started to fall off. Kallik remembered how she and Taqqiq used to ride on their mother Nisa's back. But that had been fun, one of the games on the ice with her brother that Kallik missed so much. This was more like the time Toklo had carried Lusa on his back after she was struck by the firebeast. They had been so afraid that Lusa would die, and now they were in another desperate race—this time to save Ujurak's life.

Ujurak shifted slightly, and Kallik rested her muzzle on his leg to keep him in place. She could feel how cold he was. She had always thought of flat-face skin as pink, but Ujurak was pale as snow, with a blue tinge like ice under the moon. He was still deeply unconscious, his head lolling.

"His spirit is ready to go," she whispered in horror.

"He'll be okay," Lusa tried to reassure her. "The flat-face healer will know what to do."

But Kallik couldn't share Lusa's optimism, or her confidence in the skill of flat-faces. She had watched Nisa and Nanuk die, even though she would have given anything to save them. Now Ujurak was fighting for his life.

As the bears trudged past the lone flat-face hut where they had first seen the cub, the first drops of rain began to fall; within moments it became a downpour. Wind drove it into their faces; their fur was soaked and the caribou trail they were following became a river of mud.

Toklo let out a growl. "This is all we need!"

The rain was bouncing off Ujurak's unprotected body, plastering his remaining fur close to his head. Kallik clamped her jaws on a howl of distress. She knew that the fragile cub needed warmth and shelter; instead the rain might be washing away his last chance of life. She couldn't even see if he was breathing anymore.

When they finally rounded the last curve of the valley and

came within sight of the flat-face denning area, there was no one to be seen.

"They're all keeping dry in their dens," Kallik murmured.

"So what do we do with Ujurak?" Toklo asked. "We need to get him into shelter, fast."

"That's where the little cub came out," Lusa said, pointing with her snout toward one of the wooden dens. "The healer must live there."

Without replying, Toklo veered from the caribou trail and plodded up to the door of the den. He crouched down; very gently Lusa and Kallik pulled Ujurak off his back and let him lie on the ground in front of the door. Kallik realized that he was still breathing, but his breath seemed shallow and quick.

"Come on," Toklo said, rising to his paws again. "Let's get out of here. We don't want the flat-faces to spot us."

He bounded off toward the shelter of a rocky outcrop at the edge of the caribou trail. Lusa raced after him. Before she joined them, Kallik let out a long, low-pitched howl.

"Help! Our friend is hurt! Come quickly!"

Then, without looking back, she followed the others. As soon as she reached the rock where they were hiding, Kallik poked her head out of cover to see what was happening. The door of the flat-face den stayed closed.

"What if the flat-face isn't there?" she whispered to Lusa, who was peering out beside her.

"He is. He's got to be!" The small black bear spat each word out through gritted teeth.

Still there was no movement from inside the den. Pain

gripped Kallik's belly as she saw how small and vulnerable Ujurak looked, huddled on the ground with rain running down his bare, pale skin.

Silaluk! Kallik prayed. *Do something, please! Ujurak* can't *die!*

CHAPTER TEN

Lusa

Lusa peered out from the shelter of the rock and across the open ground to where Ujurak's limp body lay motionless in front of the closed door, the rain beating down on him. *Come on, flat-face! Where are you?*

Beside her she could feel tension quivering through Kallik; her friend's gaze was fixed on the door as if she was willing it to open. Behind her, Toklo's voice came in a soft, wordless grumble.

We've done everything we can, Lusa thought. *It's up to the flat-faces now.*

A sharp sound came from the flat-face denning place; every hair on Lusa's pelt prickled as the door of another den swung open and the gray-furred flat-face came out. He strode across the open space toward his own den and stopped abruptly when he spotted Ujurak lying in front of the door. Stooping down, he laid one of his paws on Ujurak's chest. Then he raised his head and glanced around; Lusa found it hard to read flat-face expressions, but she thought he looked confused.

"Take him inside!" Toklo growled behind her. "Why are you messing around like that?"

For a moment Lusa wondered if the flat-face was going to leave Ujurak there, dying in the rain. Did flat-faces care for strangers who weren't part of their herd? Then she let out a gasp of relief as the flat-face slid his forelimbs underneath Ujurak and lifted him up. He pushed the door open with one shoulder, carried Ujurak inside the den, and shut the door behind them.

"There!" Kallik exclaimed with satisfaction. "He'll be okay now, won't he, Lusa?"

It was Toklo who replied, "I don't know. I still don't trust flat-faces."

His doubts couldn't quench the hope Lusa had begun to feel as soon as the flat-face took Ujurak in. "These flat-faces aren't like that. Ujurak said so," she reminded him. "He said they had animal spirits."

"That's just a load of cloudfluff," Toklo retorted.

Lusa guessed Toklo just didn't want to allow himself to hope in case they lost Ujurak after all. She pressed herself comfortingly against his side, wishing she could give him some of her trust.

"The flat-faces in the Bear Bowl looked after us," she told him. "I told you they took care of my mother when she was sick? She was so ill, I thought she was going to die. But when they brought her back she was well again, just the same as always."

"The flat-face wouldn't have taken Ujurak in if he didn't

want to care for him," Kallik added hopefully.

Toklo just grunted.

Lusa stared at the closed door of the healer's den, wishing she knew what was going on inside. She thought about her dream on Smoke Mountain, when her mother had come to her and told her that she had to save the wild. When she woke, Ujurak had known all about it.

They had never spoken about the dream since, but Lusa had known from that moment that Ujurak was even more special than they realized. The spirits wouldn't let him die. The whole of the wild needed him too much.

Closing her eyes, Lusa tried to send out a message to Ujurak. *The flat-faces will look after you,* she told him, hoping that he could hear her. *We'll wait for you until you're better, so we can keep going to save the wild.*

Lusa felt new strength welling up inside her like a mountain spring. Somehow she knew that Ujurak would receive her message. Letting out a long sigh, she opened her eyes again. "I'm starving!" she announced. It seemed as if days had passed since they had persuaded Ujurak to join the flock of geese in the hope of catching one of them. "What about you?"

Toklo nodded. "We need to hunt," he murmured reluctantly, "but—".

"But we can't go off and leave Ujurak," Kallik finished for him. "Not when we don't know if he's going to be okay."

As the bears glanced uncertainly at one another, Lusa raised her snout and sniffed. She could pick up whiffs of interesting scents, and she realized how quiet the denning place was, with all the flat-faces indoors because of the rain.

She gave Kallik a friendly shove with one paw. "Don't worry. Flat-face dens are always good for a few scraps of food, if you know where to look."

Toklo frowned. "I'd rather hunt our own prey."

"No, Lusa's right," Kallik said. "This will be easier, and we can stay close to Ujurak."

Toklo shrugged. "Okay. But don't blame me if the flat-faces catch us."

By now twilight was gathering. The rain still hissed down around them, and the doors to the flat-face dens stayed firmly closed. Cautious, but still confident, Lusa led the way across the denning area, looking for the shiny containers full of rubbish that flat-faces always kept at the back of their dens.

The faint sound of music and flat-face voices came from the bigger den that the healer had left. Lusa crept up to a lighted window and peered inside. Rows of flat-faces sat at tables, with little piles of meat in front of them. They were talking loudly and baring their teeth at one another in a friendly way.

As one of the flat-faces rose to his feet, Lusa drew back into the shadows, shoving Toklo and Kallik away from the window. A moment later the flat-face opened the door and stepped out, pulling a pelt over his head, and ran across the rainswept ground to another den in a distant corner.

"Let's get on with it!" Toklo hissed in her ear. "They'll spot us if we hang around here."

Lusa knew he was right. She set off again, still looking for the flat-face rubbish containers. To her surprise, she couldn't see any. "What do they do with their rubbish?" she muttered angrily. "Don't they know there are hungry bears around here?"

As they came to the end of a row of flat-face dens, Toklo halted, sniffing at the air. "What's that?" he asked.

Lusa joined him and took a deep sniff. The most delicious smells tickled her nostrils; they seemed to be coming from a small den a little ways from the end of the row. "We've *got* to have some of that!" she exclaimed.

"Be careful," Kallik warned her as she padded up to Lusa's side. "There's the smell of fire, too. It could be dangerous."

"I'll be fine."

Before either of her friends could object, Lusa gave a swift glance around to check that no flat-faces had appeared, then trotted up to the door of the small den. She gave the door a push, but it wouldn't open. Frustrated, she glared at it, then noticed a gleam of silver between the edge of the door and the frame. Something there was holding the door shut.

Squeezing her paw into the gap, Lusa gave the silver thing an experimental prod. There was a clicking sound; she almost lost her balance as the door swung inward. Smoke surged out of the doorway, while the delicious scents grew stronger still.

Lusa looked back to where her friends were waiting a few bear-lengths away. "Keep watch for flat-faces!" she called.

Then she slipped through the doorway into the small den. The air was full of smoke, stinging her eyes, but the smell guided her forward until she could make out long strips of meat hanging from wooden beams under the roof.

What's the meat doing there? Lusa wondered. *I'll never understand flat-faces!*

Rearing up on her hind legs, she managed to snag the end of one of the strips with an outstretched paw and pull it to the ground. Encouraged by her success, she tugged down a second piece. Grabbing them in her jaws, she raced out of the den and back to her friends.

"Lusa, you're brilliant!" Kallik exclaimed.

Toklo still had an air of nagging anxiety, which the sight of the meat didn't banish. "Better take it back to the rocks. The flat-faces might spot us if we stay here." He spun around to lead the way without waiting for a response.

Lusa hurried after him, dragging the long strips of meat, expecting at any moment to hear flat-faces shouting behind her. But everything was quiet.

"Here, eat," she said, dropping the meat in the shelter of the rock.

Kallik seized on one end of a strip, chewing eagerly, but Toklo still hung back. He was peering around the side of the rock at the healer's den.

Lusa gave him a gentle shove. "Come on, eat. We won't be any use to Ujurak if we're weak from hunger."

Toklo nodded reluctantly and settled down to gnaw at the other strip of meat. "Caribou," he muttered after a mouthful or two. "Tastes a bit weird, but it's good. Thanks, Lusa."

"You're welcome."

Lusa crouched down to eat her own share, enjoying the rich, tangy taste of the caribou meat. But she couldn't help noticing that Toklo was still brooding, pausing every few moments to listen and glance around, as if he was desperate for any sign that would tell him what was happening to Ujurak.

"I know what we can do," she said when she and her friends had finished eating. "Follow me."

Kallik and Toklo exchanged a puzzled look, but they followed Lusa out from behind the rocks. The rain was easing off, but by now it was full night, and the doors of the flat-face dens stayed closed as Lusa led the way around the edges of the open space, clinging to the shadows. They froze as another flat-face left the big den and sprinted past them, barely two bear-lengths away. He had his head down against the last flurries of rain and didn't spot the bears crouching in the shelter of a projecting roof.

"That was close!" Kallik breathed.

Toklo nodded. "Let's get a move on."

Lusa took the lead again, trying to slink through the darkness as if she were only the shadow of a bear, until they reached the back of the healer's den. Light streamed out of a window and cast a golden patch on the ground.

Lusa padded up to the window. Standing on her hindpaws, she rested her forepaws against the wall of the den and peered inside.

CHAPTER ELEVEN

Toklo

Toklo crept warily up to the flat-face den and peered through the shiny stuff, like solid water, that blocked the hole in the wall. A fire burned at one side; even out here, Toklo could smell strange fumes coming from it, and he blinked to chase away a sudden feeling of dizziness. But in spite of the odd smell, it looked warm and cozy inside, with flat-face pelts spread on the floor and hanging from the walls.

Lusa and Kallik pressed their noses to the window on either side of Toklo, peering into the den. Toklo studied the old flat-face who had taken Ujurak in. The flat-face had his back to the window, blocking the bears' view of Ujurak, who was lying next to the wall. Now and then Toklo caught a glimpse of one of the old flat-face's pink, furless paws as he reached out to pick up or put down some small, silvery object.

I guess he's still trying to get the line out of Ujurak's throat, Toklo thought. *His paws are very small, and much nimbler than ours. Maybe Lusa was right to bring Ujurak here, after all.*

Then the flat-face healer moved, and Toklo got a clear view

of Ujurak for the first time. Still in his flat-face shape, he lay on his back in a flat-face nest, partly covered by pelts.

"He looks dead!" Kallik whispered, her voice horrified.

Toklo didn't reply, but his belly clenched and he gritted his teeth to stop himself from howling aloud. Ujurak lay so still; his flat-face skin was a sickly gray. His eyes were closed, and Toklo couldn't tell if he was breathing.

"He's not dead," Lusa said reassuringly. "The flat-face wouldn't be trying to help him if he were."

Toklo found it hard to believe her. What did flat-faces know? Besides, if Ujurak wasn't dead now, he might die soon, and there was nothing Toklo could do. He hated the feeling of helplessness; like the geese that scattered when he tried to creep up on them, everything that was happening was flying out of his control.

Just briefly, when he had hunted the caribou alone, he had been at peace. Now he felt as though nothing would ever go right. One thought kept nagging at him, refusing to leave him alone: *It was my fault Ujurak turned into a goose. If I hadn't had that dumb idea . . .*

Hot panic flooded through him. His heart thudded as he remembered the guilt he had felt over Tobi's death and the way Oka had abandoned him; he knew he couldn't carry the weight of that guilt again.

No, it wasn't *my fault,* Toklo told himself. *It* wasn't *my fault.*

Gradually his heart steadied and the scorching terror ebbed away. *I'm not Ujurak's mother,* he told himself. *It's not my responsibility to keep him safe.*

He remembered the last time Ujurak had been injured, when the firebeast had struck him as they crossed the bridge on the way to Great Bear Lake. Then Toklo had felt as if he were the starbeast in the loneliest, darkest part of the sky. He had failed to protect Ujurak; he had felt utterly worthless.

Not this time, Toklo asserted, taking a few deep breaths. *Ujurak should be able to take care of himself. Why is he so stupid? Why does he always get into trouble?*

Suddenly a faint choking sound came from inside the den. Toklo caught his breath. "That was Ujurak!" he exclaimed. "He's not dead."

The old flat-face bent over Ujurak again. A silver claw shape flashed in his hand. Toklo's belly clenched with anxiety as Ujurak's limbs spasmed and his skinny flat-face arms flailed. Then the Ujurak-cub relaxed, and the flat-face healer straightened up, stretching out a hand to smooth back Ujurak's tangle of head-fur.

Glancing away from the window, Toklo saw the moon hanging over the forested mountain slopes. Longing gripped him, sharp as a wolf's fangs. *That's where I belong.* Endless forests were the right place for a brown bear; that was where he should be, not hiding here in the shadows, on the fringe of a flat-face denning area.

Toklo's mind flew back to when he and Tobi were tiny cubs, still living in their BirthDen with Oka. He recalled the very first time Oka had taught them how to hunt.

"See this stick?" she had said, dropping it in front of them. "I want you to pretend it's a hare. What are you going to do?"

"Chase it?" Tobi guessed, his eyes sparkling.

A pang passed through Toklo as he remembered that there had been a time when Tobi hadn't been so ill. Even though he wasn't as strong as Toklo, none of them had realized how sickly he was. Oka hadn't been so anxious about him, and Toklo had been able to love him without being irritated by his weakness.

"That's dumb, squirrel-brain!" Toklo had replied to his brother. "You can't chase a stick. This is what *I'm* going to do!"

Toklo leaped on the stick and sank his teeth into it, shaking it from side to side and finally dropping it at Oka's paws. "I killed it, didn't I?" he yelped.

"You did," Oka growled approvingly. "Come on, Tobi, you try."

Tobi jumped onto the stick, stretching out his front legs to grip it with his claws, but he slipped as he landed and rolled over on his back. The stick went flying.

"Your hare just escaped," Toklo huffed in amusement.

Oka let out an exasperated sigh. "Tobi, you're not trying!" she scolded. "How do you expect to feed yourself when you're full-grown if you don't learn now?"

Tobi sat up, shaking scraps of leaf-mold off his pelt. "I'll stay with Toklo," he replied. "Toklo, you won't let me starve, will you?"

"'Course not," Toklo barked. "I can catch enough prey for both of us. Watch!" He pounced on the stick again, and this time it snapped cleanly in two between his paws.

"No," Oka scolded. "You're both wrong. Brown bears live alone. That's the way it's always been. It's our greatest strength, that we don't need to depend on any other bears to survive. We're responsible for ourselves, and no one else."

There had been a grim determination in her tone; even as a young cub, Toklo had wondered what made her insist so strongly that brown bears must live on their own. Although now he knew it was how most brown bears chose to live, he still felt that for Oka it had been more than that, some instinct deep inside her that rejected all companionship.

Lusa wriggling next to him brought Toklo back to the present. Inside the den, the old flat-face had disappeared, leaving Ujurak sleeping in the nest, wrapped in pelts.

That flat-face is trying to help, Toklo thought. *But I still can't be sure Ujurak will be okay. I can't leave yet.*

Sighing, he glanced once more at the tree-covered mountains, silvered by the moonlight. They looked so peaceful, and his paws itched to carry him up there, under the shadows of the branches.

"Soon," he whispered, too faintly for his companions to hear him. "I'm coming soon."

CHAPTER TWELVE

Ujurak

Ujurak crouched on the floor of a cave, shadows clustering around him. His throat throbbed with pain, and a deathly weariness was spreading through all his limbs. His paws scuffled on the hard stone beneath him, but he didn't have the strength to get up. His senses swirled into a whirlpool of night.

Suddenly a blur of white light penetrated the darkness. Ujurak blinked, trying to focus. In front of him an Arctic hare had hopped through the mouth of the cave. Its snowy pelt glowed as if the moon had fallen to the earth and filled every hair on its pelt.

"Come," the hare said. "You must leave this place."

"I can't," Ujurak croaked, the pain in his throat stabbing deeper as he tried to speak. "I'm too tired."

"You must." The hare's voice grew more commanding. It turned and hopped a pace or two back toward the cave mouth. Glancing over its shoulder, it warned, "You cannot stay here."

Something about the hare compelled Ujurak to follow, as if the two of them were connected by an invisible thread.

Once again he scrabbled his paws against the stone, and this time he managed to heave himself up. His limbs felt too heavy to move; all he wanted was to sink back into the comforting darkness.

"Follow me," said the hare. "All will be well if you come out of the cave."

Ujurak staggered forward step by painful step, following the pure white light of the hare. The cave mouth drew gradually closer; Ujurak began to notice light filtering into the cave from outside.

As he struggled onward, the light grew stronger, a golden light that gradually filled his eyes, blotting out the sight of the hare. He felt cool, fresh air blowing toward him from the mouth of the cave, carrying the warm scents of summer.

At last Ujurak took the final step that brought him outside, leaving the dark cave behind him. Golden light blinded him, but from within it the voice of the hare rang out joyfully.

"Well done! There's nothing to fear now. You are safe here."

Ujurak blinked and opened his eyes to find himself lying in a nest in a flat-face den, wrapped in warm pelts. At one side of the den a fire was burning. Smoke drifted from it, tickling Ujurak's nostrils with the scents of healing herbs. He recognized one that he used to chew into a pulp and put on wounds, and another that soothed pain. Yet another scent was unfamiliar.

In spite of the fire and the pelts, Ujurak couldn't stop shivering. His throat burned as if the fire had scorched it. When he tried to remember what had happened, and to decide what he ought to do next, he felt as though he were groping his way through a fog.

Gradually Ujurak became aware of a steady mumble of words coming from one side of the bed, barely audible above the crackling of the fire. He couldn't understand the words; turning his head, he saw a flat-face sitting beside him. He was a broad-shouldered man with a lined, weathered face and long gray head-fur swept back from his forehead and tied into braids, caught at the ends with bright beads and feathers. His hands were square and looked strong. Ujurak thought he looked familiar; after a moment he recognized the man who had come out of the den where the little flat-face had gone for healing.

"You're awake," the flat-face said. He was speaking clearly now, his face creasing into a smile. "Welcome to my home. My name is Tiinchuu."

"What happened?" Ujurak asked hoarsely. "Why am I here?"

"You swallowed a fishhook," the flat-face told him. "It nearly killed you. But I visited your spirit in the form of a hare, and brought you back. Your animal spirit is strong."

He visited me . . . Ujurak thought confusedly. *Is he like me? Can he be a hare and a flat-face, too?*

He struggled to sit up, and discovered how weak he was; he couldn't resist when the healer placed one gentle hand on his shoulder and pressed him back onto the bed.

"Lie still, little bear," Tiinchuu said. "You'll soon be strong again."

Ujurak struggled to clear his head, but the heavy smell of the smoke made it hard to think. His vision kept blurring, and the room swam around him as if he were looking at it through water. A brightly colored mask on the wall seemed to leer at him, then faded back into mist.

"Don't try to talk," the healer went on. "I've taken the fishing line out of your throat, but the wound needs time to heal."

Reaching into the shadows, he showed Ujurak a small bowl that held a long length of almost transparent fishing line, with a wicked barbed hook at one end. A couple of clots of blood still clung to it. Memory drifted into Ujurak's mind: the pain in his throat and his desperate efforts to breathe.

"It's all over," Tiinchuu reassured him. "I have given you shepherd's purse to stop the bleeding, and echinacea for the infection."

Rising from the side of the bed, he moved away from Ujurak's range of vision. When he returned, he carried another small bowl with a few tiny white things at the bottom of it.

Ujurak flinched, pressing himself into his pillows. "What are they for?" he croaked.

"Don't be afraid." Tiinchuu smiled again. "There are many ways of healing, and these pills will work with the herbs to make you better."

Gently he raised Ujurak up with an arm around his shoulders. Ujurak felt that he was expecting him to do something, but he didn't know what it was.

"Take one of the pills and put it on your tongue," Tiinchuu explained after a moment. "Then you can swallow it with this water." He reached for a cup from the table beside the bed.

Nervously Ujurak picked up one of the tiny white pills; it was hard to grasp it with these unfamiliar flat-face fingers.

"It will hurt to swallow," Tiinchuu said as Ujurak hesitated, staring at the pill. "But you need to do it, and you'll feel better later."

Ujurak gave him an uncertain nod. He put the pill on his tongue; Tiinchuu held the cup for him and tipped water into his mouth. In spite of the pain in his throat, Ujurak managed to swallow.

"Good," Tiinchuu said. "That will do for now. You can have more later."

Ujurak didn't feel any different after he swallowed the white pill. But from what Tiinchuu said, it must be powerful for healing. Maybe the white stuff came from a different sort of herb, one that grew hard white berries. Ujurak would look out for it.

Tiinchuu let Ujurak lie down again and retreated from the bedside; Ujurak heard him moving around the den, the sound pulsing loud and soft as waves of heat and cold chased one another through Ujurak's body.

What happens now? Ujurak wondered. He didn't feel as if he belonged here. He longed to be outside, under the open sky, traveling with others beside him . . . *others?* Which others? Dimly he realized that he had forgotten something important. *I'm not a flat-face; I'm a . . . I'm a . . .* When he tried to remember, his memories dissolved like snow falling on water. He knew his life hadn't begun the moment he woke in this warm, fragrant den. But what had come before? The knowledge of who he really was drifted away in a fog of weariness and pain.

Tiinchuu reappeared with another cup in his hand. Aromatic steam came from it.

"Drink this," the healer said, sitting beside him on the bed. "It's wintergreen tea. It will soothe the pain and help you to sleep. There's elderberry in it, too, to bring down your fever."

He raised Ujurak's head and held the cup to his lips. The warm liquid was comforting, but Ujurak's nervousness increased at being so close to a flat-face.

"That's right," Tiinchuu murmured as Ujurak sipped from the cup. After a moment, he added thoughtfully, "You're not from here, are you?"

Ujurak shook his head.

"I thought not. Will anyone be looking for you—your parents or friends?"

Anxiety flooded through Ujurak and he struggled once again against the sleep that was enveloping him. This flat-face seemed so close to guessing his secret. *Whatever that is.*

He opened his mouth, not knowing what he wanted to say, but Tiinchuu raised his hand for silence.

"Rest, don't talk," he ordered. "There'll be plenty of time for talk when you're stronger."

Setting the cup aside, he let Ujurak lie back on the pillows and tucked the blankets more closely around him. Ujurak began to feel warmth creeping through his body, and his eyelids grew heavy.

"You should sleep now," Tiinchuu told him. "But first, let me give you these. They are charms that will help you get well."

He folded Ujurak's hand around three small carvings. Ujurak uncurled his fingers and stared at them. Three bears—brown, white, and black, tiny, but so vividly carved that they almost seemed to be alive, looking up at him with worried, questioning eyes. They had names, whispering in Ujurak's head, prompted by the shapes of the tiny carved creatures. Memories spun from the mist that filled his mind: three figures plodding ahead of him, outlined against the horizon; mountains filled with the smell of burning; swimming a great black river that pulled at his fur and tasted bitter and slimy; sleeping and hunting and walking on, on, on through scorching days and nights that passed in a flicker of shadows.

Toklo.

Kallik.

Lusa.

And Ujurak, brown like Toklo, a bear like all four of them. Pushing them onward, led by the voices that told him they hadn't reached the end of their journey, that more had to be done before the wild could be saved.

I am a bear.

Ujurak gazed up at the healer. *How could he possibly know?*

"You . . . you called me little bear," he whispered.

The corners of Tiinchuu's eyes crinkled in amusement as he pointed to the window of his hut. Ujurak saw three wet bear snouts pressed against the glass.

"Friends of yours, I think," Tiinchuu said.

Ujurak smiled as he made out Lusa's, Toklo's, and Kallik's faces, glad beyond words that they had stayed so close to him.

He closed his hand around the three carvings, thinking sleepily that it felt strange to have skinny little fingers rather than a paw. Comforted by the presence of his friends, he slipped easily into sleep.

CHAPTER THIRTEEN

Kallik

"He's alive!" Kallik yelped. "Ujurak is alive!"

"Get down!" Toklo pushed her away from the window. "The flat-face has seen us."

"Don't worry." Lusa dropped to all fours beside them. "He won't hurt us. Look how he helped Ujurak."

"Yeah," Toklo agreed. "It looks like Ujurak's going to be okay." Sounding reluctant, he added, "Maybe all flat-faces aren't bad. Of course, the healer thinks Ujurak is a flat-face. I wonder what he'd do if he knew he was a bear?"

Kallik moved a little farther from the window and looked around. The rain had completely stopped and the wind had risen, chasing ragged clouds across the sky. The moon shone fitfully through the gaps between them, and Kallik could make out the steady shining of the Pathway Star.

"We'd better get out of here," she murmured to Lusa and Toklo. "We don't want to risk the other flat-faces finding us."

"I think these flat-faces are okay," Lusa responded, padding up beside her. "The healer is helping Ujurak. He knows we're here, and he doesn't seem worried."

Toklo snorted. "Who knows what a flat-face is thinking?"

"Besides, all the flat-faces might not be the same," Lusa added.

But whatever Lusa said, Kallik found it hard to believe that they could be safe in the middle of a flat-face denning area. She shook her head.

"Okay, we'll go." Lusa sounded untroubled. "Not too far, though. We'll need to check on Ujurak later."

Kallik padded after Lusa as she took the lead to the edge of the village and farther up the caribou trail. The white bear's legs were aching and, now that she wasn't so anxious about Ujurak, she realized how tired and hungry she was. They needed to find a place to rest and something more to eat.

As they trudged past a thicket of thornbushes, an Arctic ground squirrel sprang out of the branches, almost under Kallik's paws. She launched herself after it, and managed to bring it down with a swift blow to the head.

"Well done!" Toklo exclaimed, trotting up to give the prey a sniff.

"Thank the spirits," Kallik said. "They knew what we needed."

She picked up the squirrel and carried it into the shelter of a rocky outcrop that jutted from the hillside at the edge of the trail. Lusa followed her a few moments later, carrying a couple of thorn branches that still bore some late berries. Her eyes were sparkling. "It's a feast!" she said, dropping the branches beside the body of the squirrel.

"Maybe for you, small one." Kallik gave her friend an affectionate nudge. "Toklo and I are getting so big, it's harder to fill our bellies."

Looking around for the brown bear, Kallik spotted him a few bear-lengths away, gazing up at the tree-covered mountain slopes. "Hey, Toklo!" she called. "Aren't you hungry?"

The young grizzly jumped, then galloped to the side of the trail and crouched down with Kallik and Lusa to share their prey. The night was growing colder, and though the rocks sheltered them from the worst of the wind, Kallik could still pick up the scent of ice, blown from the ocean. Peace spread through her as she ate her share; Ujurak was safe, and she knew that soon she would be able to return to the ice.

"We did it," Lusa said when they had finished the squirrel and were nibbling on the last of the berries. "We've saved Ujurak, working together. We're a great team!"

Kallik murmured agreement, but Toklo was silent. Faint apprehension tingled in Kallik's paws when she saw the distant look in his eyes.

"Ujurak isn't our responsibility anymore," he announced.

Lusa looked puzzled. "But he's still our friend."

"I know, but . . . " Toklo let his voice trail off, then took a deep breath. "Ujurak is safe now," he said. "His life isn't in danger anymore, and we have reached the end of our journey. This is a place where we can live safely, with plenty of food and shelter. It's time that I followed my own path."

"What?" Lusa yelped, her eyes wide with dismay. "You can't leave us now, Toklo. You *can't*!"

"I have to," Toklo replied.

Hesitating slightly, he reached forward and touched his nose to Kallik's, then to Lusa's. Then he turned toward the trail the caribou had followed, long before, winding up to a pass that led into the mountains. With a panicky squeal, Lusa scrambled in front of him and blocked his path.

"Toklo, please don't go," she begged.

Kallik sat frozen, watching. She didn't want Toklo to go, but she understood what was driving him. He felt the pull of the forest, just as she was drawn toward the ice.

Lusa doesn't see that, she thought sadly. Anxiety clawed at her as she wondered what would happen to Lusa when they said good-bye to each other. *How will I tell her that I* must *go back to the ice?*

Lusa and Toklo still faced each other on the trail, their gazes locked together.

"Please," Lusa repeated. "We don't *know* that Ujurak will get better."

Toklo swung around, as if he was going to head up toward the pass without any more argument. Then his shoulders sagged and he turned back.

"Okay," he said. "I'll stay for a while."

"Great!" Lusa gave a little bounce of happiness and pushed her snout affectionately into Toklo's shoulder. "Thanks, Toklo."

But it's not over, Kallik thought, as the three of them settled down to sleep under the rocky outcrop, huddled together for warmth. *Sooner or later, Toklo will leave, and nothing Lusa can say will stop him.*

CHAPTER FOURTEEN

Ujurak

Sunlight on his face woke Ujurak. With one hand he explored the unfamiliar pelts covering him and sat up in alarm when he realized that he didn't know where he was. Then as he took in the flat-face healer's den, with the fire still burning, a pot bubbling on it, and the masks hanging on the walls, he remembered what had happened: his flight as a goose, and the agony in his throat when he swallowed the fishhook. And he remembered the healer who had cared for him when he woke up here in the shape of a flat-face. Tiinchuu, who had known all along that Ujurak was a bear.

His throat still hurt and shivers ran through him every time he took a deep breath. He felt hot and cold by turns. He pulled the coverings more tightly around himself and lay back.

I have to get out of here and find Lusa and Kallik and Toklo.

A door opened in the wall opposite the fire and the flat-face healer came in. He smiled when he saw Ujurak. "You're awake," he said. "How do you feel?"

"Better, thanks." Ujurak's voice sounded like claws scraping on rock, and pain stabbed his throat as he spoke.

"Good. I've made you some more wintergreen tea." Crossing to a table by the fire, Tiinchuu poured liquid from a jug into a cup and brought it over to Ujurak. Deftly he slid an arm around Ujurak's shoulders and helped him to sit up.

"There," he murmured, holding the cup for Ujurak to drink. "We'll soon bring your fever down and have you up and about again."

Ujurak thought that the healer's eyes looked kind, and the touch of his hands was strong and sure. Gradually he relaxed, growing more confident that the flat-face didn't mean him any harm.

"What's your name, little bear?" Tiinchuu asked.

"Ujurak."

"And how did you come here?" The healer tilted the cup so that Ujurak could swallow the last drops of tea, and set the cup aside. He rearranged Ujurak's pillows so that he could sit back supported by them.

"I was certainly surprised when I found you lying naked on my doorstep," he went on. "Did you fall from the stars?"

Ujurak's eyes flew wide with astonishment. *Does he really think so?* Then he recognized the amusement in Tiinchuu's eyes and managed to smile.

"Where did you come from?" the healer asked, growing more serious.

Ujurak hesitated. "I don't know where I'm from," he confessed. "I . . . I don't remember."

"Hmm . . ." Tiinchuu moved away to get a cloth soaked with some fresh-smelling liquid. He sat down on the side of the bed and used the cloth to wipe Ujurak's face and throat. Ujurak let out a grateful sigh at the cool touch.

"You're not a boy, are you?" the healer said, with a sudden piercing look.

Ujurak thought of the dark cave that had filled with golden light, and the Arctic hare that had pulled him forward, dragged him out of the shadows to the light and the warmth. The spirit of the hare was here now; he could feel it in the man sitting beside him. *He's a hare as well as a flat-face. . . .*

"No," Ujurak said. "I'm a bear."

He braced himself for the healer to leap away in fear, or tell him that he was lying, but Tiinchuu just blinked. "And were you a bear when you swallowed the fishhook?"

"No, I was a goose."

Tiinchuu's eyes widened in surprise. "You have the spirit of more than one creature?"

Ujurak nodded. "Mostly I'm a bear. But I've been a goose, and an eagle, and a mule deer—"

"Then you're a shape-shifter?" the healer interrupted. His gaze was fixed on Ujurak's face and there was a look of fascination, almost of hunger, in his dark eyes.

"I . . . I guess so." Ujurak tilted his head to one side. "What about you? That hare in the cave . . . that was you, wasn't it?"

Tiinchuu nodded. "You have many shapes, but I have just two: a man, as you see me now, and an Arctic hare. Most of the time I live as a man, but in my dreams I become the hare and learn things I could never know in my human shape."

Ujurak remembered the feeling of peace in this denning place, the certainty he had that they would not be hunted. "Can all the flat-faces here do that?"

The healer smiled. "Flat-faces? Well, I guess that makes sense. No, little bear. I am the only flat-face here who possesses the spirit of an animal."

Tiinchuu sat back, examining Ujurak's face. "Why are you here?" he asked.

Ujurak found that question more difficult to answer; he wasn't even sure himself. "I . . . I hear voices sometimes," he stammered. He didn't feel as if he could tell the healer that he thought the voice belonged to Silaluk; surely even Tiinchuu wouldn't believe that the mighty star-bear would speak to a brown bear cub.

To his relief, Tiinchuu didn't ask him where the voices came from. Instead he got up again, went over to the fire, and ladled a thick, delicious-smelling liquid into a bowl.

"What do the voices tell you?" he prompted as he returned to the bed.

"They say . . . they say I should save the wild."

Tiinchuu let out a long breath, shaking his head. "That's a huge task," he murmured.

He sat down, dipped a spoon into the bowl, and began to feed Ujurak. The liquid was hot and comforting, tasting of caribou and herbs. Its warmth spread throughout Ujurak's body, and he began to feel sleepy again. But he didn't want to sleep; he wanted to ask some questions of his own, and find out more about where he was and the man who was caring for him.

Maybe it was Silaluk who brought me here.

"What place is this?" he managed to say when he had swallowed another mouthful.

"This is Arctic Village," Tiinchuu replied, holding the spoon for Ujurak again. "We are the Caribou People. We like to live here among the animals in the Valley of the Caribou. This is the Last Great Wilderness."

Ujurak was beginning to feel a little stronger and finding it easier to talk. "I've heard that name before," he said. "Some . . . someone I met told me about it." No need to mention that Qopuk was a bear.

Tiinchuu nodded. "The people here—" he began, and broke off at the sound of a loud, drawn-out clattering from outside.

Ujurak sat up again, his heart beginning to pound. *What's that? It's louder than a firebeast!*

Tiinchuu calmed him with a hand resting briefly on his shoulder. "I have to leave you for a while," he said, rising to his feet. "You should try to sleep."

"Where are you going?" Ujurak asked.

"Today the village is expecting visitors from far away," the healer replied. "And it sounds as if they've arrived. I have to go meet them." His tone was grim; Ujurak realized that he wasn't looking forward to the meeting.

"Visitors?" he echoed.

"There are people who respect our ways," Tiinchuu explained. His dark eyes were somber. "But there are others who don't want the wilderness to stay wild."

"What others?" Ujurak asked hoarsely.

"Hunters who do not respect the animal spirits as my people do," Tiinchuu said. "Men who want to cover the wilderness with roads and houses. And others . . ." He frowned. "Others who want to rip the heart out of the earth for their own profit."

Ujurak's eyes widened. He didn't understand what Tiinchuu meant, but it sounded terrifying.

"Don't worry," Tiinchuu said. "While there is breath in my body I will fight the change that is coming, and I'm not the only one."

CHAPTER FIFTEEN

Toklo

In his dreams, Toklo found himself in a thick forest. Branches arched overhead and rustling in the undergrowth betrayed the presence of prey. He let out a growl, rearing up to score his claws down the trunk of a tree.

This is my territory! Better not mess with me!

A mule deer stepped out of the bushes and stood in a clearing just ahead of him. Toklo bunched his muscles, ready to hunt it down, but as he bounded forward he seemed to fall over his own paws. He woke to find himself underneath the rocky outcrop with Lusa and Kallik beside him and faint dawn light seeping across the sky.

Toklo sat up, yawning and giving himself a vigorous scratch with one paw. *That was a weird dream!*

Beside him, Kallik huffed out a breath and opened her eyes. When she saw Toklo, she heaved herself to her paws. "I'm glad you're still here," she murmured.

Toklo nodded. "For now."

He was relieved that Kallik seemed to understand that he

couldn't stay forever. Soon he would have to take the path of a brown bear into the forest, but he knew that however much he tried to explain, he would never make Lusa see that it was the only choice he could make.

"I'm hungry. Let's hunt," he said out loud.

Padding out into the valley, he snuffed at the air for the scent of prey, and spotted a rabbit nibbling at the long grasses on the edge of a pool. Kallik saw it, too; with a brief nod she glided forward, skirting the rabbit in a wide circle so that she could come at it from the other side.

When she was in position she jumped forward with a fearsome growl. The rabbit started up, saw her, and fled straight into Toklo's paws. He killed it with a blow to its spine.

"Great kill!" Kallik said, bounding up. "We should try that again sometime." Then her eyes grew shadowed, as if she remembered that they wouldn't have many more chances to hunt together.

Toklo picked up the rabbit and carried it back to where Lusa was still sleeping. As he approached, the little black bear grunted, stirring, and passed her paws over her face. "Morning already!" She yawned, scrambling up. "We'd better go back to the flat-face dens and see how Ujurak is doing." Her eyes shone as she turned to Kallik. "Maybe he'll be ready to come back with us today!"

"Hang on," Toklo said. "Eat first."

"Oh, thanks. I'm starving!" Lusa's eyes shone as she tore a mouthful from the rabbit. Toklo could see that she had put their argument of the night before out of her mind. He guessed she had managed to forget that he was going to leave.

When they had finished eating, Toklo and Kallik followed Lusa as she bounded eagerly back down the trail toward the flat-face denning area. Toklo's belly churned as he worried about being spotted by the flat-faces, and he was relieved when Lusa slackened her pace as they approached the dens.

"We know we can trust the healer," she murmured, "but—"

"*You* trust the healer," Toklo interrupted. "I'm not so sure."

"I think Toklo's right," Kallik put in. "He helped Ujurak because he's in the shape of a flat-face. But how does he feel about bears?"

Lusa shrugged. "I suppose you could be right. In any case, it's true that we can't be sure about the other flat-faces. We'd better be careful they don't see us."

It was not long past sunrise, but already one or two of the flat-faces were walking between the dens. Toklo, Lusa, and Kallik ducked into the shadows under an overhanging roof as a flat-face walked past with a large, shiny object dangling from one paw. Loud noises issued from it, and a high-pitched sound was coming from the flat-face's mouth. As he passed another of the dens the door opened and the female who Ujurak had said had a goose spirit appeared and called out to him.

While they were talking, Toklo, Kallik, and Lusa slipped quietly around the back of the dens and headed toward the one where the healer lived. Toklo crept up to the window and stretched up his paws to brace himself so that he could peer through. Lusa squeezed up beside him and Kallik joined him on his other side.

Inside the den Toklo saw that Ujurak was sitting up, propped against the flat-face pelts. The healer sat on the bed beside him, feeding him something from a bowl. Toklo could hear that they were talking to each other, though he couldn't understand the flat-face words.

"Look, he's better!" Lusa yelped. "He'll be able to come back to us soon."

"Yes, he's fine now," Toklo agreed. With a long sigh he stepped away from the window of the healer's den, dropping down onto all four paws. "Ujurak is safe," he said as Lusa and Kallik followed him. "His life isn't in danger anymore. It's time that I followed my own path."

"What?" Lusa's eyes stretched wide. "Last night you said you would stay!"

"I said 'for a while,'" Toklo reminded her. "But now that I know Ujurak's okay, I can leave. I'm not responsible for him anymore." Toklo knew he had done more than enough by bringing them this far. Now it was time to do what his mother had said, and live on his own.

"But . . ." Lusa's voice choked. "I'll miss you."

Kallik padded up and rested her muzzle on the little black bear's shoulder. "A time always comes for parting," she murmured. "I had to learn that when Taqqiq left. It's no use trying to hold on to someone when they want to be somewhere else." Looking deep into Lusa's eyes, she added, "Let him go."

Lusa said nothing, her dark eyes still full of misery, but she stepped back and stood at Kallik's side.

"Thank you, Kallik," Toklo said. His heart ached at the thought of leaving his friends, but he knew this was what he had to do. "The spirits go with you both," he added.

"And with you," Kallik responded.

Lusa nodded sadly. "Good-bye, Toklo."

Toklo turned and headed off up the caribou trail. At the far side of the flat-face denning area he stopped to look back. Lusa's black pelt had been swallowed up in the shadows, but he could still see Kallik, gazing steadily after him.

Toklo reared up on his hindpaws for a moment in a final farewell. Then he turned and headed off alone, into the mountains.

CHAPTER SIXTEEN

Kallik

"I hope Toklo will be okay," Kallik murmured when the brown bear had disappeared up the valley.

"I'm worried about him," Lusa whimpered. "Why did he have to go off on his own?"

Kallik shrugged. "It's what brown bears do. But I'm going to miss him."

She turned back to the healer's den to take another look at Ujurak. But as she pressed her nose to the shiny clear stuff in her efforts to get a better look, the air was split by a terrible clattering noise.

Kallik sprang away from the window. Turning toward the sound, she saw a metal bird hovering farther down the valley. It was heading for the denning place. For a few moments it clattered above the dens, its metal wings whirling, then swooped down toward a stretch of open ground.

"What is it?" Lusa yelped, her voice shrill with fright.

Kallik's heart was pounding and her breath came harsh

and fast. Memories exploded in her mind, of her terrifying flight with Nanuk underneath that other metal bird, the one that had fallen out of the sky. She remembered the fire, the sudden rush of freezing snow, and watching Nanuk die, leaving her all alone.

"They take bears away!" she replied to Lusa, fighting panic.

"We've got to hide," barked Lusa as they watched the metal bird settle on the ground, its whirling wings slowing to a stop.

Clinging to the shadows, they crept toward the edge of the denning place and then made a dash for the outcrop of rocks where they had hidden with Toklo the night before. From there they peered out at the metal bird.

Its side slid open and three male flat-faces got out. They wore black pelts and carried thin, square objects in their paws; sniffing, Kallik picked up a harsh, unnatural tang, and her pelt prickled with disgust.

"I've never smelled flat-faces like these before," she whispered to Lusa. More acrid scents came from them, scents like nothing Kallik had ever smelled in the wild.

"Who are they?" Lusa asked, but Kallik couldn't find an answer.

The three flat-faces stood together for a moment, talking in soft voices. They looked nothing like the flat-faces in this denning area; their pelts were different and their head-fur was short and sleek. Kallik wondered if the metal bird had brought them from far away. She wished it would take them back again.

Suddenly the doors of several dens were flung open and some flat-faces came out. Kallik shoved Lusa back into the cover of the rocks. "Don't let any of them see us," she hissed.

"Maybe they're going to fight one another," Lusa suggested. "Like brown bears do if strangers come into their territory."

Kallik poked her snout from behind the rock to see the flat-faces who lived there going up to the strangers and holding out their front paws to be shaken. It didn't look like they were angry that the other flat-faces had come.

The flat-faces led the visitors into one of the biggest dens. The healer emerged from his den and went to join them.

"It's some sort of flat-face gathering," Kallik reported to Lusa. "I wonder what it's for." She kept her gaze fixed on the door where the flat-faces had disappeared. Could the healer have guessed that Ujurak wasn't a real flat-face, and then told those others, who had come in the metal bird to take him away?

We should never have brought Ujurak here, she thought. *But he was dying! What else could we have done?*

"We have to get Ujurak out of there," Lusa declared. She was obviously thinking the same thing. "Quickly, while all the flat-faces are talking."

Kallik looked around for any flat-faces that were still outside, but the spaces between the huts were empty. She guessed that most of them were in the big den. "Let's go," she whispered.

They raced across the open ground and halted in front of the door to the healer's den. Lusa studied it.

"Be quick!" Kallik urged her.

"Keep watch," Lusa hissed, not taking her eyes off the door. A moment later she squeezed one paw into the gap between the door and the door frame, and wriggled it around. For a long time nothing happened; Lusa was muttering under her breath, while Kallik's pelt prickled with fear that one of the flat-faces would come out and spot them.

At last Kallik heard a click. "Got it!" Lusa puffed, pushing the door open.

Every hair on Kallik's pelt stood on end as she followed Lusa through the door. This was totally wrong: Bears didn't go into flat-face dens! But Lusa didn't look scared, only cautious, and Kallik couldn't let her rescue Ujurak alone.

Looking around, she spotted the shiny gap in the wall that they had peered through. Her heart pounded; she hated the feeling of being shut in, with flat-face stuff all around her. But the air was full of the tang of herbs and caribou meat, soothing after the harsh scent of the metal bird.

"We have to hurry," Lusa said. "We don't want the flat-faces to catch us in here."

Kallik glanced anxiously back at the open door, hoping any passing flat-face wouldn't notice anything wrong. Then she followed Lusa over to the nest where Ujurak was lying. There was hardly enough room for them to squeeze through the flat-face stuff that filled the den. Kallik brushed against a wooden slab standing on four flimsy legs; a round white thing fell off the top of it and smashed on the floor, sending sharp little fragments bouncing into the corners. Kallik's heart thudded, but no flat-faces burst in to find out what the noise was, and she managed to reach Ujurak's side without knocking anything else over.

He looks so small! Kallik thought, pity welling up inside her at the sight of the skinny flat-face cub half buried in the flat-face pelts. Ujurak's face was white, except for a spot of red on each cheekbone, and his tangled fur was slicked against his head. But he was breathing evenly, his eyes closed in sleep, and he seemed quite peaceful.

"Do you think he's strong enough to come with us?" Kallik whispered.

"He's got to be." Lusa raised a paw and shook Ujurak's shoulder. "Ujurak! Wake up! We have to get out of here!"

Ujurak let out a grunt and burrowed deeper into the pelts without opening his eyes.

"Ujurak!" Lusa gave him another prod. "Wake up!"

This time Ujurak's eyes flickered open. For one startling moment he gazed at Lusa and Kallik as if he didn't know who they were.

He can't have forgotten us! Kallik thought in dismay.

Then recognition flooded into Ujurak's face. He reached out and plunged a paw into Lusa's fur, exclaiming something in flat-face talk. His voice was hoarse, and it seemed to hurt him to speak.

He can't talk to us anymore! Kallik realized. *What if he doesn't understand us, either?*

"Do you remember where you are?" Lusa asked him urgently. "In the flat-face dens beside the caribou trail?"

Ujurak looked puzzled. Lusa exchanged a frustrated glance with Kallik, and then went on, as if somehow she could communicate her desperation to Ujurak, even though they couldn't understand each other's language.

"A metal bird landed here. Some new flat-faces got out, and now they're all having a gathering in one of the big dens."

"We need to leave now," Kallik added, her fear rising with every moment they spent inside. "Something's going on, and it's not safe here anymore."

Ujurak sat up, looking from Lusa to Kallik and back again. His face had cleared, and when he spoke again it was with bear words, though his voice was hoarse and difficult to understand. "Yes, I remember."

Unsteadily he got out of bed and tottered over to the fire, where some flat-face pelts were hanging on a wooden frame. Slowly he put on the pelts; they were too big for him, and he had to roll them up so they didn't hang over his skinny paws. Kallik noticed that he slipped something small into a pouch in one of the pelts.

"Why does he need all that flat-face stuff?" she asked Lusa. "If he changed back into a bear, he would have his own pelt."

Lusa shrugged. "Maybe he's not strong enough to change yet. It's better that he takes these pelts to keep warm while he's still a flat-face."

Ujurak turned back to the bed, stripped off one of the pelts that lay there, and wrapped it around his shoulders. Slowly, still unsteady on his hindpaws, he crossed the room to the door and peered out.

Crowding up beside him, Kallik saw his eyes widen as he spotted the metal bird. The sound of voices was coming from the big den; Ujurak pointed at it and looked at the bears, a question in his eyes. "In there?"

"That's right," Lusa said impatiently. "Now let's go, before they come out and catch us." She gave Ujurak a nudge, trying to get him moving.

Ujurak ventured out into the open, padding softly on bare pink paws.

"At last!" Lusa muttered, turning down the valley, back in the direction of the plain. "Hurry up!"

But Ujurak didn't follow her. Instead he sneaked along the line of dens until he reached the big one where the gathering was taking place. He edged open the door and listened for a moment. "Wait for me," he whispered.

"No!" Lusa gasped as she watched Ujurak slip inside and close the door behind him.

Kallik shot a horrified glance at Lusa. "What is he doing?"

"I don't know." Lusa's frustrated growl was quite unlike her. "I think being a flat-face has turned his brain to fluff."

Swinging around, she headed for the rocks where they had hidden before. Kallik bounded after her, huffing out her breath in relief as they reached the shadows they cast, out of sight of the flat-faces.

"We can't leave him there," she whispered.

Lusa nodded. "I know. But we can't get him out without being seen. All we can do is wait."

CHAPTER SEVENTEEN

Ujurak

Ujurak closed the door of the big den behind him and slipped into the shadows. Waves of heat and cold swept over him, and he was afraid he was going to be sick. The wooden floor felt hard and cold under his bare feet, and he pulled his blanket closer around him.

The den was one big room with a raised platform at one end. Three flat-faces in black clothes were seated there, along with three of the villagers. Tiinchuu the healer was one of them; Ujurak hadn't seen the other male flat-face or the female before.

Benches were set out in the main part of the room, below the platform. More of the village people were sitting there, with a few younger males on their feet, leaning against the wall; they were all so intent on the platform that no one had noticed the arrival of Ujurak. He thought he caught a flicker in Tiinchuu's glance, as if the healer had spotted him lurking there, but he didn't give Ujurak away.

One of the strangers rose to his feet, a fistful of papers in one hand. "This is our proposition," he began. "You know that there are vast reserves of oil underneath the Coastal Plain. The company I represent wants to drill for it, and they're prepared to offer you a fair price for the rights."

His voice was quiet and he smiled as he talked. Ujurak thought that he looked kind. It sounded as if he was offering something that the villagers would want. So why had Tiinchuu looked so grim when he left his den to come to this meeting?

"We'll give you more money than you've ever seen in your lives," one of the other visitors added.

The villagers glanced at one another and murmured to their neighbors, hiding their mouths with their hands. Ujurak could see that most of them didn't like the idea. They kept repeating the word "oil" as if it was something important.

Ujurak frowned, puzzled. *What's money? What's "oil," and why do these men want it?*

He shivered. Pain had begun banging in his head like a woodpecker rapping on the trunk of a tree. The voices of the flat-faces pulsed loud and then soft in his ears, and he missed the next few words.

" . . . a poor living here," the man in black was saying when Ujurak could listen again. "You need jobs. You need hospitals and all the benefits of modern development. Allowing the oil companies onto your land will give you all this."

Tiinchuu, who had been sitting with his eyes fixed on his clasped hands, looked up. "Senator, we are not poor," he stated calmly. "Not in the things that matter. We drink clean water and breathe pure air. The spirit of the land is strong. We—"

The male flat-face Tiinchuu had called "Senator" let out an irritated snort, and gestured with his fistful of papers as if he were flicking away a fly. Ujurak didn't think he looked quite so kind now.

"We are rich in our hearts," Tiinchuu finished, ignoring the visitor's reaction. "Not even the oil companies can put a price on that."

"Just a minute." One of the younger males standing by the wall of the hut took a step forward. "You're not speaking for all of us, Tiinchuu. It's hard to make a living here, and not all of us want to struggle for the rest of our lives."

"He's right." Another young male at the far side of the hut sprang to his feet. "And the Senator's right. We have families to think of. I worked for an oil company in the east, and life was better there."

"Then what did you come back for?" someone called out.

"You know why he came back," another villager replied, sounding annoyed. "To look after his parents."

Ujurak could hardly make out the last few words as comments rose from every part of the room. Someone else yelled, "Sit down!"

"We have a right to be heard!" the first young man protested.

Ujurak shrank into the shadows as the angry voices rose. *What if they start fighting? Will they get out their firesticks?* A hubbub of voices rose around him, and he lost track of what the flat-faces were saying. But he could smell the adrenaline scents of anger and fear.

Ujurak could sense the mounting impatience of the three black-clad men as they listened to the villagers' arguments. The Senator spoke again. Ujurak missed what he said because another wave of heat swept over him. His knees felt weak, and he leaned back against the wall to stop himself from falling.

"You hypocrite!" The female villager on the platform sprang to her feet and faced the Senator, glaring at him furiously even though her head reached only to his shoulder. Ujurak was reminded of Lusa standing up to Toklo. The Senator looked taken aback, as if he hadn't expected any of the villagers to defend themselves so fiercely.

Then Tiinchuu spoke, more calmly than the others. "The oil under our land won't last forever. What will happen to us when it has run out? What will we eat when the caribou no longer migrate past our village? Our ancient ways will be forgotten."

"You don't speak for the whole tribe," the Senator said. "Times have changed."

Tiinchuu shook his head. "I do not claim to speak for everyone. Here, every single one of us has a voice, and we will hear it. We'll take a vote," he went on calmly. "Raise your hands if you want to allow the oil company to develop our land."

For a moment, no one moved. Then the young men who had spoken in favor of the oil raised their hands, along with a few of the other villagers. They looked at one another almost guiltily, as if they realized that few people agreed with their view.

Tiinchuu nodded. "And now those who don't want the oil company to come here."

It was as though a forest sprouted in the hut as most of the villagers raised their hands. "That seems clear enough," Tiinchuu said to the strangers.

The Senator's mouth twisted into a hard, flat line. "I expected this. I know how stubborn you people are. You've refused to allow drilling before, so it's no surprise that you've refused again. I'm sorry, but if you won't give us access, we'll have to take it."

Ujurak felt the villagers around him stiffen in shock.

Tiinchuu's eyebrows lifted. "What do you mean?"

"We came here for oil, and we *will* have it. The good of the whole country is at stake."

Ujurak felt a jolt of fear in his belly. The Last Great Wilderness wasn't safe after all. These flat-faces obviously thought they had the power to destroy it, in spite of anything the villagers could do.

"Save the wild!" he called out hoarsely, but none of the flat-faces heard him.

The villagers were springing to their feet, shaking their fists at the men on the platform.

"You can't do that!"

"The land is ours!"

"Get out of here, and don't come back!"

The men ignored the shouts of protest. The Senator thrust his papers back into a square pouch, then beckoned to the other two to follow him out of the hut.

Ujurak pressed himself into the corner of the room as the visitors swept toward the door. But there was nowhere he could hide properly. The Senator halted, looking shocked. His cold gray eyes softened.

"Who is this?" he demanded, pointing at Ujurak.

Ujurak flinched as the villagers all turned to stare at him.

"I don't know. I've never seen him before," the woman with the goose spirit answered, craning her neck to give Ujurak a closer look.

To Ujurak's relief, Tiinchuu pushed his way through the crowd and laid a hand gently on his shoulder. "I found the boy unconscious on my doorstep," he told the strangers. "I've treated his injuries, and he's getting well. I'll take him back to rest now."

He began to propel Ujurak toward the door, but the Senator thrust him aside. "This is monstrous!" he exclaimed. "This boy is seriously ill; I can tell that just by looking at him. He needs urgent medical care."

"He's getting all the care he needs." There was an edge to Tiinchuu's voice.

The Senator let out a sigh. "I mean modern facilities—the kind that *you* don't have."

Ujurak let out a cry of terror as the Senator stepped forward and picked him up. Tiinchuu grabbed the man's arm, but his companions pushed the healer away.

"I'm going to see the boy gets the help he needs," the Senator said, thrusting at the hut door with one shoulder and carrying Ujurak out into the open. "As for the rest of you people, it's time you woke up and joined the real world!"

CHAPTER EIGHTEEN

Lusa

Lusa poked her head out yet again from the shelter of the rocks. "They've been in there an awfully long time," she whimpered. "I hope Ujurak is okay."

She saw her own anxiety reflected in Kallik's eyes as the white bear peered over her shoulder. "Maybe we should never have brought him to the flat-faces."

"If we hadn't, he'd be dead by now." Lusa was at least certain about that. "I know he doesn't have to be afraid of the flat-faces who live here. It's these new ones I don't like." She wrinkled her nose at the harsh scent of the metal bird, suppressing a shiver as she remembered the three strangers in their sleek black pelts.

"Should we go look through the gap in the wall?" Kallik suggested, jerking her head toward the big den.

Lusa was tempted, but she guessed that with so many flat-faces inside, they were sure to be spotted. "I don't think—" she began.

A crash interrupted her. The door of the den had been

flung open, slamming back against the exterior wall. The three visiting flat-faces strode out into the open. Lusa's belly lurched in terror when she saw that one of them was carrying Ujurak in his arms.

Ujurak was struggling feebly, crying out something in a thin flat-face voice. Lusa didn't understand what he was saying. Then his gaze fell on Lusa and Kallik, and he stretched out one arm toward them. "Lusa! Kallik! Help me!"

"He's calling to us!" she exclaimed. "They must be taking him away. Kallik, we might never see him again!"

Suddenly Lusa didn't care about being seen by the flat-faces. She burst out from behind the rocks, letting out a fearsome roar as she hurtled toward the strangers. "Stop!" she shouted. "Don't take him! Leave him alone!"

The flat-faces stared at her in horror, then ran for their metal bird.

"Stop!" Lusa shouted again. "Ujurak belongs with us!"

The flat-faces ignored her. They reached the metal bird and climbed aboard, bundling Ujurak in with them. Loud growling like the noise of a firebeast came from inside the bird; the metal wings on top began to spin with a chopping, huffing noise. Wind swept across Lusa, buffeting her fur, as the bird rose slowly into the air.

Scrambling to her paws, she bounded after the metal bird. "Come back! Come back!" Her calls were drowned out by the clattering of its wings. "He's our friend!"

As the metal bird rose higher, Lusa became aware of shouting from behind her, and she realized that the villagers were pouring out of the big den, surrounding her. She felt trapped by the noise and scent of flat-faces. Panic surged through her from her snout to the tip of her tail and she let out a growl. "Get back! Leave me alone!" she snarled, lashing out with her forepaw in the hope of scaring them off.

A yell of alarm came from somewhere among the flat-faces. Lusa heard Kallik calling, "Lusa! Lusa!" but she couldn't see her friend through the crowd of flat-faces.

Desperately Lusa searched for a way of escape. Then she recognized the healer who had helped Ujurak. He pushed his way to the front of the crowd, opening up a gap. Lusa charged through it and saw Kallik waiting for her near the rocky outcrop.

"Come on!" the white bear barked. "We've got to get out of here."

As she ran toward her friend, Lusa spotted the metal bird again, growing smaller as it flew off above the mountain slope, heading along the ridge that ran parallel with the coast. She hurled herself after it. She had already lost Toklo, the bear she had left the Bear Bowl to find, and now she was losing Ujurak, too. She realized that although she had imagined herself living the life of a wild bear, alone in the forest, she had never really thought about what that would mean. Now all she knew for sure was that she didn't want to lose her friends. Her heart pounded with fear.

"Quick, Kallik," she begged. "We've got to follow them."

Not waiting for Kallik's response, she hurtled across the valley and began to scramble uphill, determined to keep the metal bird in sight. Lusa's breath came in huge gasps as she forced herself to keep going, thrusting herself up the steep slope.

"Lusa, slow down!" Kallik called after her. "It's no use!"

Muscles screaming, paws scraping on the rough ground, Lusa forced herself on, up the mountain slope. The metal bird was still ahead of her. Lusa charged down into a gully, then up the slope on the other side, dodging rocks and scrubby bushes. She could hear Kallik struggling behind her.

Pausing for a moment, gasping for breath, she saw that the metal bird was growing tinier and tinier in the sky, pulling away from her in spite of all her efforts.

"No!" she choked out.

She scrambled farther up the slope, through a clump of stunted trees, until she reached a plateau not far from the summit. The metal bird was nothing more than a dot against the clouds. A flight of birds swarmed across Lusa's view; when the sky cleared again, the tiny speck had disappeared.

"They've gone!" Lusa wailed, collapsing onto the ground. "We've lost Ujurak! Oh, Kallik, it's not supposed to end like this."

Kallik flung herself down beside Lusa, chest heaving as she fought to breathe. She was too exhausted to speak, but Lusa could see the despair in her eyes.

I've failed! I've failed! Lusa wanted to whimper. *There were four of us yesterday. And now there are only two.*

CHAPTER NINETEEN

Ujurak

Ujurak lay on his back on a kind of bed in the belly of the metal bird. His stomach lurched as the bird lifted into the air. He tried to call out to Lusa again, but his throat still hurt and his voice was too weak to carry.

What will happen to Lusa and Kallik now? Will the villagers hurt them? And where's Toklo?

He struggled to sit up, to look out of the metal bird's windows, but he was too dizzy to keep himself upright. His throat was on fire, and his skin felt as though ants were crawling all over it.

An arm went around his shoulders, raising him; Ujurak shrank away with a cry as he realized the Senator was sitting beside him. Was he going to start shouting like when he was talking to the villagers in the big den?

But when the Senator spoke, his voice was gentle. "Take it easy, son. You're going to be just fine. Here, drink this."

He held a water bottle to Ujurak's lips. Ujurak gulped the

cold liquid gratefully, feeling it begin to quench the fire in his throat.

Sitting up like this, resting against the Senator's shoulder, he managed to get a glimpse out of the window, but all he could see were clouds and sky. Lusa and Kallik must be far behind, he realized, left in the village.

"Lie back now," the Senator said when he had finished drinking. He gently pushed Ujurak back so that he was lying flat on the seat again; he tightened a blanket around him and arranged a small pillow under his head. "That's it."

The metal bird bobbed in the air, making his stomach lurch. Ujurak groped for the three carved bears that Tiinchuu had given him and gripped them tightly. Their edges felt hard against his frail flat-face fingers. *I'm a bear!* he thought, fighting back panic. *Bears don't fly. . . . Bears don't fly. . . . How will the others ever find me now?* When he changed into a goose or an eagle, he had always felt a pull that drew him back, even if he couldn't remember why. But he couldn't control his flight when he was inside the metal bird. *What if it never comes back down to land?*

Then he began to gain control of his fear. The metal bird had landed once; it was bound to land again, sooner or later. *I have to stay alert, so I'll be ready as soon as there's a chance to escape.*

Gazing around, he realized the two flat-faces who had gone into the big den with the Senator were seated behind them at the back of the bird. Two more flat-faces were sitting in seats in front of him. They wore bulky pelts in bright colors, with hard black things sticking out of their heads. They kept reaching out their paws to prod at the surface before them, pushing and pulling at shining bulges at the front of the bird, where lights blinked on and off.

"Try to rest," the Senator said.

Ujurak could hear a growl coming from deep inside the bird, and the rhythmic beating of its wings overhead. He had flown before as a gull, a goose, and even an eagle, but his sensations now were completely new. He couldn't feel any wind around him, and he didn't have to make any of the movements of flying: none of the swooping and gliding, no need to find air currents and let them take him upward, banking way above the ground.

Instead everything around him was still. He tried to imagine the metal bird flying high in the air, over the mountains, or maybe across the sea. He could tell that the bird was like a firebeast, not really alive, but he'd never seen a firebeast rise up from its BlackPath and fly off through the air.

Where are they taking me?

The Senator leaned forward to talk to the two flat-faces in front. "You'd better let the medical center know we're on our way."

One of the men glanced back and raised his hand to the Senator, the thumb pointing upward. Then he began to talk, too quietly for Ujurak to follow what he was saying. Another voice replied, sounding crackling and far away.

Ujurak leaned forward to see where the voice was coming from. But there was no one hiding at the front of the metal bird. The voice was coming out of nowhere, yet none of the others seemed to think there was anything strange about it.

The Senator looked down at him, smiling. "What's your name, son?" he asked.

"Ujurak."

"Where are you from?"

Ujurak stared at him. He couldn't answer that question in a way that would make any sense to the Senator.

Now the Senator was looking puzzled. "Where are your folks? Your mom and dad?"

At least Ujurak understood that question, even if he wasn't sure of the answer. "They're dead, I think."

"You don't have a mom?" The Senator scratched his head. "Are you American?" he asked. "You don't sound American."

That was another question Ujurak didn't understand; he lapsed into silence again.

The Senator shook his head with a smile. "What a mystery you are, young man," he said. "You're sick, you don't have any folks, but you're not scared, are you? Not a bit." He shook his head again, looking away from Ujurak. "Some kid," he muttered.

As he finished speaking, Ujurak felt the metal bird begin to drop. The note of its growling changed.

"Where am I going?" he croaked.

"We're going to get you fixed up," the Senator told him, smiling again.

That's not an answer, Ujurak thought. Out of the window he could see tall white buildings as the metal bird sank past them, and then he felt a jolt as it touched down on the ground.

Well, we're here. Wherever here is.

CHAPTER TWENTY

Toklo

A breeze rustled through the tops of the trees as Toklo padded over a bed of cool pine needles. Somewhere in the distance he could hear the gurgling of a stream. He drew in a long breath full of fresh forest scents, and let it out in a sigh of satisfaction.

This is the right place for a bear to be.

Traveling without taking any particular direction, he reveled in the sensation of being alone. He didn't have to listen to Lusa's chatter anymore. He didn't have to stand and wait while Ujurak examined a stone that might tell them where to go. He didn't have to look into Kallik's eyes and glimpse the hard, empty, icy wastes she longed for.

Toklo was thinking instead about carving out his own territory. He stayed alert for scratch marks on trees that warned of the presence of other grizzlies, but he didn't see any. *Pretty soon,* he thought as he clawed some berries from a bush and gulped them down, *as soon as I've found the right place, I'll set some scratch marks of my own.*

As he wandered farther into the forest, he realized that he

didn't feel as if he was exploring. Instead his surroundings had a strange familiarity. *That's it!* he thought, halting in surprise. *I feel as if I've come home.*

"Fluff-brained or what?" he muttered to himself, even while a warm sensation of comfort and safety was coursing through him from his snout to his tail. He had moved around so much with his mother and Tobi that he had never felt that he was at home before. They were always moving on, always padding restlessly from den to den, trying to find a place where they wouldn't be disturbed by bigger bears who didn't want them on their territory. This place felt more familiar, more reassuring than anywhere Toklo had been for a long time.

I remember that kind of bush, he thought as he ambled on, passing a thick shrub with dark, glossy leaves. *Oka told us it's no good to eat.*

His ears pricked as he heard the sound of a bird hopping on a branch above his head. *"Look at the bird over there."* Oka's voice seemed to sound in Toklo's head. *"That means there'll be juicy maggots at the bottom of the tree, if we can get there first."*

Toklo padded over to the tree and sniffed, turning over the scraps of bark and twigs that littered the ground. Soon he exposed a cluster of fat white grubs, wriggling in the light. He licked them up with his tongue and crunched them. *Delicious!*

Farther on, he heard the splash of a stream, and he stood on a jutting gray rock to gaze down into the peat-brown water. He remembered Oka teaching him and his brother not to stand on the green, moss-covered rocks. *They're too slippery. You could fall.*

Toklo took a drink from the stream, then leaped across it and journeyed on. Memories were crowding in on him now, and he began to run, feeling sheer joy in the bunching and stretching of his muscles and the sensation of wind in his fur. Bushes slapped lightly against his pelt, and his ears filled with the song of the forest. He could almost sense two bears running alongside him, one large, the other much smaller.

Oka! Tobi! I've come home!

A bird shot upward right underneath Toklo's paws, chattering crossly at him as it landed on a branch. Toklo halted, panting and glancing from side to side to make sure that no other bears had spotted him being so foolish. *Oka and Tobi are dead. It's just me now.*

Toklo took a deep breath and dug his claws into the ground. *That's fine. I'm glad to be alone.*

He was pleased with what he'd seen of the forest so far. There wasn't a big river where he could catch salmon—or at least he hadn't found one yet—but there were streams to drink from and plenty of signs of other prey. He picked up a trace of ground squirrel scent, and his jaws watered at the thought of succulent newkill.

As Toklo emerged into a clear patch on the hillside, he heard a thrumming noise from above the trees. His fur prickled as he cast a wary glance into the sky and spotted a metal bird skimming over the treetops. Then he relaxed as the sound died away, leaving the forest peaceful once more.

Dismissing the metal bird from his mind, Toklo gazed at

the forest around the grassy meadow. *All this could be my territory,* he thought. *My home.*

A raucous cry from behind him startled him out of his thoughts. He turned to spot a woodpecker clinging to a tree trunk a couple of bear-lengths away. Its pale head and spotted feathers stood out clearly against the rough bark.

"Er . . . hi there," Toklo muttered, a bit embarrassed to be talking to a bird. "Do you know you're in my territory?"

"Chawk!" the bird replied.

"I guess you don't know, or care," Toklo went on. "But it's true." All those moons of traveling, all the bare and hungry places he had passed through, had brought him here to this place, where he could be a true brown bear. "Not a black bear. Not a white bear," he informed the bird. "A brown bear. The way I was always meant to be."

"Chawk!" said the bird.

As the harsh cry died away, the forest seemed to grow still around Toklo. In the silence, a shiver passed through him. *The forest is very big. It'll take me ages to explore. . . .*

"But that's okay," he said aloud, trying to sound confident. "I've got plenty of time."

The first thing, he realized, was to make a den. A proper den, not just a temporary place to shelter under a bush or beside a rock. He tried to picture what Oka had done when she had built them a den. Toklo remembered his burning resentment that he had to stay and learn what to do while Tobi was allowed to go off and chase beetles.

Furious with Oka and his brother, Toklo hadn't paid much

attention. He had never imagined that Oka would leave him so soon.

She didn't mean to do it. She loved me. Lusa said so.

He wondered if Oka had realized even back then that Tobi would never live to build a den of his own.

Shaking his pelt, Toklo realized that he knew how to build a den. He had listened reluctantly, distracted by Tobi's happy cries, but he had listened all the same. He sniffed around the roots of the trees at the edge of the clearing, watched by the woodpecker with its head cocked to one side.

These aren't the right trees, he told himself. *Oka said to find one that doesn't shed its leaves in the cold season, so it shelters the den from rain and snow.*

He pushed a few bear-lengths farther into the forest until he came to a row of dark-needled pines growing along the sloping bank of a stream. The woodpecker darted along behind him, as if it wanted to see what he would do.

This is a good place, Toklo decided. *There's water, and bushes near the stream that would be good for hunting. There might even be mountain goats in the clearing.*

Toklo rejected the trees at the bottom of the slope, knowing that if there was heavy rain the stream would rise and flood his den. He found a good thick tree a little farther up, but its roots were so tangled that he knew he would never be able to make the hole big enough. Finally, near the top of the slope, he found the perfect spot beneath a tree whose low-growing branches almost swept the ground, to give extra shelter. He padded around it until he worked out where he would be protected from the prevailing wind, and where he would get the most warmth from the sun during the day.

There's so much to think about! But that's okay, because making a den is what bears do.

Still watched by the woodpecker, Toklo started to dig. He was surprised how hard it was to force his claws through the roots of grass and the hard-packed earth. Oka had made it look so easy, with her huge paws and sharp claws.

My claws are blunt, Toklo thought, drawing back from the beginnings of his hole to examine them. *Oka used to sharpen her claws on a tree where deer had stripped the bark. I guess I'd better do that.*

He set off again. He had to pad many bear-lengths farther into the forest before he spotted a tree where the bark had been peeled away, exposing the gray trunk beneath. Reaching up as high as he could, Toklo scraped and scraped until his paws were sore and his claws ached.

"That will have to do," he panted.

Looking up at the tree, he suddenly forgot about his throbbing paws. *I've marked a tree! This is really my territory now.* Pride filled him up like rainwater in a curved leaf as he examined the scratches: high up to show how tall he was, deep to show his strong, sharp claws. *No bear will mess with me now!*

On his way back to his den site, Toklo marked a few more trees, reaching as high as he could with his front paws. The woodpecker still followed, chattering with annoyance as if it didn't like the marks Toklo was making.

"Tough!" Toklo told it. "This is my territory now, and these are my trees."

Back at his chosen tree, he started digging again. He worked faster now, but it was still hard going. His legs ached and his claws felt as if they were going to drop off. Earth showered everywhere, making his eyes stream and his pelt itch.

At last Toklo realized that the light in the forest was changing to red. The sun was going down. His den was still only a scoop no deeper than his belly.

I'm starving! he thought, backing out of the hole and spitting out earth. *I've got to take a break from digging and find some prey.*

Wincing as he put his sore paws to the ground, he shambled down the slope to the stream and jumped from rock to rock until he found a small pool.

Toklo leaped in, relishing the cool shock of the water as it rinsed his fur. Tiny silver shapes darted away from him. Revived by the water, Toklo pounced, slapping his paw down on one of the fish and feeling it wriggle against his pad. Thrusting his snout into the stream, he bit into the fish and swallowed it.

The fish was small, but its taste tingled in his mouth. Toklo waded farther into the pool, managing to catch more of the tiny fish, until the survivors had all fled into the unreachable shallows around the edge or into crevices among the rocks.

Finally Toklo heaved himself out of the stream, too tired to hunt anymore. He padded back upstream and climbed the slope to curl up in his unfinished den. Satisfaction surged over him. He didn't care that the den wasn't finished. It was his, in his own territory, and he had eaten prey he had caught himself.

The den felt cold without Kallik, Lusa, and Ujurak curled up beside him, but Toklo wriggled deeper into the hole, out of the chill night wind, and was comforted by the familiar scents of earth and trees and half-buried roots. Soon his eyes closed and he slept.

The next morning Toklo bounded out of his den, determined to get on with his digging, but his paws were sore, and the muscles on his shoulders felt as if they were on fire. When he started to scrape at the earth again he found it was much harder to make progress. He kept coming up against roots and had to push his snout into the hole and bite through them.

I'm fed up with this! he thought, backing out of the den with a long, gnarled root in his jaws. He dropped it and pawed at his mouth to try to get rid of some of the dirt. *I'm going to take a break and explore some more.*

He set off up the mountain, the morning sunlight filtering through the trees and warming his fur. Before long he came upon a deer trail, the scent strong and recent, and farther on he picked up traces of ground squirrels.

When he reached the top of the ridge the forest was denser, the trees mostly the same dark pines as where Toklo had made his den. Sometimes he had to push his way through undergrowth, making a path for himself. The air was quiet and hushed, with few birds calling. Toklo found that he was looking around for the woodpecker.

Bee-brain! he scolded himself. *It's only a stupid bird.*

There was a bitter chill in the air in spite of the sunlight, and where the rays didn't penetrate, the earth beneath Toklo's paws crunched with frost. Beginning to feel thirsty, he looked for a stream, but he couldn't find one or hear the sound of running water anywhere.

I don't want this part of the forest in my territory, he decided.

Leaving scratches on a few trees, he headed back toward his den, padding along the ridge to descend by a different path. Farther along, he followed the scents of grass and clear air and emerged in an open meadow. Rabbits were feeding a few bear-lengths away.

Toklo tried to creep up on them, but his sore paws made him clumsy. The rabbits started up and fled, their white tails bobbing through the grass. Toklo gave chase, but his muscles ached so much that they easily outdistanced him.

Huffing in annoyance, Toklo gave up and padded back toward the trees. Before he reached them, he almost tripped over the body of a ground squirrel. Its pelt was slashed as if a hawk had killed it and then dropped it. Toklo sniffed it warily; it smelled fresh, and he tore into it.

"It's not as good as prey I caught myself," he mumbled around a mouthful. "But it's better than nothing." *And it shows this is a good territory,* he added to himself. *There's plenty of prey here to feed me.*

His belly comfortably full, Toklo settled down in the shade at the edge of the trees and snoozed with his nose on his paws. A grunt roused him; blinking, he raised his head to see another brown bear nosing its way out of the trees a few bear-lengths away. It was a young male, a bit smaller than Toklo, with powerful muscles and a frosting of gold on the surface of its fur. So far it hadn't seen him.

"Hey!" Toklo growled, standing up. "What are you doing here?"

The other bear whipped around. His fur bristled. "Why do you want to know?"

"This is my territory," Toklo told him. "Didn't you see the clawmarks?"

The other bear huffed scornfully. "What, those little scratches? I thought they were made by a ground squirrel."

A tide of fury started to mount inside Toklo. *My clawmarks are strong and powerful!*

"I think you must be blind," he snarled. "You can't see what's in front of your snout."

"You're blind yourself if you think your clawmarks will scare me!" the newcomer retorted.

"Watch it!" Toklo took a pace forward. "Get out of here or I'll rip your miserable pelt off."

"You can try." The other bear showed his teeth. "Where did you come from, anyway?"

"That doesn't matter." Toklo padded forward until he stood nose-to-nose with the stranger. "I'm here now."

"And so am I. I didn't climb all the way up this ridge to go back because some ground squirrel tells me to."

Toklo swiped a paw through the air, close enough to ruffle the other bear's fur. "This is *my* territory," he snarled.

"Oh yeah?" Anger flared up in the newcomer's eyes. "Actually, I think it's *mine*."

With a roar of fury, Toklo reared up on his hind legs and fell onto the other bear, carrying him off his paws and rolling him in the grass. The other bear fought back fiercely, fastening his teeth into Toklo's shoulder until Toklo had to break away, panting.

The two bears circled each other, low growls coming from their throats. Then the other bear darted in, gave Toklo a nip on the leg, and jumped back before Toklo could respond.

With another roar Toklo leaped at the newcomer. He remembered his fight against Shoteka on the island in Great Bear Lake. This young brown bear was so much smaller, it should have been much easier to defeat him. Instead Toklo found that he couldn't use his speed and nimble size against the clumsy strength of his opponent because the stranger was just as fast as he was.

Toklo found himself fighting desperately with teeth and claws, trading bites and slashes with the intruder. He struggled to keep his footing on the loose stones that rolled beneath his hindpaws.

I can't keep this up much longer, he thought as he lashed out again, raking a paw down his opponent's side. Then new determination surged up inside him. *This is the home I've been looking for all these moons. I'm not going to let him drive me out!*

Toklo summoned the strength to hurl himself at the other bear again. This time the bear jumped backward and stood glaring at him.

"This isn't the end," he spat, his sides heaving as he fought to catch his breath. "You're a stranger here. I can tell by the way you smell, and your fur's too dark for these parts. These mountains will never belong to you." He began to pad away, then paused and glanced back over his shoulder. "I'll see you again," he warned.

"Not if you know what's good for you!" Toklo called after him.

He watched the bear retreating toward the other side of the ridge until the trees swallowed him up. Then he turned and began limping back to his den. He was bruised and bleeding. Sinking into the hole, he licked his wounds, wondering what herbs Ujurak would have used.

There was something with a yellow flower. . . .

But Toklo was too exhausted to go looking for it. Curling up in the shelter of the den, he let himself drift off to sleep.

CHAPTER TWENTY-ONE

Ujurak

The beating of the bird's metal wings gradually grew slower and came to a stop. One of the men in the front seat slid open a panel in the side of the bird and jumped down to the ground. A blast of cold air came in through the gap, carrying unfamiliar scents that made Ujurak wrinkle his nose.

"Okay, Ujurak," the Senator said. "This is where we get off."

Looking out through the window, Ujurak saw that the metal bird was standing on a wide stretch of flat ground, with a large flat-face den at one side. The ground was covered with the same sort of hard stuff as a BlackPath. Several BlackPaths led away from it, and in the distance a white firebeast was snarling along one of them as it headed toward them.

The strange scents made Ujurak's head swim. He could smell the metallic scent of the bird, and a tang on the wind that reminded him of firebeasts. From the Senator, who still sat close beside him, Ujurak picked up the soft aroma of his pelts and a spicy scent that came from his face. But there was no scent of earth or water or green things growing.

I wonder where they're taking me.

In his mind he pictured his friends bounding across the mountains to find him, with Toklo in the lead. Trying to ignore his weakness and the pain in his throat, he managed to smile. *Come quick, my friends,* he thought.

Under cover of the blanket, he slid a hand into his pocket and pulled out one of the charms the healer had given him in the Arctic Village.

The white firebeast snarled to a halt where the BlackPath led onto the flat ground not far from the metal bird. Two male flat-faces jumped out of it and one of them pulled open doors at the back. The other strode over to the bird and looked in through the door.

"You must be Ujurak?" he said.

Ujurak nodded. The male looked friendly enough; he was tall and lanky, with a mop of red fur on top of his head.

"Hi, Ujurak. I'm Tom," he said. "We're going to take care of you from here, okay?"

With the Senator's help maneuvering him through the door, Tom picked up Ujurak and carried him to the firebeast. On the way, Ujurak opened his hand and let the tiny carved bear drop to the ground.

Please, spirits, guide my friends to me.

Tom lifted Ujurak through the doors at the back of the white firebeast and laid him on a bed inside. Ujurak gripped the blanket tightly, struggling with fear. There were no windows here, and in a moment they would close the doors and he would be shut in.

Are they feeding me to the firebeast?

The Senator leaned in through the open doors, smiling down at Ujurak. "You're in good hands now," he said. His voice was kind, so different from the harsh tones he had used in the big den in the village. "Don't worry about a thing. We'll get you fixed up. Try to relax."

Ujurak was slightly reassured. "I will," he whispered.

The Senator reached out and ruffled his head-fur. "I'll check in on you later."

Ujurak tried to smile, sensing that the Senator needed to feel he had done the right thing by taking him away from the Arctic Village. He didn't want to make the Senator angry again.

The Senator stepped back, glancing at the flat-face called Tom. "He's some kid," he said.

Tom nodded, then stepped into the back of the firebeast with Ujurak. The second flat-face pushed the doors shut. A moment later the firebeast growled into life and Ujurak felt it move off.

He wasn't sure how long the journey took. Once he was used to the sound and movement of the firebeast, it was quite soothing, and he was so exhausted that he dozed off for a brief while.

He roused when the firebeast halted again, and the inrush of cold air as the doors were opened brought him back to full consciousness.

"Here we are, kid," Tom announced.

Ujurak struggled to sit up, but Tom pushed him gently

back onto the bed. "Lie still," he said. "You don't have to do a thing."

Surprise surged through Ujurak as Tom and the other flat-face lifted the whole bed out of the firebeast and started to trundle it along. Ujurak realized that it had small round paws, a bit like the huge black paws of the firebeasts.

A bed with paws! Wait till I tell the others!

Moments later, Tom pushed the bed up to the doors of a huge white stone den. Ujurak craned his neck to stare; it was bigger than any other den he'd ever seen before. Its walls were filled with shiny squares, reflecting the pale gray sky.

"Welcome to the Eisenhower Medical Center," Tom said.

Ujurak's belly fluttered with the beginnings of panic. He'd be cut off from his friends for sure once the flat-faces took him in there. He fumbled in the pocket of his pelts and managed to drop another of the carved bears to the ground before he was swept inside the doors, which closed behind him with a hiss.

Warmth and light enveloped Ujurak as Tom brought his bed to a halt. Sniffing, Ujurak picked up a mixture of unfamiliar scents: He could smell traces of blood and fear, and even death. His skinny flat-face paws clenched hard as he tried to stay calm.

Two flat-face females dressed in white pelts headed for Ujurak and looked down at him as they reached his bedside.

"Welcome," one of them said. "Don't worry about a thing. We're here to look after you."

For a moment the women and Tom talked together, their

voices too soft for Ujurak to make out what they were saying. While he waited, he looked around. The walls of the huge den were white, like the outside. Off to one side, more flat-faces were working inside a kind of cage made of the same transparent stuff that was in the gaps in the wall. Chairs lined the walls, and there was a table that held a huge bunch of flowers; the flower heads were the biggest Ujurak had ever seen, and their colors were much brighter than the flowers he knew in the wild.

Flat-faces even have special kinds of flowers!

A touch on his shoulder distracted him; Ujurak looked up to see Tom smiling at him. "I gotta scoot now, Ujurak," he said. "I'll see you later." With a last squeeze of Ujurak's shoulder, he strode away, his feet making little squeaks on the floor.

One of the females bent over Ujurak, adjusting his blanket. "So you're the mystery boy," she said with a smile.

The other female was smiling, too. "Hey, Ujurak," she said in a kind voice.

One of the women took hold of his bed and pushed it down a long passage; the other flat-face walked beside her. They talked to each other, their voices quick and light. Unable to follow what they said, Ujurak stared around as he was wheeled along. Through open doors he spotted other flat-faces lying in beds, covered with white blankets.

It's peaceful here, he thought, trying to push down the last traces of his fear. *There's nothing to be afraid of.*

Near the end of the passage the flat-face pushing his bed wheeled it into a tiny room with metal walls; the door slid shut behind them, leaving him trapped there with the two females. His feelings of peace faded abruptly; his heart began to race with alarm and he tried to sit up.

Are they keeping me a prisoner here?

"Take it easy, Ujurak," one of the females said. "It's only the elevator."

She touched something on one of the walls, and Ujurak thought he could sense movement, though he couldn't see anything. Then the door slid open again and the female pushed him back out into the passage—but it was a different passage! Ujurak's eyes stretched wide in wonder. *These flat-faces are amazing!*

Farther down this new passage the female pushed him into a much smaller room, with a bed and a window hung with more of the brightly colored pelts. "There," she said. "Now we can have a good look at you."

Gently the two flat-faces took off the pelts Ujurak had taken from the village, and dressed him in a different set, made of a fine, soft fabric, pale green like young leaves. Then they helped him into the bed and covered him with white blankets.

Once he was settled, one of the women left. "I'll see you later, Ujurak," she promised with a wave of her hand.

The other woman bent over him and took his wrist; she held it for a few moments while she stared at some flat-face thing pinned to her pelt. "Hmm . . ." she murmured as she released him.

Ujurak watched curiously as she picked up a long black

thing like a flat snake and wrapped it around his arm. He knew about healing as a bear, and he had learned a bit about flat-face healing from the healer in the village, but he had never come across anything like this. *How is this snake-thing going to help me?*

The female was doing something that made the snake tighten around his arm. Ujurak's heart began to pound with alarm. *Is it going to crush me?*

"It's okay," the female said soothingly. "It only takes a minute."

As she finished speaking there was a long sighing sound from the snake and the pressure on Ujurak's arm relaxed. He blinked in confusion as the female put the snake away again.

What was that all about?

"Now open your mouth," the female said as she bent over him again. "Let me have a look."

Obediently Ujurak made his jaws gape as wide as he could.

"What happened to you, young man?" she asked.

"I ate a fishhook," Ujurak rasped.

The woman's eyes opened wide with surprise. "You did, did you? Hang on a minute."

She left the room, and returned a moment later with a male flat-face; he was short, for a flat-face, and his head-fur was gray and wispy. "Let's see your throat, Ujurak," he said.

Ujurak opened his mouth again, and the male flat-face peered into it with a tiny, bright light on the end of a stick. "It's healing well," he said after a few moments. "Did they give you any medicine for it in Arctic Village?"

"Yes, a lot." Ujurak wanted to make sure that these flat-faces knew how well the healer had looked after him. "I was asleep some of the time, so I don't know everything that Tiinchuu did. But I remember echinacea for the infection, and elderberry for fever."

The male nodded, his eyes bright with interest. "Good. Very good. Anything else?"

"There were little white things called pills. I had to swallow them with water."

The flat-face nodded again. "I think we'll give you some more of those pills," he said. Turning to the female, he added a few words Ujurak didn't understand.

What does he mean? Ujurak wondered as both the flat-faces went out, leaving him alone. But he was too exhausted to worry for long. For a few moments he struggled to keep his eyes open, but the bed was so comfortable that he gradually relaxed and sank into sleep.

CHAPTER TWENTY-TWO

Kallik

Kallik opened her eyes and peered out blearily across the mountain slope. She still felt exhausted; her muscles shrieked a protest when she tried to move, and her belly cramped with hunger. Her pelt pricked with fear, but there were no threats nearby, nothing but the empty ridge and the lonely cries of birds.

Managing to sit up, she looked around and saw Lusa lying close by her, mud streaking her black pelt. She was so still that Kallik's heart began to pound in panic, until she spotted the gentle rise and fall of her friend's chest.

Seeing her, Kallik remembered the terror of the day before, when flat-faces had carried Ujurak away in the metal bird, ignoring Lusa when she had tried to stop them.

"You were very brave, my friend," she whispered, nosing Lusa's shoulder. "But it didn't do any good."

She remembered their frantic chase, scrambling up the mountain slope with the metal bird high above and falling farther behind with every desperate pawstep, until at last they lost sight of it.

"Ujurak . . ." Kallik murmured. "What are they doing with you? Will we ever see you again?"

Lusa stirred, then sat up with a gasp.

"Lusa?" Kallik said. "Are you okay?"

For a moment Lusa stared at her as if she didn't recognize her; then her eyes cleared and she relaxed. "I'm fine, Kallik," she replied. "I just had a weird dream. We were trying to chase the metal bird, and it changed into Ujurak." She hesitated, scuffling her paws in the marshy grass. "We've lost him, haven't we?"

"I guess we have," Kallik whispered.

She didn't want to talk about their friend. Lusa sat and hunched in on herself, her eyes gazing into the distance. Kallik couldn't bear to see her look of desolation.

"Come on," she said, giving the little black bear a nudge. "We need to eat. Let's go look for some food."

For a moment she thought Lusa was going to refuse. Then the black bear let out a sigh. "Okay," she agreed listlessly.

A stiff breeze was blowing along the ridge, but sunlight lit the valley slopes in front of them.

"Suppose we go down a bit," Kallik suggested. "It'll be warmer there, and we can get out of the wind."

Lusa trailed behind her as Kallik led the way down the slope into the next valley. At the bottom a lake reflected the sky; around its edge trees and long grass offered the bears some shelter where they could forage among the berry bushes.

Kallik kept a lookout for the best berries and guided Lusa toward them. They had foraged together like this countless

times before, but now Kallik couldn't hide from herself that
something was missing. The berries seemed tasteless, but it
was too hard to work up the enthusiasm to go hunting for
other prey. *We need Toklo and Ujurak,* she thought. *We should be
four, not two.*

A pebbly spit of ground jutted out into the lake. Kallik
padded along it to the end and gazed down into the water,
wondering whether she could catch a fish. But she didn't see
any flash of silver; the water was clear and empty.

Dipping her snout to take a drink, Kallik turned back to
see Lusa standing forlornly at the edge of the lake. She quickened her pace to return to the black cub.

"I can't see any fish," she reported. "Are you still hungry?
We could look for grubs under some of these stones." She
pointed her snout at a scattering of flat rocks a little farther
around the lake.

Lusa shrugged. "If you want."

The sun rose in the sky and began to sink again as the two
she-bears halfheartedly searched for grubs. Later, their bellies
full, Kallik and Lusa sat beside the lake, watching the shadows
lengthen.

"We should find somewhere to den for the night," Kallik
said. "Maybe there'll be a sheltered spot among the trees."

"I guess we can look," Lusa replied.

Kallik led the way into a nearby copse and discovered a
small hollow under the roots of a tree. She and Lusa squeezed
into it together.

"Try to get some sleep," Kallik urged Lusa. "Maybe things

will be better tomorrow." But she knew that her words were empty, and Lusa wasn't deceived.

Kallik felt as though she were lying on every sharp pebble, every pointed scrap of twig, in the whole wilderness. Sleep was impossible; though Lusa was crouched beside her with her paws over her nose, Kallik could tell that the little black bear wasn't asleep, either. Stars began to appear through the branches of the tree above her head, clustering so thickly that the sky looked white through Kallik's half-closed eyes.

"Kallik?" Lusa sat up suddenly, startling Kallik out of a doze. "Kallik, I've made up my mind. I'm going to look for Ujurak. I can't let the metal bird take him away. No bird can fly forever, so I'll follow the way we saw it go, and find it wherever it landed." She hesitated, gazing deep into Kallik's eyes, then added, "I'll understand if you don't want to come with me. I know you want to go back to the ice, and . . . and I wish you luck there. . . ." Her voice trailed off miserably.

"What are you, fluff-brained or something?" Kallik nosed Lusa's shoulder. "Of course I'm coming with you."

Joy flooded into Lusa's eyes, and she sprang to her paws. "Really? You're sure?"

"As sure as I've ever been."

"Then let's go!"

As Kallik followed Lusa back toward the lake, she thought about how quickly she had made the decision to look for Ujurak. She had felt the pull of the ice so strongly for so long, and she had been ready to find her own path there, without the others. But since Ujurak had gotten injured, she had felt the bond with her friends grow stronger than the draw of the ice. *Ujurak needs our help, and now Lusa needs me.*

Kallik and Lusa trudged side by side through the darkness. All was silent except for the sighing of the wind and the occasional cry of a night bird. At last, exhausted, they stopped to rest on the crest of a hill, with dawn a pale silver line on the horizon.

"I hope we're going the right way," Lusa murmured.

"This is the direction the metal bird was flying," Kallik pointed out. "It has to come down to earth sooner or later."

Lusa let out a faint sigh. "Kallik . . ." she began. "There's something I want to tell you."

"Yes?"

"You remember my accident, back on Smoke Mountain? When the firebeast struck me?"

Kallik nodded.

"I had a dream afterward. My mother came to me and told me something I didn't understand. And I still don't understand it."

"What was it?" Kallik prompted. She wasn't sure why Lusa wanted to talk about this now, but her curiosity was pricked.

"She told me I had to save the wild."

Kallik stared at her. "Do you know what that means?"

"No," Lusa replied, shaking her head. "But I know it has something to do with Ujurak. He had a dream that told him the same thing. And do you remember when he said our journey wasn't over? Well, deep down, I feel just the same." She let out a bewildered huff of breath. "But I don't know what I'm supposed to do, without Ujurak."

"We'll find him," Kallik assured her. She couldn't quite agree with her friend that their journey wasn't over yet; she had always believed that her own journey would end on the ice. But she wouldn't abandon Lusa, or Ujurak, whatever it took to find him again.

Huddled together, the she-bears dozed on the hilltop until the sun had risen above the horizon. The pale sky gradually deepened to blue, dotted here and there with small puffs of white cloud; the wind dropped to a gentle breeze.

When they went on, Kallik felt her spirits lighten. Lusa seemed certain that they'd find Ujurak, and her chatter gave Kallik a new surge of optimism.

"I wonder what Ujurak will be when we find him," Kallik said. "Wouldn't the no-claws be scared if they saw him changing into a brown bear?"

Lusa let out a little snort of amusement. "Or a goose, so he could fly away!"

"That would be great," Kallik replied. "Then *he* could find *us!*"

"I wonder what Toklo is doing now," Lusa murmured.

"Oh, chasing prey, scratching marks on trees, just being a brown bear," Kallik said. "You know that's what he always wanted."

"Chasing all the black bears away," Lusa went on with a huff of amusement. "Or maybe he's caught a caribou at last!"

"And now he's sitting in a cave, roaring at passing squirrels," Kallik added.

Crossing a stream, they followed its channel down a long slope covered with tough, springy grass. The sun was high overhead, dazzling on the water. Kallik's belly growled; it seemed a long time since the berries she had eaten on the previous day, when they had been too tired and discouraged to forage properly. It didn't seem right, just being with Lusa. There was an emptiness around them that couldn't be filled with hunting or talking about Ujurak.

"I wish Toklo were with us now," she whispered.

"So do I," Lusa replied.

CHAPTER TWENTY-THREE

Lusa

Following the stream around a spur of the hill, Lusa and Kallik came
to a place where the land fell away more steeply in front of
them. The stream cascaded down in a series of small water-
falls and joined a wider river in the valley below.

As they drew closer, Lusa could see that the river flowed
fast and deep, the water foaming around boulders that poked
out of the current. The opposite bank was steep and rocky,
and it seemed a long way away.

"That looks dangerous to cross," Kallik commented as
they drew to a halt on the bank. "Do you think we should go
upriver or downriver?"

Lusa hesitated, snuffing the air and glancing undecidedly
up- and downstream. "Ujurak was best at this," she murmured. "He always seemed to know which way to go." She
padded forward until she stood on the very edge of the bank,
with water rushing along past her paws. "Remember what he
used to do?" she continued. "You have to look at all the pos-
sibilities and see how you feel about them."

While Kallik looked up and down, Lusa examined the two directions carefully. Upstream the river was a narrow, raging torrent, foaming around rocks, with thornbushes crowding close to the water's edge. Where she and Kallik were standing, the water glided along more quietly, but a little way downstream it divided around a rock. The sharp black outline stuck up out of the river like a bear's paw, with the current pounding it and gushing around it in a tumult of white foam.

Lusa's paws tingled. There was a sign here, if she could just work out what it was.

"I've no idea," Kallik confessed, breaking into Lusa's thoughts. "What do you think? Which way will lead us to the metal bird and Ujurak?"

Thoughtfully Lusa pointed her snout upriver. "That way looks narrow and shaded," she said. "And the current is too fast around the rocks. It doesn't feel right to me. And downriver"—she turned and pointed again—"look at that rock! It's as if it's blocking the way. We shouldn't be going up- or downriver."

Kallik was gazing at her with doubt in her eyes. "Lusa," she said, "you're not telling me we have to swim across here, are you?"

"Yes!" Lusa felt a sudden surge of confidence. *I'm right! This is what we have to do.* "I know it's not perfect," she began, "but unless we cross here we might have to travel skylengths before we find a better place. And look at the way the sun is shining on the water, making a sparkling path. The spirits are telling us that's the way we have to go."

Kallik caught her breath. "Yes! I see it, too! You are clever, Lusa."

Lusa shrugged, feeling a little embarrassed. "I'm just trying to work out what Ujurak would have done. Let's go!"

She bunched her muscles, ready to jump in, then hesitated, remembering the huge river they had crossed with Toklo and Ujurak. She had almost drowned then. . . . She swallowed nervously. *I'm a black bear,* she reminded herself. *We're the best swimmers of all the bears. And this river is nowhere near as wide as the other one.*

But she still couldn't forget the feeling of the black water closing over her head, her ears roaring with bubbles, and her nose and mouth filling with something that made it impossible to breathe. . . . She shivered.

"What's the matter?" Kallik asked. "We can find a different way if you want."

Lusa forced herself to shake her head. "I'm fine," she insisted. "We've seen the signs, so we know this is right."

In her heart she was certain that whoever had sent the signs to Ujurak had also sent this one to her. She had to trust in that power, and accept the guidance.

"Let's go!" she barked.

"Wait!" Kallik shouldered Lusa away from the edge of the river.

"What's the matter?" Lusa asked, confused. "I'm okay, honestly."

"I know," Kallik told her; she was keeping herself between Lusa and the river. "And I'm willing to give this a try. It's

just . . . well, look at the current. I think if we want to go across
the river, it's no good to swim straight across. We have to swim
as if we want to go upriver. The current will drag us the other
way, and we should end up where we want to be."

"But won't crossing like that take longer?" Lusa asked,
impatient to be moving.

"Yes, and it will be very tiring. But at least we won't get
washed away."

Lusa studied the fast-flowing water. She imagined a stick
floating out from the bank and shooting downstream as soon
as it reached the middle of the river where the current was
strongest. To reach the shore directly on the other side, the
stick would have to start higher up along the bank, to be carried down as well as across. "Okay, we'll do it your way," she
said.

She launched herself into the river, striking out forcefully
against the current. Immediately she felt its strong pull, tugging at her legs. But she kept on paddling determinedly, with
Kallik swimming at her shoulder, nudging her upstream. Lusa
huffed and puffed as she fought the drag of the river, almost
swimming sideways as she tried not to get swept away. Gradually they drew closer to the opposite bank.

Just as she was beginning to think that the danger was over,
she heard a yelp from Kallik. "Lusa! Watch out!"

Lusa glanced over her shoulder to see a fallen tree branch
being carried downstream, turning over and over in the white-
tipped water. She was swimming straight into its path.

Pumping her legs desperately, Lusa tried to swim out of the

way of the branch, but she was too late. The branch crashed
into her and she was sent tumbling down the river, her legs
flailing as she tried to stay upright. Her head went under the
swirling water. She fought her way back to the surface, but she
had lost her sense of direction. All she could see was water
bubbling past her snout.

A moment later all the breath was driven out of Lusa's body
as the current flung her against something hard. Half dazed,
she realized that she was pinned against the huge rock she had
noticed earlier.

"Kallik! Help!" she choked out.

Lusa fought against the current, struggling to pry herself
away from the rock, but all the terrifying power of the river
was trapping her there. There was no escaping the crushing
weight of the water. It roared in her ears, nose, and mouth; she
could feel her strength draining away by the instant. She tried
to breathe and took in a mouthful of water.

I'm going to drown!

Then she felt strong claws fastening to her pelt. Peering through the surge of water, she made out the drenched
white shape of Kallik by her side. The white bear was pushing
her across the face of the rock. Lusa felt the current gushing
around the side as it caught her, and Kallik held on to her as it
dragged them both away downriver.

"Swim!" Kallik gasped.

For a few moments Lusa was too exhausted to obey. She
pawed feebly at the surface, Kallik's claws keeping her above
water. The frothing waves surrounded them, battering over

their faces and their backs; Lusa was sure that any moment now they would sink and not come up again.

Then she caught sight of a tree on the bank. Its branches were bathed in golden rays of sunlight. Calm suddenly swept over her, as if some great bear had laid a gentle paw on her head. Somehow she forced her aching legs to begin paddling again, and tried to keep the opposite bank in sight as she struggled across the current.

You told us to cross the river, she thought. *You won't let us drown.*

At last, Lusa could feel the scrape of rocks beneath her thrashing paws and managed to stand with the river surging around her shoulders. Kallik gave her a push and guided her to a gap in the rocky bank, where they could scramble up a slope of shale.

Lusa felt as if her body were one huge bruise as she clambered out of the river. Her fur was plastered to her sides, and she shivered in the bright sunshine as she gasped and coughed up mouthfuls of water.

Bending her head, she whispered, "Thank you. Thank you . . ."

"That's okay," Kallik said, pushing her snout into Lusa's shoulder. "You managed fine in the end."

"I was thanking Arcturus." Lusa staggered into the shade of a bush and collapsed, her sides heaving as she gulped in air. "He gave us the signs to lead us across the river. I had to trust the signs to lead us the right way, not somewhere we'd drown." She looked up at her friend, who just gave her a confused nod. "But thank you, too, Kallik. I wouldn't have made it without you."

Kallik stumbled to her side and curled up next to her. "I'll always be here for you, my friend," she murmured.

Lusa knew they should get up and continue searching for Ujurak. But the sun was warm on her fur, and the roar of the river faded to a comforting murmur. Kallik was dozing at her side; at last Lusa gave up the struggle to stay awake, and let herself sink into darkness.

CHAPTER TWENTY-FOUR

Toklo

Sunlight angling through the trees woke Toklo. He blinked sleepily, then let out a startled yelp and opened his eyes wider. He was staring into Ujurak's face!

"Cloud-brain!" he muttered to himself a moment later. It wasn't Ujurak's muzzle he was looking at, just a knot in the trunk of a nearby tree. *It doesn't even look like Ujurak!* he scoffed, hauling himself out of his den and shaking earth from his pelt. *That's just the sort of bee-brained thing Lusa would think!*

Lusa believed that when bears died, their spirits went into trees. Toklo's belly lurched. *Ujurak isn't dead,* he told himself. *That flat-face was making him better.*

To push the thought out of his mind, he rubbed himself against the knotted bark, giving his pelt a good scratch. His wounds from the previous day's fight were still painful; his muscles ached and his belly was growling for prey.

Cautiously he sniffed the air. *No sign of that other bear. Good! I taught him a lesson he won't forget!*

Feeling stronger, Toklo looked around. The forest was very

quiet, and he wondered where the woodpecker had gone. "I wish he'd come back," he muttered, and immediately felt foolish. *That's totally squirrel-brained, missing birds!*

But it stops you from missing Kallik, Lusa, and Ujurak, a small voice whispered inside his head.

Toklo tried to shake off the thought as if it were a troublesome fly. He struggled to recapture the way he had felt the day before, when the forest was an exciting place to explore, and he was proud to be a bear, marking out his own territory. But somehow he didn't want to venture any farther today.

I'll stay here and finish off my den, he decided.

But when he started to scrape at the hole again his claws hurt too much to keep on digging out the hard-packed earth. Frustrated, Toklo paced up and down for a while, trying to decide what to do. His belly was bawling even louder now, but there didn't seem to be any prey close by his den.

I'll go this way, he said to himself at last, setting out in the opposite direction from the meadow where he had encountered the other bear.

As the sun climbed higher in the sky, he worked his way deeper into the forest, crossing a wooded spur that thrust out from the ridge. A stream tumbled down to the valley bottom, and Toklo splashed through it, grateful for the bubbling water on his sore claws, and its icy coolness when he stopped to quench his thirst. Strength began to return to his muscles as he scrambled up rocks and bounded down slopes covered with lush undergrowth. The trees cast their shade over him, filling the air with the murmuring of their leaves.

He still hadn't found any prey when he came to another stream where berry bushes were growing close to the water on the other side. As he waded across to the opposite bank he heard a rustling sound among the bushes. Another bear was in his territory!

"Get out!" Toklo roared, charging toward it.

He skidded to a stop as a small black bear scrambled out of the bushes, staring at him with fear in its eyes. It backed away, letting out a terrified whimper, and Toklo took a pace backward. Suddenly he could see Lusa gazing at him from the dark, frightened eyes of the other bear. Sensing that it wasn't about to be attacked, the black bear whipped around and fled.

As the little bear scuttled away, a scoffing voice spoke behind Toklo. "Ooh! You're so brave! No black bears in *your* territory!"

Toklo spun around to see the other brown bear emerging from behind a nearby tree.

Wincing inwardly, Toklo let out a growl as he stepped forward. "What do *you* want?" He bared his teeth. *If he wants another fight, he can have one!*

But the other bear didn't move toward him. "I'm just exploring," he said. "Hunting. Watching."

"But this is my territory," Toklo reminded him.

The brown bear snorted. "No, it's not. I told you, you don't belong here."

Rage began to mount inside Toklo. "I've built a den!" he protested.

"What? That little scrape in the earth back there? I thought that was a ground squirrel hole." The brown bear's eyes were gleaming with mockery. "Do your ears fit in? At least your head will be above water if it floods."

Toklo's fury overflowed. He leaped forward and the other bear swiped at him with a paw, catching him with a blow on the side of the head. Surprised at the smaller bear's strength, Toklo stepped back, his ears ringing.

"There's more where that came from," the intruder growled.

Toklo stared at him. He didn't want to admit that he was reluctant to start another fight. "Can't we share the territory?" he blurted out. "There's plenty of prey."

"You don't get it, do you?" the brown bear huffed scornfully. "There's less prey every season, less territory, and more bears fighting over what's left. Flat-faces steal more and more, and if we bears try to fight back, they *always win*. This mountain can't support the bears that were born here, let alone strangers."

Toklo stared in confusion. *But this is the Last Great Wilderness! There's supposed to be plenty of prey.*

The brown bear padded up to him and thrust his snout into Toklo's face.

"Not even the *mountain* wants you here," he snarled. Turning, he headed into the undergrowth without a backward glance.

Glaring furiously after him, Toklo waited for him to get well away, then padded in the direction of his den. The sun had gone; clouds were covering the sky, as dark as the thoughts that were crowding in on Toklo.

When he reached his den, he stood on the edge of the hole and looked down. *The bear was right,* he thought wretchedly. *That miserable scrape isn't a den. It's not even deep enough for a ground squirrel!*

But he knew that it wasn't his den that really troubled him. It wasn't even the loneliness of living on his own, though it was harder than he had ever imagined. What threw Toklo's thoughts into turmoil, as if bees were buzzing inside his head, was what the other bear had said about the mountain.

He says the territory is shrinking because of the flat-faces. And that's exactly what Ujurak has been telling us all along.

Thinking back to his journey with his friends, he knew that he missed the sense of a shared destiny, the companion-ship of bears who were prepared to work together, and not just fight. *I even miss Lusa's annoying chatter, and the way Ujurak sees signs everywhere!* He felt sorry for the other brown bear, who had no choice but to fight for every pawstep of territory, every mouthful of prey.

But you're no better now, he reminded himself, facing up to what he had lost. He felt as if part of his insides had been ripped out.

Ujurak was certain there was a chance to change everything, Toklo thought, crawling into his inadequate den. *But you threw away your opportunity to be a part of it.*

As the daylight faded, Toklo stared unseeing into the shadows of the forest. "Oh, Ujurak," he murmured. "Did I abandon you too soon?"

CHAPTER TWENTY-FIVE

Lusa

Lusa was looking down into the Bear Bowl. She could see Yogi scrambling up the Bear Tree, while King slept in the sun. Her mother and Stella were nosing through the fruit that the flat-faces had brought.

This is weird, Lusa thought. *Why aren't I down there with them?* With a jolt of sadness she knew the answer to her question: *Because I don't belong with them anymore.*

So where am I? she wondered. Looking around, she saw that she was standing above the Bear Bowl, surrounded by flat-faces. Fear shivered through her. *They'll catch me and take me back!* Then she realized that though she could see the flat-faces, she couldn't hear them. Their mouths were open as if they were talking and huffing out the sounds that showed they were pleased, but they were completely silent. And none of the flat-faces seemed able to see her.

This should be fun! Lusa thought. *I could do anything I like, and they'd never know!*

But all she wanted to do was look down at her family in

the Bear Bowl. She saw Ashia leave Stella and amble across to settle down in the shade underneath the ledge. She put her nose on her paws and closed her eyes.

"Hello, Ashia," Lusa whispered. "It's me, Lusa. Are you dreaming about me, like I'm dreaming about you?" Ashia's ears twitched as if she had heard Lusa speak. "I'm okay, you know," Lusa went on. "I've got friends now, and I've learned how to live in the wild. You don't need to worry about me."

As Lusa gazed down at her mother, Ashia suddenly seemed to be drawing farther and farther away, until the whole of the Bear Bowl was only a dot in a blaze of sunlight that swallowed up everything else. Lusa let out a terrified cry as she realized she was falling, falling. . . .

She landed on the ground with a bump that jarred every one of her bones. Her eyes flew open. She still lay under the bush where she had crawled the day before after her escape from the river. Her body hurt as if she had really fallen from the sky. Rain hissed softly down; the bush wasn't thick enough to shelter her, and raindrops trickled through her pelt to her skin. Raw cold gripped her like the claws of a giant grizzly.

Kallik lay curled up next to her, snoring. Lusa watched her for a moment, reluctant to disturb her, then gave her a tentative prod with one paw. They had already lost time; they had spent a whole night under the bush and now a new day had dawned. They had to move, to keep on searching for Ujurak.

Letting out a grunt, Kallik opened her eyes. "You okay?" she asked Lusa.

"I'm fine." *Sore, exhausted, and scared, but still fine.* "Thanks to you, Kallik."

Kallik shook her head as if she were flicking off a troublesome fly. "Great spirits!" she muttered. "I feel as if I've been pounded by a grizzly."

Shakily she heaved herself to her paws; Lusa did the same, wondering if her legs would support her. The struggle in the river had weakened both of them, she realized. *Will we make it?* she wondered. *Can we keep going until we get to the place where they're keeping Ujurak?*

Side by side Lusa and Kallik padded to the riverside and lapped a few mouthfuls of the water.

"Which way now?" Kallik asked. "Do you know where the metal bird went from here?"

Lusa sighed. "I'm not sure anymore, but I think it's this way." She pointed with her snout. "Otherwise, why did the spirits tell us to cross the river?"

"That makes sense," Kallik agreed, trudging off in the direction Lusa indicated.

Lusa followed, splashing and slipping through the mud as she and her friend scrambled up the hillside at the far end of the valley and started down the other side. Her belly was shrieking with hunger, but in all the bleak landscape she couldn't see anything to eat.

"I'm starving," she grumbled, half to herself.

"Me too," Kallik said. "And there's not even a sniff of prey."

Lusa snorted. "I bet all the prey is too sensible to be out in this rain. They'll be hiding in their burrows."

"I wish we were, too, but we can't." Kallik sighed. "If only it would stop."

Far from stopping, the rain was growing heavier, pouring down in a silver-gray screen that blotted out their view of the land ahead. The she-bears stumbled on, their belly fur caked with mud and their pelts soaked and dripping, clinging to their frames. Lusa couldn't remember ever being so cold and tired.

We've got to find food, or we can't go on.

She peered through the rain until she spotted a scattering of boulders poking out of the ground. Grunting with effort, she turned one over; her belly growled at the sight of worms and grubs wriggling around in the soil she had exposed.

"Hey, Kallik! Over here!"

The white bear splashed toward her, and together they licked up the grubs, turning over all the stones that were small enough to move. There weren't enough grubs for either of them to feel full, but having something in her belly made Lusa feel better.

Later they found a few berries, though Lusa guessed other bears had already scoured the bushes, leaving just the smaller, shriveled fruit.

"We really need meat," Kallik muttered. "Where's Toklo when we need him?"

A long way away by now, Lusa thought. "Yes, he'd be able to catch something," she said aloud. "He was always better than us at scenting prey."

The gray daylight finally faded. Lusa and Kallik spent the night uncomfortably squashed together in the scant shelter of an overhanging rock. By the following morning the rain had stopped, though clouds still covered the sky.

"Today should be easier," Lusa declared, crawling out of their makeshift den and shaking her pelt to air it and get rid of the debris stuck to it. She still felt stiff and tired, but the pain of her bruises was beginning to fade and strength was returning to her legs. "At least it's dry."

"And we can see where we're going," Kallik agreed, emerging to sniff the air at Lusa's side.

But the landscape ahead didn't give much hope of prey. Rough open land stretched in front of them, scattered with ponds fringed with reeds. And even though the rain wasn't falling anymore, the ground underpaw was still muddy; Lusa's paws sank into it at every step.

"There won't be any prey in this," she muttered.

"I suppose we might find a frog or two," Kallik said with a sniff of disgust.

She had hardly finished speaking when a rabbit burst out of the reeds beside a pool and pelted across the grass. Lusa let out a yelp and hurled herself after it, with Kallik a pawstep behind. But Lusa's legs still felt weak and shaky, and the rabbit easily outstripped them. She halted with a growl of frustration when she saw it dive down a hole.

"We're hopeless!" she exclaimed.

As the day wore on, they didn't spot any more prey. The ground was still too wet, and there was no sunlight to entice the creatures out into the open. Lusa's legs were starting to ache, and she wondered how long she could keep going.

I'm not giving up! If Kallik can do this, so can I!

A stiff breeze began to blow, breaking up the clouds to let a gleam of watery sunlight through. It carried with it the scent of more rabbits; Lusa sniffed hungrily, but all she could see was a scattering of holes in the sandy bank they were passing. Like all the other prey, the rabbits were sheltering in the warmth of their burrows.

"I wish we were on the ice," Kallik murmured, her attention on the horizon, where the ocean lay hidden behind a ridge of broken rock. "I could hunt better there than on the land."

Lusa halted, staring at the rabbit holes. "Show me," she suggested.

"What?" Kallik looked puzzled.

"Pretend those rabbit holes are seal holes," Lusa explained, pointing with her snout at the bank. "Show me what you would do."

"Okay." Kallik blinked, excitement creeping into her voice. Lusa guessed she had never expected to be able to use her ice skills on land.

Picking out a rabbit hole a little way away from the others, Kallik went on. "That's a hole in the ice, okay? We're going to creep up to it and crouch down beside it and wait. We have to be very quiet and not move around, or the seal—sorry, the rabbit—will realize we're there."

"Okay, let's do it," Lusa whispered.

She followed Kallik as the white bear crept over to the hole and lay down beside it with her muzzle on the ground. Lusa could hardly believe that a bear as big as Kallik could move so quietly. She did her best to copy her friend, easing herself to the ground on the opposite side of the hole, pleased when she didn't make a sound.

"This is fun!" she exclaimed, wriggling to get comfortable. "It's almost like playing with Yogi in the Bear Bowl!"

"Shh!" Kallik hissed.

Lusa mouthed, *Sorry!*, and settled down to wait.

Soon Lusa felt that the moments were dragging by. *I never expected it would take as long as this. I can't believe Kallik is so patient!*

She was convinced that some sort of bug was crawling around in her fur, but when she lifted a paw to scratch it Kallik gave her such a fierce look that she froze into stillness again. The wind blew cold through her pelt, and a blade of grass tickled her nose so that she wanted to sneeze. She wished they could give up, but she didn't dare suggest it while Kallik was so focused on the hole.

Lusa was staring at her paws when a tiny scrabbling noise came from inside the burrow. When the rabbit popped its head out, all she could do was stare at it. She had waited so long that she had forgotten what to do.

While she was still staring, Kallik pounced. One large white paw swiped the rabbit across the neck, then dragged it out of the hole.

"That was brilliant!" Lusa barked, springing to her paws. "Great catch!"

"It was your idea," Kallik replied, but she sounded pleased.

With the rabbit dangling from her jaws she padded along the bank until she came to a shallow cave, just big enough for them to shelter from the wind and share their prey. Lusa followed and squashed in beside her, water flooding her jaws as she took in the rich, warm scent of rabbit. She forced herself not to gulp down all her share at once, aware that it might have to keep her going for a long time.

"Wouldn't Toklo be surprised?" she said between mouthfuls. "I wish we could show him how to hunt like that."

"Me too," Kallik replied sadly.

Lusa nodded. "But we can show Ujurak," she insisted. "We'll catch up to him soon. We're *not* going to let the flatfaces keep him."

CHAPTER TWENTY-SIX

Toklo

A spatter of rain roused Toklo in the middle of the night. The forest was dark; clouds had covered the sky and no gleam of moon or stars pierced the branches. Wind made the leaves thrash and set the branches to creaking.

At first no more than a few drops of rain fell, but gradually it grew heavier, sweeping on the wind into Toklo's inadequate den. He squashed himself into the bottom, but his back was still exposed, and the branches of the tree gave him very little shelter. The rain began to soak his pelt, and tiny streams of water trickled into the den until he was crouched in a puddle.

This place is no good after all, he thought irritably. *Tomorrow I'll have to start searching all over again.*

As soon as dawn light started to filter into the forest he left the den that had taken such effort to dig. The rain became heavier and heavier. His fur was waterlogged, weighing him down, and at every pawstep he picked up clods of mud that made it hard to walk. His paws felt unsteady on the sodden ground, and he kept slipping into muddy holes. He was trying to search for shelter, but he could hardly see because of the water streaming down his face.

"I'm bee-brained to be out in this," he grumbled, shaking his head in a vain attempt to get the rainwater out of his eyes. "I should be dry in a den, like any sensible bear."

But he felt too wet and tired to start digging another den now. Besides, he had other, more urgent needs. He couldn't remember when he had his last proper meal, and hunger was tearing at him like claws.

I'll never catch anything while this rain keeps up, he thought wretchedly. *All the prey will be hiding in their holes, and the scents are washed away.* He sniffed as if to prove his point; all that he could smell was water, and the rich decaying scent of leaf mulch.

He was making his way along a slope where the trees thinned out toward the top of the ridge. Down below, the forest looked thicker, and Toklo guessed there might be more chance of shelter there. But as he veered down the slope he trod into a mudslide; he hadn't seen it because of the driving rain. His paws shot out from under him and he rolled down the slope, flailing for a grip on the ground. Mud plastered his fur and filled his nose and mouth. He kept on scrabbling helplessly at the squelchy ground until he landed with a thump against the trunk of a tree.

Half stunned and exhausted, Toklo lay where he had fallen for a few moments, the rain sluicing through his fur. Part of him wanted to give up and lie there, but he knew that could be a big mistake. If more mud fell down the mountain, he could be buried alive. His muscles shrieked as he staggered to his paws; letting out a groan, he stumbled into the shadow of the trees.

The thicker foliage overhead kept some of the rain off him, but the ground underpaw was soaked and the undergrowth snagged his pelt and sent showers of water over him as he brushed past. He still couldn't scent any prey.

Eventually he spotted a huge old tree with a cleft in the trunk, and forced his weary paws to head for it.

Shelter! It might not be big enough for a den, but it'll do until the rain stops.

But before he reached the hollow tree, Toklo heard a roar of rage behind him. Something heavy slammed into him and knocked him off his paws. For a moment his face was smashed into the thick layer of leaf mulch that covered the forest floor. Twisting his neck, spitting out a mouthful of rotting leaves, Toklo saw a huge grizzly looming over him.

"Wha—?" he gasped, dazed.

"This is *my* territory!" the grizzly snarled. He bared his teeth and planted a paw on Toklo's shoulder, pinning him to the ground. "No bear trespasses here."

"I'm sorry, I didn't—" Toklo began, only to break off as the bear gave him a sharp cuff on the side of his head.

With a massive effort Toklo pushed him away and scrambled to his paws as another blow landed on his back. His head was spinning, his eyes dazzled, and though he lashed out a paw in self-defense he was too dizzy to put any force behind it.

"Get out, now!" Snarling with rage, the other grizzly thudded into Toklo, pushing him farther down the hillside.

"Okay, okay, I'm going!" Toklo protested, slipping and scrabbling as he tried to get a firm pawhold on the muddy slope. "Keep your fur on!"

Half running, half sliding, he fled through the trees, glancing once over his shoulder to see the big grizzly standing on his hindpaws, watching him go. His roar of fury echoed through the forest; Toklo could still hear it even when the bear was out of sight.

He didn't slow down until he thought he must have passed the edge of the grizzly's territory. Panting, he stopped and looked around, relaxing when he couldn't spot any trees with scratch marks.

As Toklo sniffed the air he picked up the scent of a Black-Path. He could hear the distant roaring of a firebeast and caught a glimpse of its glittering color through the trees ahead of him. Cautiously he padded forward, pushing his way between clumps of fern and thornbushes until he reached the BlackPath that sliced through the forest in a straight line. It was quiet now. He listened, but the only sounds were the rain and the shaking of the trees in the wind.

Then he heard the sound of another firebeast, growing rapidly louder. Roaring, it swept past Toklo as he scrambled away from the edge of the BlackPath. The firebeast's huge black paws sent up a spray of tiny stones that stung Toklo as they showered over him.

"Ouch!" he yelped.

Running beside the BlackPath, raised a little way off the ground, was a long silver-gray tube. Toklo sniffed it suspiciously; it had a strong smell of firebeasts. It reminded him of the tube beside the Great River, where firebeasts and flat-faces had been digging up the ground, except this one was smaller, about as high as his shoulder.

Toklo's head and shoulders still stung from the blows the big grizzly had given him, and his pelt was clumped with wet soil and debris.

Fed up with splashing through mud and struggling through undergrowth, Toklo began to pad along the edge of the Black-Path, relieved to be on firmer ground. He leaped back when the next firebeast roared past him, terrified that it would crush him beneath its rolling, hissing paws. To his relief, it didn't turn toward him, but he was still pelted with stones and soaked by the surge of water that came from it.

I've had enough of this!

The shower of stones clattered on the metal tube, drawing Toklo's attention back to it. He gave it another cautious sniff. Though the top of it was curved, it looked wide enough to balance on, and it was raised well above the mud.

Why not? It's worth a try.

Heaving with his forelegs, Toklo managed to scramble onto the top of the tube and stood there for a moment until he was sure he could balance. Then he began padding along it, setting his paws down carefully so that he didn't slip on the rain-wet surface. It made him nervous to be so close to a flat-face thing, and the strong smell of firebeasts made him choke, but at least he wasn't floundering through mud any longer. And the tube reminded him of the games he used to play with

Tobi, balancing on fallen tree trunks when they were little cubs.

None of the firebeasts paid him any attention, and Toklo grew more confident as he realized that they couldn't get at him while he was raised above the BlackPath like this.

Then an even louder roaring came from up ahead, and one of the biggest firebeasts Toklo had ever seen swept into view. He stopped to watch it as it bore down on him. Its huge paws pushed waves of rainwater aside as it growled along. As it passed Toklo, it flung up stones from its paws, clattering over the tube and stinging Toklo's side like a swarm of hornets.

Toklo reared away, and his paws slipped on the smooth surface of the tube. He let out a roar of shock and fright as he toppled sideways and crashed into the undergrowth.

"Bee-brain!" he huffed after the departing firebeast. "Watch where you're going!"

Struggling to his paws, he gagged on an even stronger reek of firebeasts, and realized that he had fallen into a sticky black pool. Drops of it were seeping from the tube, dripping onto the ground and puddling in a hollow beside the BlackPath. It was smeared all over Toklo's fur, so that as he backed away from it the disgusting smell came with him.

It stinks! Growling in anger, Toklo pawed at the stuff to clean it off his fur, but that just transferred the sticky liquid to his paw. *Yuck! What is it? It's slimy and disgusting and it's making me feel sick! What do I have to do to get rid of it?*

His belly heaving with every breath, Toklo left the Black-Path behind, wandering down a slope into the trees and scraping his flank against the trunks in an effort to rub off the horrible stuff. Pain shot through one of his forelegs when he put weight on it, and he realized that when he fell he must have hurt it.

He kept an eye open for more scratch marks on trees, but apart from that Toklo limped along aimlessly. He hadn't eaten all day, but when he tried to sniff for prey again, the stench of the black stuff on his pelt made it impossible to locate anything. He was growing exhausted; it was becoming harder and harder to put one paw in front of another. The pain from his injured leg grew worse.

Darkness was falling and still the rain didn't let up. Toklo was stumbling along now, head down, unaware of where he was going. Then he suddenly smelled the scent of prey, even stronger than the stench of the black stuff, coming up from the ground in front of him. He had nearly padded over the half-eaten remains of a rabbit.

Toklo wondered if the big grizzly had killed the rabbit. He glanced around before he crouched in front of it and gulped it down in a few famished bites. It wasn't enough to soothe the pangs of his hunger, and as he was nuzzling around among the debris to see if he had missed any scraps, the sky seemed to open up and the rain fell down even harder than before.

"Great spirits!" Toklo groaned. "Have you got a grudge against me, or what?"

In the last of the light he spotted a hollow under the roots of a tree a few bear-lengths away. Limping over to it on three legs, he crammed himself into the narrow space, laid his nose on his paws, and thankfully let himself slip into unconsciousness.

Water dripping on his nose roused Toklo. Blinking, he lifted his head to see that gray daylight had returned to the forest. Water pattered from every leaf and twig, but the rain had stopped.

Toklo let out a low moan. Every muscle in his body protested as he dragged himself out of the den under the roots and tried to stand. Pain shot along his spine as he put his injured leg to the ground. His fur was still wet from the rain and sticky from the black stuff that had seeped from the tube; the stench of it caught in his throat. Even the rain hadn't washed it away.

I can't go on yet, he told himself. *I need to rest.*

Moving slowly, every step an effort, he clambered to the top of a boulder and looked around. Through the trees in one direction he caught a glimpse of the BlackPath with the silvery tube beside it, and heard the distant snarls of firebeasts. There was nothing else to tell him where he might be.

I hope I'm not in another bear's territory, he thought, remembering the abandoned rabbit from the previous night. He might even have crossed back into the territory of the big grizzly who had driven him off the day before. *I can't fight or run in this state.*

He dozed on top of the boulder, gradually warming up as his fur dried out and an occasional gleam of sunlight began to pierce the cloud cover and slide through the branches above his head. Near sunhigh, he summoned the energy to climb down and scrape himself against the trunk of a tree, getting rid of the worst of the foul-smelling stuff that was sticking to his pelt. To his relief, it came off more easily now that it was dry and hard.

Moving around had eased some of the stiffness in his injured leg. It wasn't as painful now, but Toklo was still doubtful about trying to travel any distance on it. He spent the rest of the day wandering close to the boulder, finding some berry bushes that helped to quiet his rumbling belly.

As night fell, he curled up in the same cramped den under the roots. *This isn't a good place to stay,* he decided as he drifted into sleep. *Tomorrow I'll look for somewhere better.*

Waking the next day, he realized that the sky above the trees had cleared and sunlight was striking down into the forest. He felt hungry, but the day's rest had given him new strength, and the pain in his leg had settled into a dull ache.

Toklo felt a lot more cheerful as he climbed through the trees until he had left the Black Path far behind. As he rounded a thicket of thornbushes he surprised a squirrel nibbling on a nut among the roots of a tree, and killed it with a swift blow to its spine. Gorging himself on the warm prey, he shoved the hardship of the last few days out of his mind.

I'm a brown bear! I can cope with anything.

Eventually he emerged on the top of a ridge and padded along it, enjoying the sensation of wind ruffling his fur. *This is more like it,* he thought.

At last he realized that he was coming to the end of the ridge. He guessed that beyond it he would look down on the coastal plain again: There would be geese and hares to hunt, and maybe even caribou. His jaws watered and his paws itched as he imagined launching himself at his prey and using his strength and skill to pull it down.

But as the ground fell away beneath his paws, revealing the land beyond, Toklo stopped dead and stared in disbelief. The plain lay in front of him, just as he expected, with the ocean beyond, but it was very different from how he had imagined. Instead of the rich harvest of prey he had hoped for, the whole stretch of land was dotted with flat-face structures: low, flat-roofed dens and tall towers, as far as he could see in all directions. One of the towers had a bright flame spurting from the top. BlackPaths with tubes beside them, like the one he had followed, crossed the area from one flat-face denning place to another and led away into the distance. Nothing moved except for firebeasts, crawling along the BlackPaths.

Toklo took a step backward, glancing over his shoulder in the direction he had come. *I'd better go back, even if I have to meet that grizzly again.*

But before he turned away, he heard a distant buzzing sound and spotted a metal bird rising into the sky from the far side of one of the denning places. He paused to watch as it flew toward him, the sun glinting on its hard, shiny pelt. It was flying low, heading for the stretch of open ground between the bottom of the ridge and the nearest of the flat-face structures.

Two tiny specks of movement on the ground caught Toklo's eye. Two creatures were heading away from the ridge, toward the denning place: one black shape, one white. And the metal bird was swooping down on them, its wings clattering and its claws outstretched.

"No!" Toklo roared. "Kallik! Lusa! Watch out!"

Forgetting his exhaustion, forgetting his aching leg and sore paws, Toklo plunged down from the crest of the ridge and hurtled toward the plain to save his friends.

CHAPTER TWENTY-SEVEN

Kallik

Kallik and Lusa spent the night in the cave beside the rabbit holes and woke again in the first pale light of dawn. Kallik crawled out of the den, shaking sandy soil from her pelt, and watched Lusa, who stood a couple of bear-lengths away, sniffing the air.

"Which way?" she asked.

Lusa hesitated for a moment. "I'm not sure," she confessed. "We've come such a long way; I can't remember what direction the metal bird was flying."

Kallik took a deep breath and smelled the familiar tang of the sea. Her paws itched with longing. "I think we should head for the shore," she murmured. "I might be wrong, but something seems to be telling me that's the way to go."

Lusa's eyes shone. "Maybe Arcturus is sending you a sign."

Or maybe it's just the ice calling me. But there was nothing to point them in a different direction, so they headed for the crest of the ridge. The sun rose as they trudged upward, warming their pelts. Kallik felt her muscles loosen and a tide of hope began to rise inside her; perhaps this would be the day when they were reunited with Ujurak.

The last bear-lengths that brought them to the top of the ridge were a hard scramble over loose rock that shifted under their paws. Lusa was the first to reach the crest; she stood staring out at the land beyond, as still as a bear carved out of stone.

"What is it?" Kallik called, her paws slipping on pebbles a little way below.

"You won't believe this!" the little black bear replied. "I don't believe it, and I'm looking at it!"

With a bit more effort Kallik thrust herself up the slope until she could stand, panting, beside her friend. Her claws scraped hard against the rock and her heart began to pound as she gazed out across the plain.

Where they had first come down from the mountains, so many days ago, the plain had been full of life. But in this place it was barren, crisscrossed by BlackPaths and dotted here and there with flat-face dens. The structures were odd shapes, some square, some long and flat, others round, some with odd bits of metal sticking out of them. They seemed to have been set down on the plain in a jumble, or in some weird flat-face order that didn't make sense to Kallik. Beyond them she could see the pale gleam of a river, with a BlackPath stretching across it, and beyond that the misty outline of what might be a flat-face denning area.

Kallik's hope died as she gazed at the distant gleam of the ocean; she felt cut off from it by all the flat-face muddle in between. "If Ujurak's here, we'll never find him," she said despairingly.

"We have to try." Lusa's voice was stubborn. "We—"

She broke off at the sound of a familiar clatter and buzz; Kallik spotted a metal bird like the one that had taken Ujurak flying along the line of the coast and swooping down somewhere on the far side of the denning place.

"Look!" she yelped as it sank out of sight. "That must be where the metal birds have their nest."

"Then that's where we have to start looking!" Lusa gave a little bounce. "Come on!"

"It's a long way," Kallik said doubtfully. "We'll have to cross the river."

"We'll worry about that when we get there," Lusa replied.

She led the way down the slope toward the flat-face place. Kallik couldn't share her eagerness, but she followed anyway.

Sunhigh was past by the time they reached the bottom of the ridge. Open ground separated them from the nearest BlackPath, a stretch of sparse, brittle grass dotted with clumps of thornbushes.

Kallik halted and raised her snout, sniffing the air. There was a strong reek that reminded her of firebeasts, though it wasn't quite the same. "What's that smell?"

Lusa shook her head. "I don't know, but it's disgusting, whatever it is."

She padded forward a few paces and gazed across the barren landscape toward the BlackPath and the strange flat-face structures beyond. "We've got to have a plan," she muttered.

Now that they were down on the plain, the flat-face dens looked even bigger.

"I don't see how we *can* plan," Kallik said. "We don't know what we're going to find. All we can do is look for the metal birds' nest and see if there are any clues there."

"Well, that's sort of a plan," Lusa said. "Come on."

They padded across the stretch of open ground, swerving to avoid the thorn thickets. It was bad enough walking through greasy black mud without having their pelts filled with prickles. The plain was sliced through with Black Paths, many of them with shiny tubes running alongside, and everywhere the tall flat-face dens loomed. Kallik shivered as she and Lusa trudged past, imagining hostile eyes peering down at them. But nothing moved, and Kallik wondered if they were empty.

"This is the biggest flat-face place I've ever seen," Lusa whispered, gazing around with a mixture of wonder and dread. "But where are the flat-faces? We've hardly seen any."

"Maybe this isn't where they live," Kallik suggested. "Their dens could be a long way off, near where we saw the metal bird."

"I think you're right," Lusa agreed. "There aren't any gardens, or firebeasts sleeping outside. And none of those big shiny things you get food out of," she added regretfully.

Kallik sniffed the air. "No smell of food at all. Just that horrible reek."

Before they had covered many bear-lengths, another metal bird rose from the far side of the denning area. At first Kallik was glad to see it because it helped to show them exactly where the nest was.

But instead of flying away up the coast, the metal bird flew inland toward the ridge. It stayed low, its claws almost brushing the roof of one of the flat-face dens. Kallik watched it approach with terror rising inside her.

"It's coming for us!" she yelped. "They've seen us and they want to catch us!"

She crouched down, huddled against Lusa's side. The clatter of the metal bird filled the sky; the wind of its approach flattened the grass and whipped at the branches of the thorns.

"I'm sorry, Kallik," Lusa whispered. "I made you come here. It's all my fault."

Kallik was too frightened to reply; she just pressed herself closer to her friend's warm pelt and squeezed her eyes shut tight.

Then above the growling of the metal bird she heard a bear roaring—bellowing their names through the stench-filled air. "Lusa! Kallik! Watch out!"

Kallik opened her eyes and lifted her head from the brittle grass to see a brown bear hurtling toward them, his jaws stretched wide. It was Toklo.

"Move! Bee-brains! Hide!"

He slammed into Kallik's side, thrusting her and Lusa toward a clump of thornbushes. Kallik crawled underneath, with Lusa beside her; Toklo crouched on the edge of the thicket, his snout raised as he snarled defiantly at the metal bird.

"Go away! You can't have them!"

Kallik waited, breathless with horror as she listened to the clattering of the metal bird. At last the noise faded, and when Kallik dared to poke her head out, she saw it lifting higher into the sky and disappearing across the ridge.

"It's all right," Toklo said gruffly. "It's gone. You can come out."

Kallik crawled into the open and stood up. She couldn't take her eyes off Toklo, still finding it hard to believe that he was here. He looked bedraggled, and he smelled foul, with the same bitter stench as the land around them.

"Thank you, Toklo!" she puffed, as her breathing steadied and she felt her racing heart grow calmer.

"You saved us from the bird!" Lusa had crawled out of the thicket behind Kallik and raised a paw to rub at the scratch on her nose. "You were so brave!"

Toklo hunched his shoulders, looking embarrassed, and let out a grunt.

"You really stink, though," Lusa added, giving him a sniff and jumping back with a shocked look.

"You're not so sweet scented yourself," Toklo retorted. "Anyway, it wasn't my fault. I had an accident. Look." He turned sideways and showed Kallik and Lusa traces of something black and sticky on his pelt.

"It's like the mud we've been walking through," Kallik observed. She leaned forward to smell it. "Yuck!"

"Look, can we not talk about my scent?" Toklo growled, beginning to bristle. "I didn't rescue you just to be told that I stink."

"Sorry," Lusa said, though amusement was dancing in her eyes. "We really are grateful, Toklo."

The grizzly cub snorted and shook his pelt. "What are you doing here?" he asked.

"We're trying to find Ujurak," Lusa replied. "What about you?"

Toklo grunted, flicking away Lusa's question like a fly that had landed on his ear. "Oh, I've been hunting, looking around . . . trying to find the best territory."

"Did you mark trees?" Lusa asked eagerly. "And make yourself a den? I bet you were the fiercest bear in the forest!"

Toklo shook his pelt. "We don't have to go into all that. Everything's fine. Just tell me what that little fluffball's done now."

They settled down in the feeble shelter of the thorns while Lusa told Toklo about the flat-faces who had come to the denning place where the healer lived, and how they had taken Ujurak away with them.

"I'm sure they brought him here," she finished. "This is where the metal birds come to nest. Will you help us find him, Toklo?"

"Please," Kallik added. "It can't be just chance that you turned up in time to rescue us. The spirits have brought us back together again."

Toklo huffed. "Spirits!" he muttered. "Who do you think you are—Ujurak?"

Even so, Kallik could tell that he was pleased to see them again. She wondered if he had been looking for them all this time. *Did he miss us, just like we were missing him?*

"I suppose I'd better help," Toklo went on with a sigh. "You'll only get into more trouble if I let you go by yourselves."

"Thank you!" Lusa butted Toklo affectionately in the shoulder. "We'll have a much better chance of finding Ujurak if you're with us."

"Okay." Toklo rose to his paws with an air of determination. "The metal birds obviously nest over there." He pointed his snout toward the opposite side of the flat-face place. "So that's where we have to start looking."

CHAPTER TWENTY-EIGHT

Lusa

As Lusa and her friends walked toward the river, the air grew heavier with the bitter smell. It caught in Lusa's throat, making her cough.

"I'm surprised the flat-faces can put up with this stink," she said when she had caught her breath.

Kallik shrugged. "They make it like this, so maybe this is how they want it," she suggested.

"Flat-faces are weird," Toklo growled.

They came to a BlackPath slicing across the landscape with a shiny tube running alongside it, raised up on metal supports. Lusa padded up to the tube and sniffed it.

"Ugh!" she exclaimed, jumping back. "It reeks of something like firebeasts."

"You have to be careful of those," Toklo advised, coming to stand beside her. "They leak out this horrible black stuff, and that's what's making the smell. I fell into a puddle of it, and that's when I got it all over my pelt."

"That's awful." Lusa looked along the tube in both

199

directions, relieved that she couldn't spot any leaks or black puddles. "We've got to cross this BlackPath," she added. "Toklo, is it safe to climb over the tube?"

"It should be okay," the brown bear replied. "Just as long as there aren't any firebeasts."

Lusa raised her snout and sniffed, then realized there was no point in trying to scent approaching firebeasts when the whole area smelled of them. She could hear growling in the distance, as if firebeasts were coming and going closer to the flat-face denning place, but here everything seemed quiet.

"Let's go," she said.

Toklo was first to scramble up onto the tube; he balanced on top of it for a moment, then leaped down on the other side and bounded across the BlackPath. He turned back toward the others. "Come on!" he called.

Kallik followed, hauling herself over the tube and flopping down awkwardly onto the surface of the BlackPath before padding over to join Toklo.

When Lusa tried to follow, her claws slipped on the shiny surface of the tube; she hadn't realized that being so much smaller than the others would make it a lot harder for her to clamber up. *I'm a black bear!* she told herself furiously. *Black bears are the best climbers.*

Scrabbling at the side of the tube, she wished she had gotten one of the others to give her a boost before they crossed, but she didn't want to call them back.

Better do it this way, she thought, pressing herself to the ground and crawling through the narrow space underneath. She felt her back scrape against the underside of the tube; there was a horrible moment when she thought she was stuck and would need to call one of the others for help.

Lusa dug her claws into the ground, dragging herself forward, bunching her muscles for a leap that would take her away from the tube and propel her across the BlackPath. Then she heard Toklo yell, "Wait!"

At the same moment the distant roaring of the firebeasts suddenly got louder. Lusa froze. A huge firebeast swept past her less than a bear-length from her nose, covering her with grit and mud that stung her eyes and spattered over her pelt.

"Oh, thanks!" she muttered, blinking to clear her vision.

"It's okay now!" Kallik called from the other side of the BlackPath.

Still not able to see properly, Lusa trusted her friend and thrust off with her hindpaws. She popped out from underneath the tube and felt the BlackPath hard under her pads as she scampered across. She crashed into Kallik's soft bulk and felt the white bear licking her face to get rid of the grit.

"Thanks," Lusa panted, blinking.

The BlackPath led almost directly toward the flat-face area, so Lusa and the others padded along beside it. Lights were coming on at the top of the flat-face towers, and as they trudged past one of them a vast cloud of fire burst from the top of it, the glare blotting out the stars. Her heart racing, Lusa pressed herself to the ground; Kallik crouched beside her, and she could feel the white bear shaking.

"What was that?" Kallik whispered.

"I don't know." Though Lusa tried to sound brave, her voice rose to a betraying squeak. "It's not hurting us," she added a moment later.

"Yet," Toklo snapped discouragingly.

The ground still sloped downward; ahead of them Lusa could make out the pale gleam of water.

"There's the river up ahead," she said, pausing to point with her snout. "I think this BlackPath goes across it. Toklo, do you remember that river we crossed by a BlackPath? That was before you joined us," she added to Kallik.

"I remember a firebeast struck Ujurak and nearly killed him," Toklo grunted, his gaze fixed on his paws. "I'm not risking that again."

"We could swim," Lusa agreed. "But this BlackPath is much quieter. It might be safe enough."

Toklo didn't reply, and Lusa didn't bother arguing; there was no point, until they reached the river and saw what they had to face.

The sun was going down by the time they reached the bank; the wide, flat surface of the water reflected an ominous red light. Lusa tried not to shiver. "That's a long way to swim," she murmured.

Ahead of them, the BlackPath carried straight on across the river, supported on huge tree trunks of metal. As the bears approached, a firebeast roared up from the other direction, swept over, and vanished into the distance.

"It's a long way to walk as well," Toklo pointed out. "If we were in the middle when a firebeast came along, it would get us for sure."

"I'd rather risk that than swim," Kallik said, peering down the bank to where the river lapped at the first of the metal supports. "I don't like the smell of that water. I don't want it on my fur."

Before Lusa could point out to Toklo that he was outvoted, another firebeast came growling up behind them and drew to a halt a couple of bear-lengths away. Its growl sank to a soft purr.

Toklo spun around to face it, his teeth bared in a snarl. "What does it want?" he growled, alarm flaring in his eyes. "Is it trying to hunt us?"

Kallik turned toward Lusa, looking scared and anxious; Lusa realized that both her friends were expecting her to provide the answers. She was supposed to be the expert here, the one who knew the most about flat-faces. But this place was so different from anything she had seen before, and she wasn't sure she could help them.

"Get ready to run," she said softly, "but don't move unless I tell you."

She took a cautious pace toward the firebeast, ready for it to leap into fierce, roaring life, but the tone of its quiet purr didn't change. She half expected its belly to open up to let out flat-faces brandishing firesticks, but that didn't happen either. Lusa could see only one flat-face inside.

"You aren't going to believe this," she said, "but I think he's waiting for us to cross."

"You're right, I don't believe it," Toklo grunted. "Flat-faces waiting for bears? You've got bees in your brain."

"I agree with Lusa," Kallik said unexpectedly. "If the flat-face wanted to hunt us, he would be doing it by now. Lusa, if you think we should cross, I'm willing to give it a try."

Lusa felt warmed by her friend's trust in her, knowing how frightened the white bear must be. She was frightened herself, except that somehow she didn't think that this flat-face meant them any harm. *There* are *kind flat-faces,* she told herself. *They were kind in the Bear Bowl.*

"Okay," she said to Kallik. "Off you go."

With another anxious glance at her, the white bear padded along the edge of the BlackPath and set out across the river. Now it would be easy for the firebeast to leap forward and trample her, but it didn't move.

"Now you, Toklo," Lusa said when Kallik was several bear-lengths ahead.

Toklo hesitated, and for a moment Lusa was afraid that he would balk and start arguing again. Instead he swung around with a huff of annoyance and loped after Kallik.

Lusa set off after them. As they reached the opposite side of the river they heard the firebeast's growl start up again and it started to roll toward them. The bears crouched by the side of the BlackPath, panting with fear, until it had gone past.

"There!" Lusa exclaimed, letting out her breath in a huge huff. "Wasn't that easier than a long swim?"

"You were great, Lusa," Kallik said. Toklo just grunted.

Feeling a little encouraged, Lusa led the way toward the

flat-face denning place. Now they were crossing a wide, flat plain dotted with small pools of water reflecting the last of the daylight. Toklo lapped at the nearest one, then backed away, making a face and retching. "Don't touch the water," he warned the others, swiping his tongue around his jaws. "It tastes disgusting."

As darkness fell, Lusa began to realize how tired she was. Her paws were sore and her mouth was parched with thirst, but there was no water fit to drink. She wanted to howl with hunger. The rabbit she had shared with Kallik the day before was no more than a distant memory. But she didn't want to take the time to hunt, and in any case, she hadn't seen any prey in this barren landscape, not even a bush where they might scavenge a few berries. Besides, the overpowering smell of firebeasts meant they couldn't scent anything even if they tried.

"I just hope Ujurak will appreciate what we're going through," she heard Toklo mutter.

Now and again a huge firebeast would sweep past them, its hard yellow eyes cutting through the gathering darkness. At least they could see them coming from a long way off. There was nowhere to hide—no trees or ridges of rock or even a thornbush—so they would huddle together by the side of the BlackPath until the firebeast had disappeared.

"They don't seem to take any notice of us at all," Kallik remarked when a particularly big one had passed by.

"That's a *good* thing," Toklo agreed. He had stayed on his paws, gazing up at the flare with a disgusted expression on his face. "This is hopeless," he added. "This isn't the right place for bears to be, and it gets worse with every pawstep."

"Maybe we should go back," Kallik suggested in a small voice, "and let Ujurak come to find us."

"That's bee-brained," Lusa retorted, though she touched Kallik's shoulder affectionately with her snout to soften the harshness of her words. "We don't know that Ujurak *can* come and find us. He might still be ill, or the flat-faces might be keeping him prisoner. Even if he can get away, he won't know where to look for us."

"*We* don't know where to look for *him*," Toklo pointed out.

"Yes, we do," Lusa argued. "Or at least, we've got a good idea where to start. And we're almost there."

By now they were padding past the first of the dens where flat-faces seemed to live. Lights were coming on inside; Lusa could hear the faint sounds of voices. Her pelt prickled when she spotted firebeasts crouching outside most of the dens.

"Quiet," she whispered, pointing to one of them with her snout. "I think it's asleep, but you never know."

Peering through the darkness, Lusa realized that the metal birds' nest couldn't be far away. There weren't as many dens here as she expected; they were much farther apart than in the denning places she had seen before. Some of them were raised up on stumpy little legs; she let out a faint huff as she imagined them scurrying off with their flat-faces inside.

"Sorry," she muttered as Toklo and Kallik stared at her as if she were crazy. "Come on, let's keep going."

Together they crept through the dens until they reached

an open stretch of ground covered with the same hard stuff as the BlackPaths.

"Look!" Lusa exclaimed. Ahead of them, crouching in the darkness, was a metal bird. "We made it!"

"I think it's asleep," Kallik whispered.

"Let's go check it out," Lusa whispered back. "If Ujurak is here, we might be able to scent him."

In spite of her optimistic words, she felt terribly exposed as they left the shelter of the dens and set out into the open. She couldn't see any flat-faces, but that didn't mean there weren't any lurking around, ready to leap out and drive them away with firesticks. And at any moment the metal bird might wake into clattering, snarling life.

But everything was quiet as they approached the bird. Snouts to the ground, they explored the area around it. Lusa's senses were alert for the least trace of Ujurak's scent, the tiniest indication that he had been here. But there was nothing. The heavy rain would have washed away the scent, she realized, and even if anything remained it was drowned by the stronger smell of firebeasts.

"This isn't working," Toklo growled. "We should go look somewhere else."

"Like where?" Lusa challenged. "We followed the metal bird. Ujurak must be here somewhere. We've got to keep searching."

"If we stay here too long then the flat-faces will find us," Toklo argued. "We have to leave now, Lusa."

"No, wait!" Kallik's voice was suddenly excited.

Lusa glanced across to where the white bear was nosing something on the ground a few bear-lengths away, where a BlackPath led into the metal bird nesting place. Bounding over to join her, she yelped, "What is it?"

Kallik pointed with her snout. Lying on the ground was a tiny white bear, made out of wood. Lusa bent to sniff it and picked up a faint trace of Ujurak's scent.

"It's a sign!" she exclaimed. "Ujurak knew we would come for him. Now which way do we go?" she wondered aloud.

Kallik raised her snout, gazing at the dens that surrounded the metal birds' nest. "He left the sign here, so he must have gone this way." She set off along the edge of the BlackPath where the bear had been lying, between two of the dens.

We'll soon be with you, Ujurak, Lusa thought as she and Toklo followed.

CHAPTER TWENTY-NINE

Ujurak

Ujurak opened his eyes in the peaceful white room. He wasn't sure how long he had been lying there in bed, but he could feel his strength returning. He sat up, pleased that the movement didn't make his head spin. His throat was still sore, but his body felt cool and comfortable.

These flat-faces are good healers.

For a moment he stroked the soft pelts the flat-faces had made him wear. They were clean and comfortable, but they didn't feel right. He wanted the thick brown fur that he wore when he was a bear.

Feeling hungry and thirsty, Ujurak spotted a cup on the table by his bed. The stuff it was made of was transparent, so he could see the water inside, but he wasn't sure how to get at it. He tried to stick his face inside it and lap up the water, but the glass skidded on the smooth surface of the table and tipped over. Water spilled over the tabletop and began dripping onto the floor; Ujurak bent his head and licked it up.

Beside the glass on the table was the last of his carved

wooden bears, the brown one. Ujurak picked it up and closed his fingers around it. A sharp pang of loss pierced him as he thought of Toklo and his other friends.

He remembered dropping two wooden bears on his way here, but he couldn't be certain that his friends would find them and come to rescue him. *They'll be looking,* he told himself. *I know that for sure.*

Suddenly the clean white walls and soft pelts and blankets seemed like a prison. He needed to be with his friends again, and he needed to be a bear.

"It's time to leave," he murmured.

Clambering out of bed, he crossed the room and opened the door a crack to look out, freezing when it let out a sharp squeaking noise. The passage outside was empty, but as Ujurak slid out of the door and closed it behind him, a woman in a white pelt turned the corner and headed toward him.

Ujurak recognized the nurse who had been looking after him. She had hair the color of red-gold maple leaves and kind brown eyes, like a bear's. She had told him her name was Janet.

When she spotted him she halted briefly with a surprised look on her face, then hurried up to him and put a hand on his shoulder. "Hey, Ujurak, where do you think you're going?" She was smiling and her voice was kind, but Ujurak sensed the firmness beneath. "You're not strong enough to be wandering around yet."

Ujurak wanted to resist, but an inner voice told him, *Wait. There'll be another chance later.*

Janet guided him into his room and settled him back in bed, tucking the blankets neatly around him. "There. Now you get some rest," she said.

"Where am I?" Ujurak asked, his voice still hoarse from his throat injury.

"Blackhorse," the nurse replied. "Don't worry; you're safe here."

"What's Blackhorse?"

"The name of this town," the nurse told him. "It's an oil town. It's part of the Propkin oil field."

Ujurak was still puzzled. "Oil?" He had heard the Senator and the villagers talking about oil in the meeting in the big hut, back in Arctic Village. He had known that it must be important, but he still didn't know what it was.

"Yeah, oil." For a moment Janet looked at him as if he'd said something weird. "You know, oil. The stuff you use to make engines run smoothly." She looked even more surprised. "Just where did you grow up?" she asked.

"Er . . . out on the plains," Ujurak replied; panic brushed him like a spray of leaves as he tried to think what to say. "We didn't have any engines."

"Wow, none at all?" There was a trace of respect in Janet's eyes. "I didn't know there were still villages like that. What's it like not having electricity or cars or TV?"

Ujurak gazed up at her blankly. *What are those?*

Janet bent down to give Ujurak a hug. She had a nice scent, like flowers, but it tickled Ujurak's nose, and he tried not to sneeze.

"Oh, honey, don't be scared," she said. "Everything will be fine, you'll see. Now you lie right there and get some rest, and I'll be back soon with your supper."

As soon as the nurse had closed the door behind her, Ujurak started to get out of bed. Then he stopped and lay back down.

She said she'd be back soon, and there'll be trouble if she catches me again. I'd better wait until later.

Besides, he had to admit that his brief exercise had tired him; he lay dozing until he heard the door squeak as it was opened again.

"Here we are!" came Janet's cheerful voice. "And I've brought you a little friend to cheer you up."

Ujurak sat bolt upright, looking past the nurse to see if Lusa or Toklo or Kallik was following her. But only Janet came into the room. She was carrying a tray, which she set down on the table beside Ujurak's bed.

"There! Say hi, Ujurak."

She was holding out something soft, colored a bright purple, made out of some kind of pelt-stuff. Ujurak blinked at it. The thing looked back at him with bright, glassy eyes. Four stumpy limbs stuck out from its fat body; its nose and mouth were made out of pelt-stuff, too.

"It's a bear, honey," Janet said, looking a bit surprised. "Your very own bear to keep you company." After a pause, she added, "I saw the wooden bear you brought with you, so I thought you liked them."

That's not a bear! It's purple!

But Ujurak could see that Janet was trying to be kind. "Uh . . . I do," he replied. "Thanks." He reached out and folded his hand around the bear, feeling how soft and fuzzy it was.

"Are you going to give him a name?" the nurse asked.

"Er . . . yeah." Frantically Ujurak wondered what flat-faces called their bears. He had no idea. "I'll call him Toklo," he said at last.

"That's a great name, honey," Janet said.

Yes, it is. I just hope the real Toklo never finds out.

Gently Janet took purple-Toklo away from Ujurak and set him down on the bedside table. "There, now he can watch you." She plumped up Ujurak's pillows so that he could sit up, and set down the tray on his lap.

There was a covered bowl on the tray with a spoon beside it; Janet took the cover off and warm, meaty scents drifted up to Ujurak's nostrils. He'd had this before: The flat-faces called it "soup," and it tasted good, even though Ujurak longed for something to get his teeth into. But the soup slid down easily without hurting his throat. He wished he could lap it sensibly, though, without having to use this clumsy spoon that spilled everywhere.

While he ate, Janet moved quietly around the room, clearing up the water Ujurak had spilled earlier, and checking something on a flat board at the end of his bed. When he had finished she took the tray away and wiped up his spills.

She hadn't quite finished when there was a tap on the door

and a male flat-face in a blue pelt came in. The door squeaked again as he pushed it open. He carried a square, metal box in one hand.

"Hi, Janet," he said. "I've come to fix the door."

Janet turned toward him. "That's great, Ed. That squeak has been driving me crazy."

Ujurak watched curiously as Ed opened the square thing and took out a container about the size of a fir cone. A long spike stuck out of the top. Ed stuck the spike into the space between the door and the wall, and when he swung the door a moment later, the squeak was gone.

"Thanks, Ed," Janet said. "I—" She broke off, glancing at Ujurak, and then went on, "Ed, just give me that can for a minute, please."

Looking puzzled, Ed handed the container over. Janet held the spike above Ujurak's empty soup bowl, and a few drops of a sticky black substance dripped out of it.

"Thanks, Ed," Janet said, handing the container back.

Ed still looked confused. "See you around, Janet," he said, and went out.

"Now, then, honey, look at this." Janet held the bowl out to Ujurak.

Ujurak took a deep sniff of the black liquid and reared back, staring up, stunned, at Janet. *That stuff smells like a BlackPath!*

"That's oil," Janet told him.

Ujurak bent over the bowl again. *So that's what all the fuss was about, back in Arctic Village!* Tentatively he reached out and stuck the end of one finger into the oil, then touched his finger to his lips to taste it.

"No!" Janet exclaimed. She pulled his hand away and wiped his fingers and his mouth with soft paper. "It's not good to eat," she explained, taking the bowl away. "It's poisonous."

Horrified, Ujurak stared at her. "Then why don't they leave it in the ground?"

The nurse shook her head slightly, as if she couldn't believe he'd asked that. "It's too useful, honey," she explained. "We couldn't go anywhere in trains or boats or planes, or have heat and light in our houses, if we didn't have oil." She smiled. "And it's great for getting rid of the squeaks in doors."

"But there must be something you could use that isn't poisonous," Ujurak protested.

"No, it's too late," Janet replied. "Whole towns are built on this stuff, and on the business of getting it out of the ground. Come here and look," she invited.

She helped Ujurak out of bed and led him over to the window, pulling back one of the pelts that hung there so that he could look out.

Outside it was night. Ujurak stared across a wide stretch of land covered with flat-face buildings, with BlackPaths running between them. Beyond them was a river, and beyond that stood a huge tower, metal tubes extending away from it into the distance, toward the mountains. A billowing flame burned at the top of the tower, shedding sharp yellow light into the dark blue sky.

"What happened here?" Ujurak whispered in dismay.

"This is the Propkin oil field," the nurse explained. "It's how we get oil from the ground." Smiling, she ruffled Ujurak's head-fur.

"But . . . but where are the plains?" Ujurak stammered. "Where are the mountains?"

"Don't worry; they're still there," Janet assured him. "If you look out the other way, you'll see nothing but mountains." When Ujurak didn't respond, she added, "I come from Chicago, and that's a much bigger place than this. Everywhere around here is really unspoiled, except for the oil field. And the oil has done so much good: It's brought schools and hospitals and better jobs for everyone."

Ujurak looked down at his fingers; there was still a smear of the black sticky stuff with the foul smell. *Are there really whole denning places built just to dig oil out of the ground?*

He remembered the words of Tiinchuu the healer, back in Arctic Village. *Those who would rip the heart out of the earth for their own profit . . .* The hairs rose on the back of Ujurak's neck, and he felt sick.

"Look, there's the oil-pumping tower." Janet pointed out of the window. "And there are the pipelines carrying the oil away to where it can be used."

Ujurak stared. "What's that flame?" he asked. "Is the tower on fire?"

The nurse laughed. "No, it's meant to do that. It's burning off the gases that we don't want."

"And where does the oil go?" Ujurak said. Those pipes were

huge, and there were so many of them. There must be a lot of oil to fill them.

"Oh . . . some to factories, some to ports to be loaded onto ships. But that's enough of that," the nurse added, pulling the pelt closed again and guiding Ujurak back to bed. "It's time you got some rest."

"Who are the men who brought me here?" Ujurak whispered as she tucked the blankets in.

"Important men," Janet replied. "They work for the government and the oil company."

"They want to take oil from the land belonging to the caribou people."

Janet nodded, frowning slightly as she looked down at him. "These are bad times," she said at last. "Poor Mother Nature is going to suffer. But we do need oil from somewhere."

She raised a hand to silence Ujurak as he opened his mouth to ask another question. "Look, I'll show you something. We'll use your bed as a map."

"What's a map?"

"Just look." Janet folded back the blue blanket that lay on top of Ujurak's bed, revealing the sheet below. "Imagine this is the ocean," she said, patting the blanket. "And we'll ruffle up the sheet just here, to make the mountains." Picking up purple-Toklo, she plopped him down at the edge of the blanket. "And here's the oil field!"

Ujurak tilted his head to one side, imagining he was a bird, flying above the land and the sea. "I get it!"

"There are oil fields out on the ice, too," Janet added,

pointing to a spot on the ocean-blanket.

"On the ice?" Ujurak's heart started to beat faster. *Kallík never told us about that.*

"Yes, they sure are clever, aren't they?" Janet said. "Now, can you show me where you come from, honey?"

Ujurak didn't want to answer her gently probing question. He didn't know where he came from, except that he was sure it wouldn't be on her map.

"Can you see the ocean from your home?" Janet prompted when Ujurak didn't reply.

"No . . ." Ujurak began uncertainly, thinking of Arctic Village and trying to work out where it would be. "It's in a narrow valley," he added, guessing where on the map the village might be and pointing to a gap between two of the sheet-mountains. "It's where the caribou go."

"My, I'm surprised your people are so primitive when they're so close to the oil field," Janet said.

"There's a lake here," Ujurak went on, beginning to be interested in the map. "And here's a place where the geese feed. And this is the forest."

"You know your land so well!" Janet exclaimed, her voice filled with amazement.

"Of course. It's where I come from," Ujurak replied.

"If you're so interested in maps, you should go to the Propkin Community Center," Janet told him. "It was built by the oil company before they started work." She got up and went back to the window, pointing out in a different direction. "There it is."

Ujurak could just make out the outline of another building, lower than the towers, but big and solid, with a flat green roof.

"It's great there," Janet went on. "There's a wide-screen TV, bowling, snack bars—even a clinic. The oil company has done such good things for the community! And you would just love the room where the oil company shows their plans." She returned to Ujurak's bed and sat down beside him, her eyes shining. "The walls are covered with maps of the ocean as well as the land around Propkin, with the oil rigs and new communities and roads. I'd really like to get a placement on an oil rig," she added, sighing. "Those guys are so brave! And they're keeping North America alive! If you like, I'll take you over there and show you when you're feeling better," she promised.

"Yes, I'd like that," Ujurak said, thinking, *If I'm still here* . . .

"And now it's time for you to get some sleep." Janet straightened the sheet and put the blanket back, tucking purple-Toklo into the bed beside Ujurak.

Ujurak leaned against his pillows. "Save the wild . . ." he murmured, remembering what Lusa had told him, back on Smoke Mountain.

"What was that, honey?" Janet asked.

Ujurak blinked. "Uh . . . nothing."

"Okay, then, well, get some rest." Janet picked up the tray and glanced around the room as if she was checking that everything was all right. "Good night," she said with a smile, and went out.

Once he was sure she had gone, Ujurak got out of bed and went back to the window, pulling the pelts aside to reveal the devastated landscape outside. With a struggle he managed to shift the catch on the window and push it open. Cold air flooded in, bringing with it an acrid smell.

Ujurak coughed, his sore throat protesting, as he breathed it in. *That's oil, then. It's foul!* He seemed to see the black, sticky stuff spreading out from his fingers, choking his skin, slicking his hair, filling his nose and mouth. . . . There was no escape from it.

The horror of his vision filled him with fury and he let out a roar. The soft flat-face pelts seemed to cling to him and stifle him; he couldn't bear their touch against his skin. Ripping them off, he felt his body begin to change. Ujurak let out a loud cry of relief as his transformation began.

CHAPTER THIRTY

Kallik

Kallik padded cautiously between the flat-face dens, Lusa and Toklo flanking her on either side. Her rush of confidence from finding the small white bear was fading away. She couldn't scent Ujurak any longer, and though she kept scanning the ground, she didn't see any more signs.

Clinging to the shadows, the bears kept going, but Kallik felt her fear growing with every pawstep. The smell made her feel sick, and the air shuddered with bursts of noise. The lights were harsh and unnatural, and their glare blotted out the bears' view of the stars.

Silaluk, where are you? Kallik wondered, raising her snout to peer vainly at the sky. *Are you still watching us, even here?*

The BlackPath they were following divided, and more BlackPaths came to join it. The bears had to cross; Kallik's pelt prickled as she listened for the roar of approaching firebeasts, but the only ones they saw seemed to be asleep.

The buildings became smaller as they left the metal birds' nest behind, more like the flat-face dens Kallik had seen before. Lights shone from gaps covered with pelts. Each of the dens had a small territory around it. Kallik started at the sound of a dog barking from behind a fence.

"Do you think the flat-faces brought Ujurak here?" Lusa whispered.

Kallik shrugged. "I don't know. I've lost his scent."

She let Toklo take the lead down a long BlackPath flanked by dens on either side. Lights on tall, thin trees glared, leaving few shadows where the bears could slip along unnoticed. Kallik's paws tingled.

Sounds were coming from the no-claw dens, but so far they hadn't seen any flat-faces outside. Then, about halfway along the BlackPath, the pelt across one of the gaps was suddenly swept aside. A flat-face cub was peering out: a female, with long yellow head-fur.

Kallik and the others froze, pinned under the blazing light of one of the thin trees.

"Oh, no, she's seen us!" Kallik yelped.

But the cub remained still, her face and paws pressed to the shiny stuff covering the gap. Finally she raised one of her pink paws and waved it at them.

"I think she's friendly," Lusa whispered.

"Let's not wait to find out." Toklo nudged Kallik. "Run!"

With Toklo a bear-length ahead, the bears charged down the BlackPath. Toklo led them around corners and down narrow gaps between buildings until they had left the flat-face cub far behind.

"Nobody followed us!" Lusa panted as they came to a halt in an open space.

Kallik looked around, trying to catch her breath and get her bearings. "You know something?" she said after a moment, her heart sinking. "I think we've been here before. We're going in circles."

She raised her head and gazed up at the stars. *Guide us, Sila-luk, please. We're lost!*

She jumped as Toklo gave her a shove and muttered, "Flat-faces coming, cloud-brain! Move!"

Intent on the sky, Kallik hadn't heard the voices heading toward them. Shivering, she huddled with Lusa and Toklo in the shadow of a big white den, while the group of full-grown males walked past them.

Toklo puffed out a breath when they had gone. "They didn't see us." Glancing up and down the BlackPath, he added, "We're no nearer to finding Ujurak. I think we should get out of here."

"Hey, Toklo! Kallik!" Lusa had moved farther down the side of the white den, and hadn't heard what the brown bear said. Her voice was excited. "Come look at this!"

"What now?" Toklo grumbled, but he padded over to her, and Kallik followed behind, her curiosity piqued.

"Look!" Lusa was gazing up at a row of huge metal cans with lids on the top. "Food!"

Kallik's belly rumbled; she had been trying to forget how hungry she was. "Really?" she asked hopefully.

"Really," Lusa said. "Toklo, can you tip one over? Carefully. We don't want to make more noise than we can help."

Toklo didn't move. "It's not a good idea. We need to leave now, before they catch us. Besides, who wants to eat flat-face rubbish?"

"I'm not leaving without Ujurak," Lusa responded stubbornly. "And if we're going to go on looking, we need to eat."

Toklo let out a sigh. "Don't blame me if it all goes wrong."

He drove his shoulder against the nearest of the metal cans and it tipped over. As the lid came off Lusa grabbed it with her forepaws and lowered it quietly to the ground. Flat-face rubbish spilled out of the can; water flooded Kallik's jaws as she picked up the scent of meat.

Lusa pawed excitedly through the heap of rubbish. "There's fruit, and some sort of green stuff . . . oh, and these potato sticks! Try them; they're really good."

She pushed a few stumpy bits of potato toward Kallik, and some to Toklo, then munched her own share enthusiastically. Kallik glanced at Toklo, who was giving the potato sticks a suspicious sniff, then tried one for herself. The taste was strong and salty; Kallik couldn't quite understand why Lusa liked them so much. *But hey, it's food!* she thought, swallowing the rest.

The can yielded a few scraps of meat, which Toklo and Kallik shared, while Lusa gulped down the fruit.

"Don't even think about it," Toklo said as Lusa eyed the next can in the row. "We've wasted too much time already. Now that we've eaten, we have to go."

Lusa nodded reluctantly. As they turned to leave, Kallik raised her snout for one last sniff. Beyond the smell of oil and rubbish, she could pick up the scent of blood coming from the big white den, mixed with something hard and strange. The combination made her fur bristle.

But there was another scent, too. Faint, almost drowned by the rest, but unmistakable . . . *Ujurak!*

"Lusa! Toklo! Wait!" Kallik called.

Already several bear-lengths away, her friends looked back. "What is it?" Toklo grunted.

"I can smell Ujurak!"

The other two bears came bounding back to her; Lusa's eyes glowed with eagerness as she sniffed the air. "You're right! But where is he?"

Looking up, Kallik saw that far above her head one of the windows of the den was propped open. "Maybe he's in there? Ujurak! Ujurak!"

"It's us! We're down here!" Lusa added.

But no one came to the window.

"Maybe the flat-faces are keeping him in a cage," Toklo growled.

"We've got to get inside and look for him," Lusa declared.

At the thought of entering yet another flat-face den, a shiver passed through Kallik from nose to claws. Fear lodged in her belly like a hard stone. But she wasn't going to let her friends down, and when Lusa set off along the side of the den, looking for a way in, she forced her paws to follow. She was encouraged by Toklo's bulk as the young grizzly padded beside her. *Flat-*

faces will think twice before they mess with him!

As they came around the corner of the den, they saw yellow light seeping out from around a door, but the door itself was firmly closed. Kallik and her friends paused on the edge of the light.

"Do you think we can get in?" Toklo muttered.

"I know we have to try," Lusa barked.

Feeling very exposed, Kallik followed the black bear as she set out across the lighted stretch of ground to the door of the den. About halfway there, Lusa stopped; Toklo almost crashed into her.

"Watch it!" he growled.

"Sorry, Toklo, but look what I've found!"

Lusa dipped her head and touched her nose to something lying on the ground. Peering closely, Kallik saw that it was a tiny carving of a black bear, like the white one she had found beside the metal bird. Giving it a sniff, she picked up Ujurak's scent again.

"He left this for us," Lusa said. "Now we know he has to be in here."

Determinedly she padded toward the door and stopped to study it.

"Now what do we do?" Toklo asked.

"Let me think." Lusa's eyes were fixed on the door. "I got into the healer's den. Maybe I can get in here."

As Lusa examined the door, Kallik kept watch for the approach of flat-faces. Her heart was pounding, but the

BlackPath was deserted as far as she could see.

"I'll have to—" Lusa took a pace forward toward the center of the doors and broke off with a frightened squeak. With an almost inaudible swish the door had parted in the middle, the two halves sliding aside to leave an opening.

Fear gripped Kallik and she kept very still. Beside her, Toklo and Lusa stood rigid; Kallik thought she could hear the thudding of their hearts.

"It's a trap," Toklo said hoarsely.

"Do you . . . do you think it wants to eat us?" Lusa whispered.

The faint trail of Ujurak's scent beckoned them through, but no bear moved. Kallik didn't think she could force her paws to carry her past this mysterious door that moved when no one was near it.

But as the moments dragged by, nothing happened. No angry flat-faces appeared, and the door stayed invitingly open.

"We wanted to get in, didn't we?" Lusa said at last. Kallik could tell that she was trying to sound brave, though her voice still shook a little. "Let's go."

Toklo blocked her as she tried to plunge inside the den. "Hold it, bee-brain! Let me check it out first."

Pushing past Lusa, he stuck his head inside the door, then padded all the way in. "There's no one around. Come on."

Every muscle in Kallik's body was yelling at her to run. She had been scared enough when she and Lusa had sneaked into the healer's den. This was much worse: She couldn't imagine what flat-faces would do to bears if they caught them trespassing here.

But letting Toklo and Lusa face the danger alone was unthinkable. Every pawstep an effort, Kallik padded into the den behind them. She stood in a small inner den, brightly lit, with white walls and doors leading off on all sides. Pushing down her fear, she followed her companions as they crept forward through one of the inner doors, which led into a long passage.

"How do we know where to find Ujurak?" she whispered as she caught up to the others.

"We don't," Toklo replied. "We just keep looking."

"Good plan," Lusa muttered.

They were passing closed doors on either side; Kallik guessed that they led to other little dens. She didn't think Ujurak could be inside one of them; she had picked up his scent again, once she was calm enough to check, but it was still a ways off.

Partway down the passage was another closed door; its frame was filled with the transparent stuff, and Kallik could see that the passage continued on the other side.

"Do you know how to get through there?" she asked Lusa.

While she was still speaking, the door slid open, just like the one that had let them into the den. *Is it a trap?* she wondered.

Then Kallik heard a door open behind her, followed by a loud scream. She whipped around to see a female flat-face in a white pelt standing in the doorway of one of the little dens they had passed. Instantly the flat-face ducked back inside the den, and Kallik heard the door slam.

Almost at once another door opened; a flat-face male popped his head out and withdrew again. His door also shut with a bang.

"They know we're here," Toklo snarled. "We've got to move *now*!"

Barely able to think for fear, Kallik bounded beside her friends, through the terrifying door and on down the passage. After a few pawsteps, she heard the door swish shut again. *It was a trap!*

But there was no time to think about that, or to worry about how they were going to get out again. A harsh ringing sound broke out all around them, and they ran even faster, skidding along the smooth passage's floor.

"This way!" Toklo gasped.

He led them up a steep slope with chunks cut out of it, which made it easier to climb. Ujurak's scent was growing stronger now. *But the flat-faces will catch us first!*

At the top of the slope they hurtled down another passage, only to skid to a halt as a flat-face with a firestick appeared at the other end.

"Down here!" Lusa dived down a side passage.

Kallik heard the crack of the firestick and glanced back to see a dart hit the wall before she pounded on.

"They'll put us to sleep!" she gasped. "They'll take us to the place where the hungry bears are kept!"

The passage led to another of the slopes; Kallik scrambled up behind Lusa and Toklo, desperate to leave the firestick behind. The passage above was deserted, in spite of the terrible clanging that never stopped.

Kallik's heart thudded with panic. Ujurak's scent was stronger here, but she knew they were running out of time. It wouldn't take long for the flat-faces to track them down inside their own den.

Even if we find Ujurak, how will we get him out?

Then Toklo swerved to one side, throwing himself against one of the inner doors. It burst open; Toklo tumbled into a small den, with Lusa and Kallik hard on his paws.

Ujurak's bear scent flooded over Kallik; he had been here, and not long before, but a single glance told her that he wasn't here now.

"This must have been his den," she panted.

"Yes, look." Toklo was standing beside the bed, staring down at something small and dark on the rumpled white coverings.

Drawing closer, Kallik saw that it was yet another wooden carving, this time of a brown bear. Her heart cried out with frustration as her gaze met Toklo's. *We've only just missed him! Ujurak, where are you?*

Lusa padded over to the gap in the wall and looked out. "This is what we saw from outside," she reported. "I can see the cans—there's the one we tipped over. Ujurak must have gone out this way just before we came."

Kallik followed her friend to the window and stuck her

head out. "It's a long drop," she murmured doubtfully.

"It's all right for Ujurak," Toklo complained, coming up behind her. "He can fly."

"Not if he's a bear," Lusa said. "Or a flat-face."

For a few moments their discoveries had made them forget about the pursuing flat-faces. Now Kallik jumped as she heard pawsteps thundering down the passage, getting closer and closer.

"Go!" Toklo bellowed. "Jump onto one of the cans!"

He shoved Lusa hard from behind, so that she tottered on the ledge outside for a moment, then half fell, half jumped onto the nearest can, then to the ground outside. Toklo scrambled up and leaped out after her. Kallik followed, hesitating at the sight of the drop until she heard a flat-face burst into the room behind her. As she launched herself through the gap a firestick cracked out, and the dart whizzed past her ear.

Slipping from the top of the can and hitting the ground hard, Kallik lay winded for a moment, until Toklo shouldered her to her paws.

"Move," he growled, pushing her forward and limping after her. "They'll find us if we stay here."

Lusa was bounding away, but she stopped after a few bearlengths and looked back. "Quick!" she urged. "We've got to hide."

Kallik staggered after her, still dazed. Lusa headed for a huge firebeast that crouched, apparently asleep, beside one of the buildings. She slid behind it, careful not to wake it; Toklo shoved Kallik into the gap and crammed himself in after her.

The loud clanging noise still came from the den behind them. The flat-faces' pawsteps and shouting grew louder as they spilled out of the den and into the night. Another fire-beast swept past, making a high-pitched wailing sound.

"Oh, Ujurak!" Kallik whispered. "Come find us, and then we can all get out of here."

CHAPTER· THIRTY‑ONE

Toklo

Toklo peered cautiously out from the shelter of the firebeast. Loud noises were still coming from the white building, but for the moment he couldn't see any flat-faces.

"We can't go yet," he muttered. "We'd better wait until things quiet down, and then we'll look for Ujurak."

He tensed as he spotted movement above them. Something with large wings fluttered down from the sky, and a few moments later a small brown bear cub crept out from the shadows, blinking nervously. He spotted Toklo's head poking out from hiding, and bounded across to him.

"You found me!" Ujurak yelped. "Oh, it's so good to see you again!"

Toklo stared at him. Relief flooded through him, making his pelt tingle, coupled with sheer exasperation at Ujurak's cheerful tone. *After all we've been through, he turns up as if we're in the middle of the forest chasing beetles for fun!*

"Get behind here," he snapped, reaching out a paw to give Ujurak a cuff around his ear. "Do you want the flat-faces to take you away again?"

"It's so great that you came to find me!" Ujurak chattered as he squeezed into the narrow space beside Toklo.

"Where have you been?" Toklo growled. "The flat-faces almost caught us in there!"

"I'm sorry," Ujurak said. Toklo could see he was trying to look penitent, but his eyes were shining. "I was being an owl, looking around this place, and then I saw you come out of the hospital. I'm so glad to see you."

Kallik and Lusa pressed up to him and thrust their snouts into his fur.

"Welcome back," Kallik murmured.

"I was scared we'd never find you," Lusa confessed.

"I knew you would! Did you find the little bears I left for you? Did you—"

"In case you hadn't noticed, we're in danger, bee-brain," Toklo interrupted. "There's no time to stand around. Flat-faces are hunting us."

Ujurak glanced over his shoulder as a flat-face ran past with a firestick in his hands, never noticing the four bears huddled in the gap between the firebeast and the wall. "Oh, these are good flat-faces," he assured Toklo. "They won't hurt us."

"They're firing *darts* at us, Ujurak," Toklo pointed out.

"That's right," Kallik added. "They won't kill us, but they'll put us to sleep and take us to the place where the hungry bears are kept. I know; I've been there. And then we won't be together anymore."

"We have to get out of here now." Toklo shoved past Ujurak

and peered around the end of the firebeast. He could hear voices in the distance, but there were no flat-faces nearby. "Come on; it looks quiet."

"Wait," Ujurak said. "I need to tell you something. I've found out what the flat-faces are doing. They're taking oil from the land."

"So what?" Toklo grunted. "What's oil, anyway? Will it help us find prey? If not, they can have it, as far as I'm concerned."

Ujurak turned to face him, the fur on his shoulders standing on end and the light in his eyes replaced with something harder and colder. Toklo had never seen him like this before; he only just stopped himself from taking a step back.

"Oil is stinking black stuff," Ujurak snarled. "I can smell it on your pelt, Toklo. The flat-faces want it, so they built all this to help them get it."

"But Ujurak—" Kallik stammered, coming up to stand beside him. "It's flat-face stuff. It doesn't have anything to do with bears."

"Oh, no?" Ujurak swung around to face her, quiet fury in his voice. "You've seen what it's like here. Filthy, noisy, reeking . . . Well, the flat-faces want to make everything like this. They want to put their stinking structures where the caribou come to feed."

"Why?" Kallik blinked, her gaze troubled. "What harm have the caribou done to them?"

"The flat-faces take oil from the ground," Ujurak told her. "That's what all this is for. The towers pump up the oil and the pipes carry it to where the flat-faces want it. I don't know why, but they need it badly. They're prepared to sacrifice the wild to get it. Not just here, Kallik, but on the ice, too."

"They can't!" Kallik's eyes stretched wide with alarm. "Flat-faces can't live out on the ice."

Ujurak pressed closely against her side. "I'm sorry, Kallik, but they can."

"Then what can we do about it?" the white bear asked.

"I don't know. But we must have faith." Ujurak's voice quavered. "We have come all this way for a reason. I think we have been sent here to stop it all."

"I can't believe you just said that," Toklo stated flatly. *Does the squirrel-brained cub really think that anything we do will stop the flat-faces?* "We have to leave here, and go into the mountains. You said that they're going to build their structures on the plain, so the mountains will be safe."

Ujurak shook his head; there was such certainty in his expression that Toklo gulped.

"No," the smaller cub hissed. "Once it starts, nowhere is safe. The caribou flat-faces have been protecting this place until now, but they cannot protect it any longer. Nowhere is safe," he repeated. "Oil will destroy everything you know. Flat-faces will break the ice and tear down the trees to find it. *Now* do you understand why we have to do something?"

Suddenly Lusa started forward; she had listened in silence until now, her gaze fixed on Ujurak. Toklo stepped back with a huff of irritation as she brushed past him and buried her snout in Ujurak's shoulder.

"We have to save the wild," she whispered.

Briefly Toklo wondered what would happen if he refused to go one step farther with Ujurak. Would any of the others follow him if he turned around and walked away? Remembering the days he had spent alone in the woods, he didn't want to put it to the test.

The sound of the firebeast with the wailing call, growing louder still, made up Toklo's mind for him.

"We can't stand around," he growled. "Does anyone know how to get out of here?"

"I'm so turned around," Lusa complained. "This way, maybe?"

Before they could move, two flat-faces appeared around the corner. One of them carried a firestick, and he let out a yell of amazement as he spotted the bears.

"Go!" Ujurak growled.

As the bears emerged into the open, more shouts broke out from farther down the BlackPath, and another firestick made a cracking sound.

"There are more of them!" Lusa gasped. "Run!"

The barking of dogs echoed behind them as they fled. Another wailing firebeast was bearing down on them, its eyes glaring; Toklo skidded around a corner into a narrow alley to avoid it, his friends hard on his paws.

"Why are the flat-faces chasing us like this?" Ujurak panted, trying to keep pace with the bigger cub. "Do they hate us?"

"Not all of them do," Lusa responded. "Hey, Kallik and Toklo, remember the little cub who looked out of her den and waved at us? She looked as if she liked bears." Lusa began to slow down. "I wonder . . ."

"Absolutely not," Toklo snapped. "If you're thinking what I think you're thinking, we can't trust *any* flat-faces, not even cubs."

"What choice do we have?" Lusa asked. "The forest is far away and we're lost. We don't know how to get out of here. We have Ujurak, who can talk to flat-faces, who can *turn into* a flat-face. What else are we going to do?"

"Asking *flat-faces* for help?" Kallik yelped. "Lusa, that's cloud-brained!"

"I don't know," Ujurak argued, his eyes bright. "It might be worth a try. Do any of you know where to find her?" he asked.

Toklo thought back to when he had seen the female cub. They had run away from her den, afraid that they would be pursued. He wasn't sure of the direction they had taken.

Lusa prodded him in the side with her snout. "Quick, Toklo! The flat-faces are catching up!"

As she was speaking, Toklo heard a shout behind him and glanced back to see flat-faces appearing at the other end of the alley. They had a dog with them; it let out a full-throated baying sound. What difference would it make if they found the cub? At worst, they would be caught by flat-faces—and it looked like that was going to happen anyway.

"This way!" Toklo snapped, heading off in what he hoped was the right direction. "But let me remind you: The last flat-faces you thought were nice were just *letting off firesticks* at us."

"There's the big white den!" Lusa exclaimed a moment later. "I can smell the bins we knocked over. Now it should be this way. . . ."

The bears weaved their way among the BlackPaths. Twice they had to crouch in the shadows while the wailing firebeast passed them, and once they ducked under a low-growing tree to hide from a metal bird.

Toklo began to feel as if he couldn't run anymore. He knew he was lost. The BlackPaths all looked the same. The den where he had seen the female cub was just like all the other dens in this horrible place. His legs ached from running and his chest heaved as he tried to gulp in air.

"It's no good . . ." he gasped.

"Toklo!" Kallik had drawn a few paces ahead, to the corner of another BlackPath. "I can smell our scent! We can follow it back the way we came."

"Brilliant!" Lusa put on a spurt of speed to join the white bear, with Ujurak hard on her paws. Toklo forced his legs to go on pounding after them.

Kallik led them around another corner. For the moment they seemed to have shaken off the pursuit.

Then Toklo spotted a den with a crooked tree growing beside it. The roof came right down over the door, like shaggy fur almost covering a bear's eyes. "This is the place!" he barked. "We can try, but I still think it's a bad idea."

Glancing from side to side, he led the way across the Black-Path and darted into the shadows beside the house. Padding along the wall, he reached the gap where he remembered seeing the cub. Rearing up on his hind legs, he tried to look in. There was a light in the den beyond, but pelts covered the gap.

Toklo nudged the shiny stuff with his snout. Almost at once a pink paw appeared, sweeping the pelt aside. The little female cub was gazing back at him.

"Help! Help us!" Lusa begged. "Flat-faces are chasing us."

The cub looked alarmed, backing away from the window.

"No!" Toklo roared.

"Stop it; you're frightening her," Lusa said, pushing him aside.

Toklo shook his head impatiently. "We can't make her understand."

In the distance dogs were barking and the shouts of flat-faces were becoming clearer. Toklo knew that soon they would have to start running again.

There was a faint scuffling noise behind him. Toklo turned his head in time to see Ujurak rearing up onto his hindpaws. His limbs grew thinner and his brown fur melted away. His snout shrank and his ears slid into the side of his head.

"Let me try," Ujurak said, stepping forward in the shape of a flat-face.

CHAPTER THIRTY-TWO

Ujurak

Ujurak shivered in the icy wind as he tapped on the window, giving the little cub inside a friendly smile. Her eyes widened and she stepped forward again, pressing her face and hands against the glass as she peered out.

"Open the window, please!" Ujurak called to her.

The cub hesitated. She still looked scared, but after a moment she reached out, unfastened the window, and pushed it open.

"Who are you?" she asked curiously.

"My name's Ujurak," he began. "I'm—I'm visiting here."

"I'm Maria," the cub responded. She let out a giggle, covering her mouth with one paw. "Shouldn't you have some clothes on? You must be frozen. Here, you can have this."

She stripped off a pink outer pelt and handed it to Ujurak through the window. Underneath it she wore soft pelts like the ones the flat-faces in the hospital had given to him.

Ujurak put on the pink pelt, pulling it tightly around him. Meanwhile, Maria leaned out of the window, her eyes wide as she gazed at Toklo, Lusa, and Kallik. "Are those your bears?"

"Yes," Ujurak replied. "And we're being chased by flat-faces—I mean people—who think the bears are dangerous. But they're not, I promise. Look!"

Lusa, Kallik, and Toklo were watching him carefully, trying to guess from his gestures what he and the flat-face cub were saying. Ujurak waved a hand at them and growled softly in bear, "Down! Look friendly!" At his side, his three friends crouched down; Ujurak could tell they were trying to look small and harmless. Lusa waved her paws in the air.

Suddenly Maria vanished from the window. Ujurak's heart sank. Had she gone to get full-grown flat-faces? But she reappeared a moment later around the side of the house with a small black-and-white dog in her arms. "This is Piper," she said, holding him out. "Piper, say hi."

The little dog wagged his tail and stretched out his neck to lick Ujurak's paw, giving him a good sniff. Ujurak felt Toklo stiffen next to him. *It's not prey, Toklo,* Ujurak warned him silently. The dog drew back, looking puzzled. *He doesn't know what to make of my scent,* Ujurak thought.

"I think he likes you," Maria said happily. She looked at the bears. "Can I touch them?" she asked. "I've never seen bears this close before."

"Er, sure," said Ujurak.

Maria stretched out and pressed her hand against Toklo's thick brown fur. Ujurak was sure he saw his friend roll his eyes.

"I wish I had pet bears," Maria whispered.

"Can you help us?" Ujurak asked. "We need somewhere to hide. I—I don't want the flat-faces to take my bears away."

Maria grinned. "I know a perfect place! Follow me. Piper, stay!"

She led the way around the side of the house. At the back, a stretch of grass led down to a small wooden den beside a fence. Maria flung open the door and beckoned them inside.

Ujurak stood back to let his friends go first. He spotted lights from a firebeast turning onto the BlackPath and heard the sound of voices. A dog barked.

"They're still looking for us," he muttered.

Inside the den smelled of apples and dry earth. Flat-face things made of wood and metal hung on the walls. At one side were shelves stacked with containers. Ujurak shook his head.

"We can't hide in here," he said. "They'll see us if they look through the window."

"Not in the shed, silly!" Maria told him. "Down here, in the cellar."

She pulled open a little door that lifted up from the floor of the den, revealing a small square space lined with flat slabs of stone. Ujurak wasn't sure there was enough space to fit the four of them. A damp chill rose out of the hole, and he shivered.

"I'm not going down there!" Toklo protested, peering down from the edge of the hole.

There was panic in Kallik's eyes. "We won't be able to breathe!"

"Yes, we will. It'll be okay." Lusa's voice was coaxing. "We won't have to stay there for long." She jumped down into the cellar and looked back up at her friends. "See? It's fine."

Outside, the voices of the pursuing flat-faces suddenly got louder. Ujurak jumped at the baying of a dog. "They're following our scent!" he exclaimed.

"Quick!" Maria urged them.

Toklo and Kallik were still hesitating on the brink of the hole.

"Get down there, *now*!" Ujurak's impatience spilled over. "This is our only chance to escape. Do you *want* them to find us?"

Maria let out a gasp, her eyes round with shock. "You just *roared*! Can you speak *bear*?"

"Yes," Ujurak replied.

He gave Kallik a shove and she half jumped, half fell into the cellar beside Lusa. Toklo opened his jaws as if he was going to argue, but a howl from a dog outside stopped him. He leaped down, landing on top of Kallik. The hole seemed full of a heaving mass of black, brown, and white fur.

"Are you from a circus?" Maria asked eagerly. "Are your bears magic?"

There was no time to answer her. Ujurak bundled down into the cellar, squeezing himself into a space among his friends, and Maria dropped the door on top of them. Thick darkness fell. Ujurak couldn't even see his own paws. The furry pelts of his friends squashed up against him and their mingled scents flooded over him.

"I don't like this," Kallik said in a trembling voice.

"You'll be okay," Lusa whispered.

"Shh!" said Ujurak. "I want to listen."

He could hear Maria's voice coming faintly from a distance and realized she must be speaking to the flat-faces outside the den. "Yes, the bears came through here. They went that way!"

Then Ujurak heard a male flat-face's voice, but this time he couldn't make out the words. Nearer, and more worrying, was the snuffling and whining of dogs; they sounded as if they were right up against the wall of the den.

"They can scent us," Toklo growled. "They know we're in here."

"Inside the shed?" Maria's voice came again. "Oh, no, they couldn't be. It's always kept locked."

Please don't try the door, Ujurak thought.

"Ujurak." Kallik's voice came again, quavering with terror. "I can't breathe! I've got to get out!" She raised her paws and started scrabbling frantically at the stone wall, shoving Ujurak into a corner.

"Not now!" Toklo protested.

"Just a moment or two longer," Lusa begged. "We can't let the flat-faces find us now!"

"I can't—I can't. . . ."

Ujurak could feel Kallik shaking and hear her rapid, panting breaths. He strained to hear what was going on outside. Flat-faces were shouting to one another, and a dog was barking; to his relief, the sounds soon began to die away.

"I think they're leaving," he said.

A moment later Maria pulled open the door; moonlight

filtered down into the cellar. Kallik exploded upward with a roar, and Toklo and Lusa scrambled out after her. Ujurak pulled himself up to see Maria pressed back against the wall of the den, trying to keep out of the way of the panicking white bear.

"It's okay, Kallik, it's okay." Lusa followed Kallik to the door of the den and stood close beside her while the white bear calmed down. Toklo headed outside, and a moment later Kallik and Lusa followed him.

"Thanks, Maria," Ujurak said to the cub. "We owe you a lot."

"You're welcome," Maria replied. "Where are you going now?"

Ujurak drew a deep breath. "Out of this place. Which is the quickest way?"

"I'll show you." Maria took them back to the BlackPath. "That way, if you want to avoid the oil fields," she said, pointing. "Head for the tall black building."

"Thanks," Ujurak said.

As he beckoned to his friends, he saw that Maria was looking disappointed. "Can't you stay?" she pleaded. "I'll bring you all food. None of my friends are going to believe that I had three bears in my backyard!"

Ujurak shook his head. "I'm sorry. We have to keep going." He turned to leave; Toklo was already heading down the BlackPath in the direction Maria had pointed.

CHAPTER THIRTY-THREE

Ujurak

"Don't go yet," Maria said. *"You* can't go around with no clothes on! Just wait here a minute."

She disappeared, scrambling back through her window. Ujurak fidgeted on the spot, while Toklo fretted impatiently a few paces farther down the BlackPath, and Lusa and Kallik stood close together, talking in low voices.

A few moments later Maria came back. She had a thick pelt bundled in her arms, and two heavy things the shape of flat-face paws clutched in one paw.

"Put these on," she ordered. "They'll keep you warm."

Ujurak stripped off the pink pelt she had given him earlier and put on the new one. It was too big for him, covering his paws and almost trailing on the ground, but it was heavy and warm, and he huddled gratefully into its folds. It was so much *colder* being a flat-face! *But I'd better stay a flat-face while we're here,* he thought. *I can protect the others if the flat-faces think I'm one of them.*

"Now the boots," Maria said, putting the paw-pelts on the

ground. "No," she added as Ujurak picked one up and tried to stick his foot into it. "The other way around!"

Ujurak didn't like the feeling of the paw-pelts on his paws. They were stiff and clumsy. *How can flat-faces feel the earth if they go around in these all the time?* he wondered. But he had to admit that his paws didn't feel so cold inside them.

Flat-faces need so much . . . stuff. It's much better to be a bear.

"Thank you, Maria," he said. "We'll never forget what you've done for us."

To his surprise, Maria stepped up close to him and gave him a hug. "Whoever you are, good luck," she murmured.

Ujurak smiled awkwardly and nodded. "Good-bye," he said.

Lusa padded up and nosed Maria's hand in a friendly way. Maria patted her on the snout. "Good-bye, bears. Take care."

"Come on!" Toklo called.

Ujurak turned and began trudging down the BlackPath, his steps feeling heavy in the paw-pelts. Kallik and Toklo flanked him on either side, while Lusa brought up the rear. Before they turned the next corner, Ujurak glanced back to see Maria still standing outside her house, looking after them. She raised a paw and waved, and Ujurak waved back to her before they rounded the corner and lost sight of her.

They headed toward the tall building Maria had pointed out. The wind had strengthened, blowing into Ujurak's face, its bitter cold even penetrating the thick pelts Maria had given him. As he shivered, Toklo and Kallik moved closer to him, warming him with their fur.

Though the BlackPath was quiet, Ujurak stayed alert for sounds of pursuit, wishing for a bear's sharper senses of scent and hearing. The tall building was still a long way off when he heard the roar of a firebeast rapidly growing louder. Glancing back, he saw it sweeping toward them, a whirling blue light shining from the top of its back.

"Not again!" Toklo growled.

"Quick, hide!" Ujurak ordered. "Down there!" He pointed to the end of an alleyway a few bear-lengths ahead.

The bears bounded forward and disappeared into the darkness. Ujurak was running after them when he heard a shout behind him. "Hey, you! Boy!"

His heart sinking, Ujurak halted and turned. The firebeast had drawn to a halt and a male flat-face was climbing out of its belly. He had a small firestick clipped to a tendril around his waist.

At least he's not pointing it at me!

"Boy! Come here!" the flat-face ordered.

"Me?" Ujurak tried to sound innocent. Resisting the impulse to look around and make sure that his friends were out of sight, he walked back toward the flat-face.

"What are you doing out so late?" the flat-face asked as he approached. "Don't you know bears have been spotted in town?"

"Bears?" Ujurak widened his eyes in pretend surprise. "Really?"

"Really. So it's no time to be wandering about on your own."

"I . . . er . . ." Ujurak tried to think what excuse a flat-face would accept. "I had to get some medicine for my baby sister," he said at last, hoping that the flat-face wouldn't ask to see it. "She's sick."

The flat-face grunted. "Were you at the hospital? Did you see anything of a runaway boy? Or any bears?"

Ujurak shook his head. "I didn't go to the hospital. I had to get the medicine from . . . from Maria's. Just down there." He gestured wildly in the direction they had come.

To his astonishment, the flat-face smiled and nodded. "Dr. Green, huh? He's very good to his patients. I'm sure his daughter, Maria, will make a great medic, too."

Ujurak returned the smile, relief washing over him. "I guess she will."

"Okay, get yourself home quickly," the flat-face went on, his tone friendlier now.

He turned away and got back into the firebeast. Ujurak waited until it had roared off, then headed for the alley.

Toklo, Kallik, and Lusa appeared from the shadows as he approached, their eyes anxious.

"What happened?" Toklo demanded. "What did the flat-face want?"

"He asked me if I'd seen any of you," Ujurak replied. "We've got to get out of here as quickly as we can."

He peered out from the end of the alley to check that the BlackPath was empty. Keeping to the shadows, he led the bears toward the tall building. The small flat-face dens gave way to bigger structures with blank windows or no windows at all; there was a sense of emptiness and desolation around him, and the reek of oil grew stronger still.

Lights on the outside of the buildings lit up a scatter of flat-face rubbish blowing across the BlackPath. A sheet of paper hit Toklo in the face; the wind plastered it to his head and chest.

"That's disgusting!" the grizzly cub complained, halting to claw himself free of the sheet. "It stinks of flat-faces."

"I know," Kallik agreed sadly. "I hate it here."

"Then we've just got to get out of here as fast as we can," Ujurak tried to encourage them. His paws tingled at the thought of padding over grass again, and dipping his snout to take a drink of pure river water. *But soon there might not be pure water anywhere.*

Ujurak remembered his vision in the hospital, after he had smeared the oil Janet brought him on his fingers. He had felt it streaming out from his body, swamping it, filling his mouth and nose, and flowing onward, unstoppable, until it had engulfed the whole world.

"It's going to get so much worse," he whispered.

Gradually the tall building grew closer, until the bears stood in its shadow. It reared up into the sky, taller than the tallest tree; all its windows were dark. The BlackPath curved past it, flanked on both sides by more flat-face dens. In every direction it was the same. Wherever Ujurak looked, the world was filled with structures of stone and metal.

"Well, what do we do now?" Toklo growled, swinging his head around in disgust. "This is where the flat-face cub told us to go, but we're nowhere nearer to finding the way out."

"We could be stuck here forever!" Kallik whimpered.

"No, we won't be," Lusa said. "We've got to keep looking. It can't be far now."

"Do you ever stop being cheerful?" Toklo muttered. "It's so annoying."

"Well, you can be pretty annoying yourself!" Lusa retorted.

"Don't fight," Ujurak said, moving to Toklo's side and resting a paw on his shoulder. "I'll find the way out, but first we've got to look for somewhere you can hide."

With the bears just behind him, Ujurak began to skirt around the tall building. Wind whistled past with a mournful sound, stirring up more dust and rubbish. Briefly Ujurak froze as he heard the throaty roar of a firebeast in the distance, but it faded without coming into sight. He thought this was the loneliest place he had ever been, worse than the remotest mountain.

At last, when they had trudged all the way around the building and were almost back to their starting point, Ujurak spotted a flat sheet of wood propped against the wall.

"Under there," he said, giving Kallik a shove. "Stay there until I come back."

Kallik padded off, and Lusa followed her, giving Ujurak a friendly poke with her snout as she went past. "Don't be long," she said.

"I won't," Ujurak promised.

Toklo went last, squashing himself into the small space

beside his friends. "I've never done so much hiding in my whole life," he grumbled.

Once they were safely under cover, Ujurak looked up at the top of the building and the stars beyond. He strained upward, feeling the wind start to lift him. His flat-face pelts fell away as his body changed. His legs shrank, his paws cramping into hooked claws. His sight sharpened; he could make out every crack and rough place on the side of the building. Feathers sprouted from his pink flat-face skin, and as he swept his arms upward they became wings, gleaming white in the moonlight. With a deep-toned cry, Ujurak swooped upward in the shape of a snowy white owl.

The cold night air flowed through his feathers as he flew far above the BlackPaths and the flat-face structures, but even here it was tainted with the reek of oil from below.

The lights in the buildings were tiny specks in the darkness; even the flames on the top of the tower were smaller than Tiinchuu's hearth fire. Firebeasts with their glaring eyes crawled like fireflies across the devastated land.

I have to find out what's going on, Ujurak told himself, letting his owl-sight roam from the sea to the mountains. *I have to know. Everything I can see is important.*

The map the nurse had made for him with sheets and blankets unfolded beneath him, from the ocean to the mountains, with the black fungus of the Propkin oil field blighting the land between them.

Wherever he looked, he could see dens and BlackPaths, the silver pipes threading their way across the land. And as he went on looking, something seemed to happen; movement seethed on the ground beneath, as if a bear had stirred an ants' nest with his paw.

The towers and pipes and BlackPaths were crawling outward, swallowing up the land that until then had been free of them. They crept along the coast and into the hills, flowing like a tide over the forests and the dens of Arctic Village, far into the distance, covering everything until the Last Great Wilderness had vanished.

Circling on snow-white wings, Ujurak let out a cry of despair. In his nightmare vision there were no more bears, no more caribou or geese or foxes, just pipes and noise and stinking air as far as he could see. The taint had even spread out to sea; black walls reared up out of the ice, spilling rubbish into the waves. There was no escape.

With a gasp, Ujurak snapped back to reality, blinking to chase away the horrible vision. His senses seemed sharper than ever: He could hear the engines pumping underground, sucking the oil from deep down, and then the oil gurgling through the pipes that carried it into the mountains.

Ice-cold terror washed over him; he could barely make his wings hold him up in the air. At last he knew the reason for his journey: the Last Great Wilderness needed his help.

Save the wild. . . . He thought of Lusa's dream. He remembered his own uneasiness along the journey, the fear of the creatures whose shape he had taken, that their world was being spoiled and poisoned, stolen from them by the flat-faces.

I'm here to fight, he vowed. *Somehow I'll find out what I have to do.*

A flash of moonlight blinded him; the stars whirled around him and he realized he was falling. His wings and tail feathers shrank away, replaced by fins, while silver scales flowed over his body. A spasm passed through him as he realized that he couldn't breathe. Choking, he twisted in the air. The river loomed up beneath him; he hit the water and slid into it in the shape of a fish.

No . . . Ujurak thought, fighting back panic. *This isn't right! I've got to get back to Toklo and the others.*

The fish shape was threatening to overwhelm him, a fierce hunger driving out the memory of his friends. His mouth gaped to draw in the nourishing food that he knew the river should have offered. But there was nothing . . . nothing but tainted water and emptiness where he longed to swim upstream in the company of his kin.

I've got to . . . change. . . . With the last scraps of his consciousness, Ujurak tried to force himself back into the shape of the owl, to soar over the oil field and locate the tall building beneath which his friends were hiding.

Flicking his tail, Ujurak swam for the riverbank. He felt his body grow bigger; legs burst from his body, and now there were four of them, ending in neat hooves. He could feel antlers sprouting from his head, and he looked down at himself to see the gray-brown pelt of a caribou.

Scrambling up from the river's edge, Ujurak stood at the top of the bank and looked out across the oil field. He realized that he was a pregnant female, feeling the weight of her calf heavy in her belly. He began to trudge forward, head down, instinct leading him toward the ancient calving grounds of his kin. But instead of the windswept marshes and forested hills, all he could see were BlackPaths, long silver tubes running alongside them, and the tall structures that the flat-faces had built. He lifted his head and gave a long, lamenting cry, letting out the grief of a mother with nowhere to raise her young.

No . . . no . . . With the last of his strength Ujurak fought against the transformation.

Owl . . . owl so that I can go back to my friends and lead them out of this place. Wings . . . white feathers . . . beak and claws . . .

To Ujurak's relief he felt himself shrinking again, as at last he managed to control the change and return into the body of the snowy white owl. He soared upward on silent wings, though his muscles were shrieking with exhaustion and his tiny bird heart fluttered like a leaf in a gale.

Blinking, he focused his owl-sight on the place below until he spotted the tall building where he had first transformed. He could even make out the sheet of wood beneath which his friends crouched in hiding.

From his vantage point, Ujurak could see that the building was close to the edge of the flat-face structures, just as Maria had said. *If we follow that BlackPath . . . then that one . . . we can leave this place behind.*

His heart heavy, Ujurak let himself drift downward and landed on the ground a couple of bear-lengths away from the sheet of wood. With a sigh of relief, he let his feathers melt away; brown fur flowed over his limbs as his wings changed into forelegs and his claws sprouted; his beak became a snout and he dropped to all fours in the shape of a brown bear cub.

For a moment he couldn't move; he just crouched, trembling, on the dusty ground. His limbs ached and he felt so tired he didn't think he would be able to move his paws. But the sound of a firebeast reminded him that flat-faces were still searching for him and his friends. There was no time to rest.

Stifling a groan, Ujurak forced himself to his paws. "I'm back!" he called. "I know what we have to do now."

CHAPTER THIRTY-FOUR

Kallik

Kallik emerged from her hiding place behind the wood and stretched her legs one by one. Ujurak was standing a couple of bear-lengths away; he was a brown bear again, but his pelt was bedraggled and filthy and his eyes were dark with exhaustion.

"Ujurak, what happened to you?" she whimpered.

"I'm fine," Ujurak replied, his voice hoarse. "I'll tell you later."

Kallik wasn't reassured, but whatever the trouble was, Ujurak obviously didn't want to talk about it. She padded up to him and buried her snout in his shoulder. "It's good to see you back in your proper bear shape," she said. "I hope you stay that way."

"I hope so, too," Ujurak said heavily.

"And I hope you know the way out of here," Toklo growled as he came out of hiding with Lusa just behind him. "I want to shake this place off my paws for good. And I'm hungry!"

"We'll hunt as soon as we can," Ujurak promised. "It won't be long now."

He turned and led the way along one of the BlackPaths he had seen from the sky; after a while he seemed to shake off some of his weariness, and his pawsteps grew swift and confident. Kallik followed eagerly. As they turned onto another BlackPath the wind in her face smelled cleaner. Sooner than she had hoped, the buildings fell away behind them. Her paws left the hard surface and landed on grass, interrupted here and there by rocks and clumps of low-growing foliage. She could hear the gentle sound of waves washing on the shore, and at last, beneath the ever-present taint of oil, she picked up the tang of salt water. Starlight glittered on the rippling surface and glimmered on the line of the ice.

It's coming closer! she thought joyfully, drawing in the familiar cold scent.

She longed to swim out across the narrow stretch of open water, onto the frozen sea. She longed to lose herself in the endless whiteness. But she knew that she couldn't leave her companions. *Not now, when we've just discovered what is happening to the wilderness.*

A few bear-lengths farther on, they came to the bank of the river. Glancing upstream, Kallik spotted the bridge she had crossed with Lusa and Toklo on their way into the denning place. Lights were flashing there, like a colony of fireflies, and she could hear the sound of no-claws shouting.

"They're still looking for us," Toklo observed.

"Yes, it's lucky we didn't try to cross there," Lusa agreed.

Ujurak was gazing across the river; Kallik padded up to join him. Moonlight glimmered on the rippling water, dividing into tiny streams as it neared the sea. Sandbanks and little islands looked black against the silvery surface.

"I think we can wade across here," Ujurak said, venturing a few pawsteps into the current. The water barely covered his paws.

With a last glance at the lights on the bridge, Kallik followed him, splashing through the river, enjoying the cold feel of it against her fur. Toklo plodded along steadily, his gaze fixed on the water as if he was hoping to spot a fish. Lusa bounded along, letting out a squeal of surprise when her paws slipped and she fell on her side, sending up an enormous splash.

"Thanks for soaking my fur," Toklo muttered as he gave her a nudge to help her back onto her paws.

"You're welcome," Lusa replied, shaking herself so that shining droplets scattered from her pelt.

"Hey!" Toklo leaped backward and slapped one paw down hard on the surface so that water showered into Lusa's face.

"I'll get you for that, you big lump!" Lusa retorted.

"Come on!" Ujurak had climbed onto a sandbank a little way ahead. "There's no time for playing around."

As Kallik waded through the water to join him, she thought how strange it was that Ujurak should be the one to interrupt his friends' high-spirited fun. Usually he was the first to get distracted.

He's changed since he was taken away by the flat-faces, she thought.

At last all four bears splashed their way up the slope of the river and stood on the far bank. A few pawsteps farther, the grass gave way to pebbly beach, scattered with spiky bushes.

Kallik could hear the swish of water and the rattle of pebbles as waves washed in and out. The line of foam was only a few bear-lengths away.

"We've reached the sea!" Toklo panted, flopping onto the ground.

Kallik and the others tumbled around him, their breath sounding harsh after their long trek. Kallik looked back to see the flat-face place they had left; she could just make out the tall building where Maria had directed them. She pressed herself to the ground as she heard the growling of a metal bird and spotted the speck of light swooping over the distant flat-face dens.

"It's not looking for us," she said as she watched it sinking down into its nest.

"No, we're safe now," Lusa murmured. "They won't come looking for us here."

For a few moments, all of them were silent, huddling together in the comforting darkness. The lights and noise seemed far away; Kallik wanted nothing more than to rest for a while, listening to the soft surge of the sea and breathing in the scent of the endless ice.

"I have the answer," Ujurak announced. "I know why we were brought here."

"I might have known you wouldn't let us rest for long!" Toklo muttered. "I know why *we* were brought here," he added, jerking his snout at Lusa and Kallik. "We came looking for you."

Ujurak pushed his snout into Toklo's shoulder. "I know

you did, and I'm really grateful. But that's not what I mean. Something has been guiding me," the small brown cub went on, his eyes glinting in the starlight. "Until we came to this place, I didn't know why. I thought I was trying to find a place where bears can live safely. But it's more than that."

"Something guiding you?" Lusa echoed. "Is it bear spirits?" She raised her head to gaze up at where Silaluk blazed in the cold sky. "Did they bring us here?"

Ujurak nodded, his gaze following Lusa's to the stars. "The Great Bear watches over us always," he whispered. "She has brought us here to save the wild."

"We're really going to do it," Lusa whispered. "We're going to save the wild."

Toklo glanced from Lusa to Ujurak and back again. "I've got this awful feeling that I'm about to find out what you're talking about."

Lusa turned to him. "Toklo, you remember when I was hurt on Smoke Mountain, and we all thought I was going to die?" Toklo gave her a curt nod. "Well, I had a dream. I thought I was back in the Bear Bowl, with my mother and King and Yogi."

Toklo let his breath huff out. "Not the Bear Bowl again!"

"My mother said I couldn't die. I had to come back because I had a task to do. I had to save the wild."

"You?" Toklo said disbelievingly. "All on your own?"

Lusa ducked her head. "I know . . . I thought it was impossible, too. But I'm *not* alone now. And if the bear spirits are helping us, there's nothing we can't do!"

Kallik gazed in awe at her friend. She envied her courage and her certainty. *I can't feel it like you do,* she thought to herself. *But if there's any way I can help you, I will.*

"The wild is in great danger," Ujurak went on. "The flat-faces are so desperate for oil that they'll spread their buildings and their BlackPaths everywhere. The flat-faces won't stop until everything is destroyed."

A cold wind whispered over the shingle, making them all shiver. Toklo fluffed out his fur, as if he was trying to deny that the cold outside had awoken the icy touch of fear within.

I know how he feels, thought Kallik.

"So where do we go now?" Lusa said. "What should we do?"

"I don't know," Ujurak admitted. "We wait for a sign."

Kallik took a step back as Toklo's fear and impatience erupted. "A sign!" he barked scornfully. "Oh, really? And what sort of sign are we looking for, Ujurak? Are those four big rocks over there a sign? Are these leaves a sign?" He tore a mouthful from one of the spiky bushes and shoved the spray of foliage into Ujurak's face.

"Toklo, don't—" Kallik began.

Toklo swept on, ignoring her. "Oh, look, there are four mountain peaks over there! Does that mean four bears? Oh, yes, that must mean we're supposed to go that way!"

He reared up on his hindpaws and glared up at the stars. "Hey, spirits!" he roared. "Are you there? Are you listening, star-bear? What are we supposed to do? Where should we go?"

Kallik and the others looked upward to see if his challenge

would be answered. But the stars went on twinkling as silently as before. There was no response from the spirits, no sign to tell them whether Ujurak was right.

Toklo slumped down on the pebbles. Lusa padded over to him and touched her snout to his shoulder, but he jerked away from her. "I think we should just go to the mountains," he muttered. "Leave the plains and the sea for the flat-faces to poison as much as they want."

"I don't think you mean that," Lusa murmured.

"Look!" Ujurak whispered.

Kallik glanced up, following the brown bear's gaze. Something was happening in the sky. At first it looked like a plume of smoke swirling above the ice, but it was the color of forest berries. It billowed upward, sweeping across the sky, the colors changing from red to the deep green of pine trees, then to gold and icy blue.

"So beautiful . . ." Lusa murmured.

Kallik's heart pounded. The whole sky was pulsing with light, as if rivers of color were cascading toward her, like the wings of vast birds drawing the air around them into fantastic shapes. The spirits of her ancestors were dancing above the Endless Ice, beckoning her toward them. *Are you with them, Nisa?* she asked. *Are you looking down at me?*

"Kallik, you must lead us now." Ujurak's voice broke into her thoughts.

Kallik stared at him. "Me?"

"Yes. The spirits are telling us to go onto the ice. You must show us the way."

Kallik looked up at the fires in the sky, felt the salt breeze tugging at her fur, and breathed in the scent of the ice that lay ahead.

"Oh, yes," she whispered. "I will lead you onto the ice. I will show you my home. And the spirits of the bears who have lived before—the spirit of my mother—will be watching over us with every step."

One journey—to find the Endless Ice—had ended. The journey to save the wild had begun.

Lusa

Streaks of pink and gold and green flowed across the night sky, stretching long, dazzling clouds of color between the twinkling stars. Rivers of light danced across the bears' fur as they stood on the edge of the shore and watched. They were bathed in waves of cool flame, soundless, touchless, carried in the air like wind. Lusa blinked, her black fur rippling as she shifted on her paws. She'd never seen anything like this before. Nothing in the Bear Bowl had ever been this beautiful, and nothing she'd seen on her long journey with her friends had ever been this strange.

Ujurak must be right. It had to be a sign. The fire in the sky had been sent by the bear spirits, telling them they needed to go onto the ice.

She looked out at the murmuring sea and the vast white emptiness beyond—the Everlasting Ice—and felt a tremor of fear. The rough, pebbly sand under her paws felt solid and comforting. Even though her nose was still clogged with the scent of flat-faces and the sticky black stuff that Ujurak called "oil," she could also smell fresh grass and hear the scrabbling of tiny animals not far away. A tiny splash from the river behind them spoke of fish waiting to be eaten, and even the shadows of the spiky bushes scattered around them promised some shelter from rain or snow.

But out on the ice, there was nothing at all . . . no berries, no grubs, no rabbits, no trees . . . nothing to eat and nowhere to hide, and not even any smells to guide them. Nothing but the cold, empty scent of unmoving water.

How could they save the wild there?

"Ujurak," she said, nudging the small brown bear with her nose. "You are sure about this, aren't you? That is what the sign means . . . that we have to go out there?" She nodded head at the ice.

Ujurak's eyes were dark and serious, with a strange look that suggested he could see things that Lusa never had. "I am sure," he replied. "Kallik must lead us into her world now."

Lusa glanced at their friend. The white bear stood with her snout lifted, inhaling the scents of the ice and the sea as if she couldn't breathe deeply enough. The moonlight turned her fur to dappled silver as the wind brushed across her shoulders. Her muscles quivered with the effort of staying on land when the endless ice tugged at her paws, calling her out. Lusa wished she could understand how Kallik felt. What was there to love about all that emptiness?

She had to be brave, that was all. This quest was bigger than any of them alone; Lusa knew that. Maybe it would be more exciting on the ice than she imagined. It would certainly be different from anything she'd seen in the Bear Bowl! "And if we go out there," she asked Ujurak, "we'll be able to save the wild? We can stop the flat-faces from tearing up the land and destroying everything?"

Ujurak bowed his shaggy head and scraped his claws through the sand, leaving deep scars. "I don't know," he confessed. "I don't know what we're supposed to do about the flat-faces, but I do believe that we have to go onto the ice. The fire in the sky has to mean something; I can *feel* it. Even though the land has come to an end, my journey—*our* journey—must continue."

He looked back out at the ice, and Lusa shivered. Although the night wind was bitterly cold, she knew it wasn't the only thing making her skin crawl and her paws tremble.

"Huh!" Toklo's voice snorted behind them. "If you ask me, you've all got bees in your brains." He turned and stalked up the shore toward a line of scraggly bushes.

Oh no! Lusa thought. They couldn't go without Toklo! The bears had already been separated once, when he decided to go into the mountains on the far side of the plain and lead the life of a lone brown bear. Lusa wasn't exactly sure why he'd come back; she hoped it was because he had changed his mind about leaving them. She'd missed him terribly, and even more than that, she knew that they needed him. All four of them had to save the wild together. It wasn't coincidence that they'd met and made it so far as a team. Couldn't he see that?

"Toklo, wait!" she called. "What about the fire in the sky?

It's not bee-brained—it's a sign!"

Toklo swung his large head around. His black eyes were very bright. "I'm just saying, if we're going on a journey, we'll need to eat something first."

Lusa felt a burst of joy. Toklo was coming with them! Maybe the fire in the sky had affected him more than he wanted to let on. Lusa wasn't exactly sure what Toklo believed about the stars. They didn't seem to fill him with joy, the way they did to Lusa and Kallik. But if the stars weren't watching Toklo in a kind way, what did he think they were doing?

She scrambled after him as he padded up the pebbly slope, sniffing the night air.

"Shush," Toklo scolded her. "You'll scare off all the prey."

"Sorry!" Lusa said, trying to tread more lightly. She bumped against his side, resisting the urge to bury her nose in his thick brown fur. "You're so brave, Toklo."

He huffed. "Me?"

"I know you don't have to come," Lusa hurried on. "I mean, I know you'd rather stay on the land . . . but you are really going to come with us, right? Onto the ice?"

Toklo stopped and crouched with his nose to the ground, smelling intently. Lusa pricked up her ears, wondering what he'd sensed. After a long moment, he snorted again.

"Why not?" he muttered, avoiding her eyes. "I mean, the mountain wasn't all *that* great. Too crowded for my liking. Too many bears fighting for too little prey." His shoulders rippled with muscle as he stood up. "Besides, you three would be lost without me." He nudged her teasingly.

A full moon floated in a cloudless sky, casting thick black shadows across the island. The leaves of the Great Oak rustled in a hot breeze. Crouched between Sorreltail and Graystripe, Lionblaze felt as though he couldn't get enough air.

"You'd think it would be cooler at night," he grumbled.

"I know," Graystripe sighed, shifting uncomfortably on the dry, powdery soil. "This season just gets hotter and hotter. I can't even remember when it last rained."

Lionblaze stretched up to peer over the heads of the other cats at his brother, Jayfeather, who was sitting with the medicine cats. Onestar had just reported the death of Barkface, and Kestrelflight, the remaining WindClan medicine cat, looked rather nervous to be representing his Clan alone for the first time.

"Jayfeather says StarClan hasn't told him anything about the drought," Lionblaze mewed to Graystripe. "I wonder if any of the other medicine cats—"

He broke off as Firestar, the leader of ThunderClan, rose

to his paws on the branch where he had been sitting while he waited for his turn to speak. RiverClan's leader, Leopardstar, glanced up from the branch just below, where she was crouching. Onestar, the leader of WindClan, was perched in the fork of a bough a few tail-lengths higher, while ShadowClan's leader, Blackstar, was visible just as a gleam of eyes among the clustering leaves above Onestar's branch.

"Like every other Clan, ThunderClan is troubled by the heat," Firestar began. "But we are coping well. Two of our apprentices have been made into warriors and received their warrior names: Toadstep and Rosepetal."

Lionblaze sprang to his paws. "Toadstep! Rosepetal!" he yowled. The rest of ThunderClan joined in, along with several cats from WindClan and ShadowClan, though Lionblaze noticed that the RiverClan warriors were silent, looking on with hostility in their eyes.

Who ruffled their fur? he wondered. It was mean-spirited for a whole Clan to refuse to greet a new warrior at a Gathering. He twitched his ears. He wouldn't forget this the next time Leopardstar announced a new RiverClan appointment.

The two new ThunderClan warriors ducked their heads in embarrassment, though their eyes shone as they were welcomed by the Clans. Cloudtail, Toadstep's former mentor, was puffed up with pride, while Squirrelflight, who had mentored Rosepetal, watched the young warriors with gleaming eyes.

"I'm still surprised Firestar picked Squirrelflight to be a mentor," Lionblaze muttered to himself. "After she told all those lies about us being her kits."

"Firestar knows what he's doing," Graystripe responded; Lionblaze winced as he realized the gray warrior had overheard every word of his criticism. "He trusts Squirrelflight, and he wants to show every cat that she's a good warrior, and a valued member of ThunderClan."

"I suppose you're right." Lionblaze blinked miserably. He had loved and respected Squirrelflight so much when he thought she was his mother, but now he felt cold and empty when he looked at her. She had betrayed him, and his littermates, too deeply for forgiveness. Hadn't she?

"If you've quite finished . . ." Leopardstar spoke over the last of the yowls of welcome and rose to her paws, fixing Firestar with a glare. "RiverClan still has a report to make."

Firestar dipped his head courteously to the RiverClan leader and took a pace back, sitting down again with his tail wrapped around his paws. "Go ahead, Leopardstar."

The RiverClan leader was the last to speak at the Gathering; Lionblaze had seen her tail twitching impatiently while the other leaders made their reports. Now her piercing gaze traveled across the cats crowded together in the clearing, while her neck fur bristled in fury.

"Prey-stealers!" she hissed.

"What?" Lionblaze sprang to his paws; his startled yowl was lost in the clamor as more cats from ThunderClan, WindClan, and ShadowClan leaped up to protest.

Leopardstar stared down at them, teeth bared, making no attempt to quell the tumult. Instinctively Lionblaze glanced upward, but there were no clouds to cover the moon; StarClan wasn't showing any anger at the outrageous accusation. *As if any of the other Clans would want to steal slimy, stinky fish!*

He noticed for the first time how thin the RiverClan leader looked, her bones sharp as flint beneath her dappled fur. The other RiverClan warriors were the same, Lionblaze realized, glancing around; even thinner than his own Clanmates and the ShadowClan warriors—and even thinner than the Wind-Clan cats, who looked skinny when they were full-fed.

"They're starving . . ." he murmured.

"We're all starving," Graystripe retorted.

Lionblaze let out a sigh. What the gray warrior said was true. In ThunderClan they had been forced to hunt and train at dawn and dusk in order to avoid the scorching heat of the day. In the hours surrounding sunhigh, the cats spent their time curled up sleeping in the precious shade at the foot of the walls of the stone hollow. For once the Clans were at peace, though Lionblaze suspected it was only because they were all too weak to fight, and no Clan had any prey worth fighting for.

Firestar rose to his paws again and raised his tail for silence. The caterwauling gradually died away and the cats sat down again, directing angry glares at the RiverClan leader.

"I'm sure you have good reason for accusing us all like that," Firestar meowed when he could make himself heard. "Would you like to explain?"

Leopardstar lashed her tail. "You have all been taking fish from the lake," she snarled. "And those fish belong to River-Clan."

"No, they don't," Blackstar objected, poking his head out from the foliage. "The lake borders all our territories. We're just as entitled to the fish as you are."

"Especially now," Onestar added. "We're all suffering from the drought. Prey is scarce in all our territories. If we can't eat fish, we'll starve."

Lionblaze stared at the two leaders in astonishment. Were ShadowClan and WindClan really so hungry that they'd been adding fish to their fresh-kill pile? Things must be *really* bad.

ERIN HUNTER

is inspired by a fascination with the ferocity of the natural world. As well as having great respect for nature in all its forms, Erin enjoys creating rich mythical explanations for animal behavior. She is also the author of the Warriors series.

Visit Erin Hunter online at www.seekerbears.com and www.warriorcats.com.

For exclusive information on your favorite authors and artists, visit www.authortracker.com.

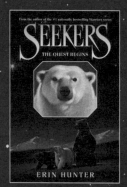

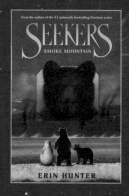
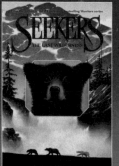